AF172617

Old Gold
The Cruise of the "Jason" Brig

by

George Manville Fenn

Double9
BOOKS

Old Gold
The Cruise of the "Jason" Brig
by George Manville Fenn

Copyright © 2024

All Rights reserved.

No part of this publication may be reproduced, stored in a retrieval system, or transmitted in any form or by any means, electronic, mechanical, photocopying or Otherwise, without the written permission of the publisher.
The author/editor asserts the moral right to be identified as the author/editor of this work.

ISBN: 978-93-64283-98-4

Published by

DOUBLE 9 BOOKS
2/13-B, Ansari Road
Daryaganj, New Delhi – 110002
info@double9books.com
www.double9books.com
Tel. 011-40042856

This book is under public domain

ABOUT THE AUTHOR

George Manville Fenn was a very productive author of novels, a writer, an editor, and an educator from England. He was born on January 3, 1831, in Pimlico, London. He mostly learned on his own; he taught himself Italian, French, and German. During the years 1851–1854, he went to Battersea Training College for Teachers and then became the head of a state school in Alford, Lincolnshire. In the early 1850s, Fenn started to write short stories and pieces for newspapers and magazines. The Old Forest Ranger, his first book, came out in 1856. Afterward, he wrote more than 100 books, many of them for teenagers and young adults. He was one of the most famous writers of his time, and his books were well-liked and read by many people. He also worked as a reporter and writer for Fenn. Among the newspapers and magazines, he worked for was The Boy's Own Paper, which he ran from 1866 to 1874. He worked hard to make children's books better and was a strong supporter of education and reading. The Englishman Fenn passed away on August 26, 1909, in Isleworth.

CONTENTS

Chapter One
Over Yonder

It was very, very hot. That is to say, it was as hot as it knows how to be in Johnstown, Guiana, which means a damp, sticky, stifling kind of heat. The sun made the muddy river look oily, and the party of three seated under the great fig-tree which shaded the boarding-house by the wharf seemed as if they were slowly melting away like so much of the sugar of which the wharves and warehouses and the vessels moored in the river smelt.

Let us be quite correct: it was more the smell of treacle, and the casks and sugar bags piled up under an open-sided shed all looked gummy and sticky; while the flies—there, it was just as if all the flies in the world, little and big, had been attracted to hum, buzz, and in some cases utter useless cries for help when they had managed to get their wings daubed with the sweet juice and strove vainly to rise in the air.

Captain David Banes, a weather-beaten sailor of about forty, took off his Panama hat, drew a yellow silk handkerchief out of the crown, and dabbed the drops off his face, brow, and the top of his head, which looked as if it had been rubbed and polished till all the hair for a broad space had been cleared away.

Then he said: "*Phe-ew!*" put the handkerchief back, and nursed his hat upon his knees, as he stared across the rough table, upon which coffee and breakfast-cups were standing, at the sun-burned gentleman who looked something like a modern yachtsman, though it was a good seventy years ago.

The latter looked back at him half-smilingly, took out a handkerchief and wiped his face, and glanced across at another sun-burned individual, to wit, a young man something like him in face, who was driving away flies from the sugar-basin, at which interference with their sweet pleasure they buzzed angrily, and the moment a spoonful of sugar had been taken out settled back.

"It's hot, Brace," said the second personage.

"Yes, I know," said the young fellow, smiling. "I found that out myself."

"Ay, youngster," said the captain, "and it don't want a man o' genous to find that out. I always say this is the hottest place there is, for I never found a hotter. I dessay it is worse in our cook's oven, but I never tried that."

He looked first at one and then at the other, as if he expected them to laugh; but as they did not he screwed up his face, coughed unnecessarily, and then said:

"Yes, it is hot, gentlemen. Wants to be if you mean to grow sugar."

"And coffee, captain," said the second personage; and just then there was a dismal creaking sound made by a windlass, a musical *yo-yo-ing* came from a vessel moored to the wharf, and a big sugar hogshead was wound up to a certain height, the crane which bore it was swung round, and as the wheels creaked the great hogshead began to descend slowly towards a gaping hole in the vessel's deck, while the captain swung himself round as if bound to follow the motion of the crane and the cask of sugar, and then lowered himself imitatively by bending his back till the cask disappeared, when he started upright, banged the table with his fist, and exclaimed sharply:

"I don't believe they're using a bit of dunnage, and if they don't the first storm they get those hogsheads'll be rempaging about in that hold, and if they don't mind that vessel'll sink, to the bottom of the sea, the sea. She'll sink to the bottom of the sea!"

He half sang the latter words, with a merry look upon his face; but it did not sound like singing, for his voice was not musical, and he turned then to his young companion.

"Know that song, squire?" he said.

"No," said the lad, smiling in turn. "Is it a song?"

"Yes, and a good one too. That's 'The Mermaid,' that is."

"But we did not come here to breakfast and discuss old songs, captain," said the second personage.

"That's a true word, sir; and we— Hullo! there you are again, are you? Anyone would think you wanted to know. See that chap, sir?"

"Oh, yes, I've seen him several times; and he does seem as if he wanted to know something. He has been watching me about ever since my brother and I have been here."

"So he has me, sir. He's one of those chaps who take a lot more interest in other persons' affairs than they do in their own, and if he comes poking his long thin sharp nose in my business he'll be getting himself into trouble."

It was a long thin nose, and on either side was a very sharp black beady eye, which did not set off or improve a thin, wrinkled yellow face, as the owner sauntered by with a roughly-made cigar in his mouth, the smoking of which seemed to necessitate the sucking in of the smoker's cheeks, as he gazed eagerly at the seated party and went on.

"He's a slave-driver; that's what he is, for a guinea," said the captain sourly. "So that's your brother, is it, sir?"

"Yes, this is my brother," was the reply.

"Thought he was. Be just like you when he's a dozen years older."

"I doubt it, captain. You don't suppose I shall stand still during the next twelve years?"

"No, of course not, sir."

"But this is not business, captain."

"No, sir, it isn't," said that individual angrily; "and if I'd known that I was going to be played such an unbusinesslike trick you wouldn't have caught me off Johnstown in my brig, I can tell you. I was as good as promised a full cargo of sugar back to Bristol, and I'm thrown overboard for the sake of saving a few dirty pounds by the agents here. But it ain't my business."

"And my proposal is, captain?"

"Well, I dunno, sir. You've come to me in a very pleasant, straightforward sort o' way to make me what sounds like a good offer. But, you see, we're strangers; I don't know you."

"And I did not know you till yesterday, when I was making enquiries about a vessel."

"That's right, sir. Well, you see, I'm a business man, and I always speak out straight what I mean."

"Speak out then, captain."

"Who may you be?"

"There is my card," was the reply, and a slip was taken out of a pocket-book and pushed across the table, to be picked up by the captain, who read:

"'Sir Humphrey Leigh, Pioneers' Club, Pall Mall.' Humph! Pall Mall's in London, isn't it, sir?"

"Yes."

"Then now I know your name, sir. But do you know anyone here, sir?"

"The bankers will be my reference, and, what will suit you better, captain, credit your account with any sum you and I agree shall be paid to you for the use of your ship."

"Yes, sir, that's all very straightforward and nice; but, you see, before I close with you there's the what for!"

"What for?"

"Yes, sir; I can't go blindfold into a bargain like this. I want to know who you are and what you want to do. In plain English, sir, what are you up to?"

"You know who I am, Captain Banes, and you can satisfy yourself at the bankers' that I am in a position to pay you well and to make your voyage a far more lucrative one than carrying home a cargo of sugar would be."

"That's right, sir; but I'm, so to speak, answerable for my brig and for the lives of my crew. Just have the goodness to tell me again what you want me to do."

"Take on board an ample supply of stores for a year's cruise, and then sail with me to the mouth of the Amazon."

"Yes, sir."

"And up the river as far as you possibly can, and then anchor, and man a boat to go on up the river or rivers as far as we can go."

"That's what you said yesterday, sir. But what for? What's the good of it?"

"That's my business, captain; and here is your friend coming back wanting to make it his apparently," said Sir Humphrey, for the keen-looking yellow-faced man came sauntering back and approached the table so as to pass closer to them.

Chapter Two
The Captain's Bargain

"Then he isn't going to know," said the captain, and then aloud: "Yes, sir, as you say, it's a hot country, and those who settle down to a sugar plantation must have rather a rough time of it. If you think of settling down I should advise you to look round a bit first. Don't be in too great a hurry."

By this time the yellow-faced man had passed, and the captain gave each of his companions a solemn wink.

"Let him turn that over," he said. "I like to put chaps like that on a false scent. He's a Poll Pry, that's what that chap is. P'raps he'll be wanting to sell you a plantation. But now then, sir, business. Directly I tell my mates and crew where we're going—if so be as we agree—the first question will be: What are we going for?"

"I don't know myself, captain," said Sir Humphrey.

"You don't know yourself, sir?"

"Not thoroughly. But I will be as open with you as I can. I am an Englishman of some means, and it is my wish to travel with my brother here, collecting."

"Oh!" said the captain.

"At the present time comparatively nothing is known of the central parts of South America."

"Wrong," said the captain. "I can tell you something: it's all big rivers running into one another like a net o' waters."

"Exactly, and that should make travelling in ship and boat easy," replied Sir Humphrey.

"But what's to be got by it, sir?"

"Who can tell," was the reply, "until the country is examined? We want to search. It may mean gold."

"That's good," said the captain.

"Or diamonds."

"That's better, sir."

"Or other precious stones. This is, of course, doubtful; but it is sure to mean an infinity of discoveries about the country and its flora and fauna."

"Its what, sir?"

"Well, its botany and zoology."

"Eh?"

"Its flowers, plants, and wild beasts."

"Oh, I see: you'd be hunting, shooting, and collecting a bit?"

"Certainly."

"But it's a feverish sort o' place, gentlemen, very hot. There's lot's o' dangerous and poisonous things about, and I have heard that the Injuns on the banks have a bad habit of shooting poisoned arrows from their bows, or little tiny ones from their blowpipes. Ain't it rather a mad idea?"

"That's what the sailors told Columbus," said the younger man, who had been sitting in silence.

"Yes," said his brother, "and it was not a mad thing to discover America."

"Well, no, sir," said the captain, dabbing his dewy head once more; "but you can't discover America over again."

"Of course not, but though North America has been traversed over and over again, how very little is known of the interior of South America!"

"Ha!" ejaculated the captain, screwing up his face; "if you put it in that way, gentlemen, we don't seem to know much about it, certainly: only that there's some big rivers there. I s'pose about as big as any of 'em. I did sail up one of the mouths for a bit once."

"Ah!" cried the younger man excitedly, "and what did you see? Strange wild beasts—wonderful trees on the shores—beautifully-coloured birds—great serpents—monkeys, and the great sea-cows?"

The captain's face shone as he wrinkled it up till his eyes were nearly closed.

"Well, why don't you speak?" said his questioner. "You could not go up that vast river without seeing some wonders. What did you see?"

"Water, sir: lots of it," said the captain bluffly.

"Of course," said the young man impatiently.

"We sailed up for three days."

"Yes?"

"And then we sailed down again."

"Oh, absurd! But the shores: what were they like?"

"Don't know, my lad. I never saw them."

"What?"

"Too far away on either hand. It was like being at sea off that coast, where the water's all muddy. That river and the big ones that run into it, according to the charts, from north, south, and west all seem as if they were hard at work washing all the land away and carrying it out to sea. It's bad enough here, but down south yonder it's wonderful: the water's muddy for miles away out to sea."

"Oh, but you couldn't sail far up that great river without seeing something interesting if you kept your eyes open," said the young man contemptuously.

"My eyes were wide open enough, my lad," said the captain, with a laugh. "I don't shut 'em much when I'm in strange waters, I can tell you. Too fond of David Banes, Esquire. Never was skipper of a ship, was you, squire?"

"Never," said the young man, laughing.

"Then take my advice—never you do be. Ships are shes, as you well know, and they're about the most obstinate, awkward creatures to deal with there are. Let 'em have their heads to themselves for a few minutes, and they give their bowsprits a toss, and if they don't run on the first rock they can find they rush into some outrageous current, or else go straight ashore, to get knocked to pieces by the breakers. That's the sort o' character I give a ship. I'd a deal rather sit behind a wild horse without any reins than trust myself in a ship without a good man and true at the wheel."

"Yes, yes, that's all very right, Captain Banes," said Sir Humphrey drily, "but you'll excuse me: we are not talking business."

"I beg your pardon, sir, but we are," said the captain stoutly. "I suppose you'll own that you propose rather an outrageous thing?"

"I do not look upon it as outrageous, captain; but certainly it is wild and adventurous."

"Same thing, sir. Wants thinking about, and I'm thinking as hard as ever I can. It means risk of life to my men and me."

"I will pay well to balance the risks," said Sir Humphrey.

The captain smiled grimly.

"I don't want to drive a hard bargain, sir," said the captain, rather sternly now. "I only want to say that I don't know what pay you could offer me and my crew that would balance the loss of our lives. I s'pose you're a man of property?"

Sir Humphrey shrugged his shoulders, and smiled at his brother.

"Then look here, sir," said the captain, "if you'll reckon all you're worth, multiply it by ten, and then do that again and offer it to me for my life, I won't take it—there!"

"No, captain, I don't suppose you would," said Sir Humphrey, smiling. "But if you feel disposed to undertake this journey, and in an honest business-like spirit set down what you consider would be a fair payment for the use of your brig and the services of yourself and crew, I have no doubt that I shall close with you at once."

"And about what we get during the voyage—gold and silver and precious stones?"

"Or more likely strange specimens of unknown animals, plants, and curiosities, captain. Well, of course they would belong to me."

"Yes," said the captain thoughtfully; "that would be only fair. But there's another thing, sir: I've got a medicine-chest, and I know how to mix up a powder or a draught for the men in an ordinary way; but I don't think anyone ought to go right up country like you talk of doing without having a doctor on board who could physic for fevers and stop holes and plaster up cuts, and deal with damages generally. It wouldn't be fair."

"You would have such a person on board, captain, for I have studied medicine and surgery, and practised for six years busily before I succeeded unexpectedly to my property and title, and then determined to see more of the world in which we live."

"H'm!" said the captain, looking from one to the other thoughtfully; "I don't like knocking about in strange places begging for a cargo, and I don't like driving my brig through the sea light in ballast. You've took me at a weak time, sir."

"Stop!" said Sir Humphrey sternly. "I don't want to take advantage of any man at a weak time and bribe him into undertaking a task over which he would repent."

"I'm not that sort of chap, sir," said the captain shortly. "If I make a bargain I stick to it, and I answer for my lads."

"That is what I want," said Sir Humphrey. "There are plenty of foreign and native skippers that I could engage; but I want a staunch Englishman whom my brother and I can look upon as a trusty friend: one who, if it came to a pinch, would fight for us as we would fight for him: a good sailor, patient, enterprising, but at the same time cautious and thoughtful, while ready to take as well as give advice."

The captain smiled grimly at the younger man, and gave his head a jerk in the direction of Sir Humphrey.

"He wants a good deal for his money, young gentleman," he said, "and I'm afraid he won't get a skipper with all that stuff in him unless he has him made to order. Look here, sir," he continued, turning upon Sir Humphrey almost fiercely, "I'm a very ordinary sort of man, and I can't strike a bargain with you, promising all sorts of things of that kind. I've got a well-found vessel, and if there's water enough I can make my crew sail her anywhere; but I've got a bit of a temper if people cut up rough with me, and don't do their duty honest. That's all I can say, I think. You want a superior sort of skipper altogether, and I don't like you any the worse for that. We've had a very pleasant chat or two, and it's been a pleasure to me to meet a couple of English gentlemen out here, and there's no harm done. I wish you and your brother good luck."

"Stop!" said Sir Humphrey; "let us understand one another. You refuse to enter into an engagement with me?"

"Yes, sir. I couldn't honestly promise to do all you want. I'm not such a perfect man as you've made up your mind to get."

"And you don't like the risk of such an expedition as I propose?"

"I never said so, sir," cried the captain bluffly. "It's what I should like."

"Then why not go?"

"Because, sir, I tell you I am not the sort of man you want. I dessay I could do a bit of fighting if I was put to it. Anyhow, I should try if anyone began to meddle with me or those who were with me, but—oh, no, you want too much."

"Brace," said Sir Humphrey, turning to his brother, "speak out frankly. It is dangerous to be hasty in choosing one's companions, but I want to know what you think of Captain Banes."

"He's just the very man we want," cried the young man, flushing.

"Thankye, my lad, thankye," said the captain, clapping the young fellow on the shoulder. "That's honest, for your eyes say it as well as your lips. But you're a pretty sort of fellow to drive a bargain! Why, you're asking me to raise my terms because you want me. That's not business."

"Never mind about that, captain," said Sir Humphrey, smiling. "Hullo, what's the matter?"

"I want to go and ask that tall thin yellow chap what he means by spying round this table and trying to hear what we're talking about."

"Let the man alone, captain, and take my advice. Don't quarrel with strangers in a foreign port."

"Advice taken, sir, and paid for," said the captain, stretching out a big brown hairy hand and gripping Sir Humphrey's firmly. "Quite right. Thankye, sir. I like you better for that than I did ten minutes ago. You make me feel half sorry that I can't come to terms with you. You want too much."

"No, he doesn't," cried Brace warmly. "We want you."

"But I'm not the sort of man for you at all, gentlemen."

"A man does not know himself so well as others know him," said Sir Humphrey, smiling. "Captain Banes, I shall be sorry if we do not come to terms, for I believe we should soon become firm friends."

"Well, I've some such idea as that, gentlemen," said the captain.

"Think it over for a couple of days, Captain Banes," said Sir Humphrey. "I will wait till then."

"Nay," said the captain firmly; "a man wants to be careful, but he doesn't want two days to go shilly-shallying over such a thing as this; and if you gentlemen think that you can trust me—"

"There's my hand," said Sir Humphrey.

"And mine," said Brace, eagerly holding out his.

"And there are mine, gentlemen," said the captain bluffly; "if you think I'm your man, your man I am, and I'll stick to you both through thick and thin."

Chapter Three
The Pushing Stranger

Wise people say that one ought to get up very early in the morning, and that it makes a man healthy, wealthy, and wise.

It is a matter to be settled to a great extent by climate, and Brace Leigh wanted no urging to hurry out of—or, rather, off from his—bed just as the stars were beginning to pale, and open his window more widely, to breathe in the comparatively cool air.

His first thought was, of course, a bath or a plunge into the river for a swim.

But the latter was not to be thought of, for more than one reason. Mud was one, but that might have been borne; another reason was that certain loathsome lizardy creatures lurked about in those waters on the look-out for food.

It a pity, for the hotel was rather a primitive place, and did not boast a bath-room, nor even a good tub or a large basin, and the young fellow had to sigh and make believe with a sponge before dressing hurriedly and going out to wait for the sun's rising and the first notes of the birds.

"Morning is the time out here in the tropics," he said to himself, as he stepped out into the cool darkness, apparently the first person up that morning, for all was very still.

"I'll go down to the waterside and have a good look at Captain Banes's vessel."

He found out directly, though, that he was not the first person up, for the door was open, and as he was in the act of stepping out a peculiarly harsh, wiry voice said:

"Good morning!"

The young man felt taken aback, for he dimly made out the figure of the thin, inquisitive-looking personage who had hung about them the previous day during the interview with the captain.

"I thought you'd be up early, so I waited for you."

"What for?" said Brace sharply.

"Just for a chat. Folks get friendly when they're thrown together in an out-of-the-way place like this. I took to you as soon as I saw you. Brother up yet?"

"No, he is not," said Brace surlily.

"Ha, ha!" laughed the man. "You want your breakfast."

"Do I?" said Brace. "You seem to know."

"A man don't want to be very knowing to find out that. One always feels a bit snappish first thing. You're going down to have a look at the skipper's brig."

"Well, really —," began Brace.

"Don't be huffy, squire. It's quite natural that you should."

"And pray why, sir? I saw the vessel lying moored yonder yesterday."

"Of course, but when one's going for a voyage in a ship one likes to look at her a bit."

"Then I'm going on a voyage in that ship, am I?" said Brace.

"Of course — you and your brother. Up the Amazons, eh?"

This was said in a questioning tone, but Brace made no reply.

"Well, of course you've a right to choose, but I say you ought to go up the Orinoco. Deal more to see there, I believe. Dessay, though, there's plenty up the Amazons. They'll do."

"That's a comfort," said Brace, smiling in spite of his annoyance, for the man was as cool as he was imperturbable.

"Is it?" he said. "Glad of it. Glad too that you young Englishmen are so enterprising. As a rule you're downright sleepy and leave nearly everything in the finding out way to us Amurricans. Didn't know I was an Amurrican, did you?"

"I never doubted it from the moment you spoke."

"Didn't you, now? Well, that is curious. It's my pushing way, perhaps."

"Yes, that was it," said Brace, laughing.

"Well, there's nothing like it if you want to get ahead. So you're going up the big rivers, are you?"

"Look here, sir," said Brace: "my brother will be down soon. Wait a little while, and then you can ask him about his plans."

"No, thankye, sir," said the man. "He's short and sharp, and maybe he wouldn't like it. You're easier to deal with. Don't be huffy. Two fellows meeting out here in a place like this ought to help one another."

"I see," said Brace good-humouredly. "Now then, you want me to help you in something?"

"To be sure. That's it exactly."

"Well, sir, what is it?"

"Look here, never mind the *sir*. That's so English. Now you're getting stand-offy again, as if you thought I was a sharper with a story about being hard up."

"H'm!" coughed Brace.

"Hah! that's what you did think?"

"Well, perhaps so."

"No perhaps about it, squire. But you're wrong. I am hard up, but it isn't for dollars."

"Then what help do you want?"

"Friendly help. I'm down in a hole, and I want you and your brother to pull me out."

"Please explain."

"Don't be in a hurry. You've been too sharp for me as it is."

"How? I never saw you till yesterday, when you came hanging about our table."

"Enough to make any man hang about. It made me wild, squire, to see the ground cut from under my feet. I'm not used to it."

"I am quite ignorant of having done anything to injure you, sir," said Brace. "Will you explain yourself?"

"Oh, I'll precious soon explain. You and your brother pushed in before me and stole my skipper."

"Did what?" cried Brace.

"Stole my skipper, squire. I came here straight, after being too late over a schooner at Trinidad. Found out that Skipper Banes had been disappointed of a cargo and was just the man likely to make a bargain with me, but before I could get in tow with him you and your brother had hooked on."

"Really, I'm very sorry for you."

"Never mind the sorrow, squire: I want something more substantial than that. What do you say to tossing for him?"

"Nothing," said Brace.

"Of course I knew you'd say that. What do you say to letting me have him, and I'll take you with me, both of you?"

"Nothing again," replied Brace, laughing.

"Why not? Lookye here: I'm going up the Orinoco exploring and collecting, shooting, fishing, and hunting, and finding every precious thing there is to be found. That's just what you're going to do."

"Is it?"

"Yes, of course it is: only you two say Amazons, while I say Orinoco."

"You seem to know all about our affairs, sir," said Brace stiffly.

"Yes, I do, pretty tidy," said the American. "Come, what do you say? You and your brother can pay half, and we'll share everything we get. What do you say to that?"

"You had better explain your position to my brother, sir," said Brace quietly; "that is all that I can say."

"That means your brother won't come unless he can boss the whole show."

"Yes, that's it," said Brace, laughing. "It's a way we English have."

"That's true, but then, you see, we Amurricans have got the old AS blood in us."

"AS—Anglo-Saxon?" said Brace.

"That's the stuff; sir, and all the best of the British race in us along with our own qualities. It came out over the row with George Three, and it's come out more and more ever since. We like to boss the whole show too, and we do it."

"Or try to."

"Yes, and try wins, squire. But look here, I suppose you're right. That's what your brother will say. He has made his plans and he don't want any Yankee meddling in them, eh?"

"Well! But I believe he will put it in a more gentlemanly way."

"Fine words won't better it, squire, and the disappointment will be as hard as ever. Look here: I want to go, and I'll pitch over the Orinoco and make it Amazons and go with you. Now then, what do you say to that?"

"Do you want the plain truth?"

"I want the words of an English gentleman," said the American sharply.

"Then I must say that I feel sure he will decline."

"Why?"

"You are a perfect stranger."

"Can't help that."

"Well, I'll be frank," said Brace: "he would not like it because of a certain English feeling of exclusiveness."

"Yes, that's it, squire; and that's where you Britishers go wrong. But look here: do I speak plain? I'll pay a fair half of all it costs—straightforward dollars."

"My brother would not be influenced by money. But there, take no notice of what I say. He will be down soon: ask him."

"But I want you to back me up, squire."

"I can't do that, sir. Can't you see that it would be very unreasonable?"

"No," said the American shortly; "can't see anything, only that I want to go in that captain's vessel, and I don't mind whether it's up the Orinoco or the Amazons. I wouldn't mind if it was only up this bit of a river here to where the gold grows. They say there's plenty up there."

"Then go up this river and seek it," said Brace, "and you'll soon get over this disappointment."

"Maybe," said the American; "but it's getting light now: the sun comes up quickly in these parts. Let's go down to the waterside and have a look at the skipper's boat."

Feeling that it would be a welcome change in the conversation, Brace walked with him to where they could get a good view of Captain Banes's brig, whose taut rigging and shapely sides began to show plainly now in the early morning, a flash of sunlight seeming to have fallen just beneath the bows on the head of the white painted figurehead beneath the bowsprit; but it proved to be only the gilded Phrygian cap which the carvers had formed, while as they walked up, admiring the trimness of the well-kept vessel the while, there was another gleam of sunlight, but only on the gilt name "Jason."

"Ah," said the American, "'Jason': that had hold of me as soon as I saw it. He was the chap who went after the golden fleece, wasn't he?"

"I believe so," replied Brace.

"Yes, that's it; and if I'd had that ship I might have got a cargo of golden fleeces, or other things that would have done as well. You'll have to back me up, squire. I feel as if I must go."

"Impossible, sir. Charter another boat. You are prepared for such a voyage, I suppose?"

"Prepared?" exclaimed the American. "I've got a dozen cases ashore here where I'm staying, full of guns, ammunition, tackle, and all sorts. My servant's got 'em in charge. There's not too much of anything, and nothing but what's likely to be useful to a man going to where he's surrounded by savages and wild beasts."

"Then you take a great interest in exploration?" said Brace.

"Interest? I should think I do, sir. I'm a regular Columbus, Marco Polo, and Captain Cook rolled up into one. Only just wish I'd a dozen smart chaps instead of only one. I'd go off in a boat, capture that brig, and sail right away."

"To be followed, caught, and put in prison for piracy," said Brace, smiling contemptuously.

"Eh?" said the American. "Yes, I suppose that's about the size of it."

"Ship ahoy, there! What cheer, oh? Morning, sir," came from the brig, and Captain Banes, who had just come on deck, took off his hat and waved it, but stopped suddenly as he made out who was Brace Leigh's companion.

"Morning, skipper!" cried the latter.

"Morning, sir, morning," shouted the captain gruffly, and then, turning sharply round, he began to give orders to the crew, which were immediately followed by sounds of holystone upon the already white boards, and splashing of water as buckets came over the side and were hauled up again.

"Don't seem as if he's going to ask us aboard," said the American.

"No," replied Brace, smiling. "Which way are you going, sir, because I am going to stroll along by those sugar-warehouses and back to the hotel on the other side."

"That's just my way; so I'll walk with you. Ah, here's the sun. Going to be another stinging hot day."

"It's hot already," said Brace, whose cheeks were beginning to tingle at the man's persistency.

"Yes, it is hot, and—I say, ain't that your brother coming this way?"

"Yes," said Brace eagerly, and he uttered a sigh of relief as he felt that an unpleasant business would be brought to an end at once.

He soon saw that there was a frown on his brother's brow, and Sir Humphrey's voice told plainly what he felt upon the stranger attacking him at once about the business he had in hand.

He heard him courteously to the end, and then, with a few words of sympathy for the disappointment he was causing, plainly told the applicant that his proposal was quite out of the question.

"Humph!" said the American. "Well, I don't like it, mister. I've come all this way to go up one of these rivers, and I don't mean to be put off. They're as free for me as for you."

"Quite so," said Sir Humphrey, "and you will go your way while I go mine."

"Ye—e—es, but it seems a pity. I like you two gentlemen, and I don't think you'd find much harm in me."

"I have nothing against you, Mr—Mr—"

"Don't you mind about the 'mister.' My name's P Franklyn Briscoe, squire, and I should like to be friends with you."

"So you shall be," said Sir Humphrey, smiling, "for I promise you I will not quarrel."

"Then you'll make a bargain of it?" cried the American eagerly.

"Decidedly not, Mr Briscoe," said Sir Humphrey firmly. "Make up an expedition of your own, sir: and I wish, you success."

"But we should do so much better, squire, if we joined hands."

"Possibly, sir, but I must decline to enter into any kind of partnership."

"With a stranger, eh?"

"Well, yes, with a stranger. Once more, sir, I wish you success."

"I'm a very useful sort of man, squire."

"That I do not doubt; but I prefer to take my own journey my own way."

"Wouldn't stop to pick me up, I suppose, if you found me drowning or starving, eh?"

"I hope I have an Englishman's share of humanity towards a fellow-man in distress, sir," said Sir Humphrey coldly; "but on your own showing you have a goodly supply of necessaries and ample funds for prosecuting your journey."

"Well, yes, tidy."

"Then once more good morning. Come, Brace, my lad, I daresay we can get some breakfast now."

Sir Humphrey bowed to the American and turned away, followed by his brother, after the latter had saluted the stranger, who stood looking after them.

"All right," he said. "People don't take to me don't like my ways, I suppose: I thought I was as polite as a man could be. But if you keep on whittling you're sure to get through the stick: whether it take a long time or a short time, PFB, my friend, depends upon the blade. Now, is your blade a sharp one, or will it only cut cheese if you put a lot of strength into the stroke? Well, we shall see."

Before the brothers had finished their meal Captain Banes was ashore, and an earnest conversation ensued about ways and means.

"Let's see," said the captain; "what about your luggage and stores? You haven't much, gentlemen?"

"Indeed, but we have," said Brace: "tons."

"Oh, that's nothing."

"I think you will say it is something when you see," said Brace. "We have stores of all kinds to last for a couple of years if necessary."

"Then you have plenty of ammunition, I suppose?"

"Plenty," said Sir Humphrey. "In fact, we brought everything we could think necessary. When will you have it on board?"

"Some time this afternoon, gentlemen. I shall warp in alongside the wharf so as to get it under hatches easily. The sooner it's aboard the better. I'll give orders to the mate, and he'll see to that while I arrange about what fresh stores are necessary. That won't take long."

"Then you propose sailing soon?" said Sir Humphrey.

"Yes, sir, as soon as you like. We can settle our little business affairs in five minutes, or I can take your word. That's enough for me."

"Thank you, Captain Banes," said Sir Humphrey gravely; "but I should prefer you to draw up a business letter that would be binding upon us both."

"Very well, sir: it shall be done."

"But what about your mate and the crew?" said Brace.

"Oh, I had a talk to them last night, sir."

"You mean that they are willing to come?"

"They all look upon it as a holiday, sir, and are as pleased as can be."

"But they've not seen us yet," said Sir Humphrey.

"What, sir?" cried the captain, laughing. "They all came ashore as soon as I'd told 'em about you, and crept up to the open window of the room where you two gentlemen sat talking by the lighted lamp."

"Indeed?" cried Brace. "I did not hear them."

"Only came one at a time, sir, and they'd no shoes on."

"Well, what did they say?" cried Brace.

"Like to hear, gentlemen?"

"Of course," cried Brace.

"They're good trusty lads, gentlemen, but, like all British sailors, a bit plain-spoken. P'raps Sir Humphrey here mightn't like it, though I answer for 'em that they meant no harm."

Brace looked merrily at his brother as if asking a question.

"Oh, yes, speak out, captain," he said.

"Well, gentlemen, they all agreed that they thought Mr Brace here would turn out a regular trump as it would be a treat to follow."

"Come, that's a good character," cried Brace; "eh, Free?"

"The poor fellows don't know you yet, Brace, my boy," said Sir Humphrey drily.

"Oh, my chaps aren't far wrong, sir," cried the captain, smiling.

"Well, what did they say about me?" asked Sir Humphrey.

The captain's eyes twinkled, and he cocked one of his eyes at Brace; but he did not speak.

"Was their report so very bad?" said the young man.

"Yes, sir; pretty tough," replied the captain.

"Never mind," said Sir Humphrey, "so long as it was honest. What did they say, captain?"

"Said they didn't quite know what to make of you, sir; but they all agreed that you looked a bit hard in the mouth, and bull-doggy—that's what they called it. The first mate said, too, that he quite agreed with them, for he could see that if ever it came to a fight with any of the natives, two-foots or four-foots, you'd never flinch."

"I hope not," said Sir Humphrey; "but I also hope we may never be put to the test."

"But—"

The captain stopped.

"Oh, there's a *but*," said Brace merrily. "It would have been quite a decent character if it had not been for that *but*."

"What was the *but*, captain?" asked Sir Humphrey.

"He couldn't say how you'd come up to the scratch if it was trouble with the long twisters that swarm up the rivers and in the damp forests of these parts."

"Snakes?" suggested Brace.

"That's right, sir: boa constructors, as the showman said they was called, because they constructed so many pleasing images with their serpentile forms."

"Well," said Sir Humphrey, "to be perfectly frank, I don't know myself how I should behave under such circumstances, for I have a perfect dread of serpents of all kinds. The poisonous ones are a horror to me."

"Or anyone else, sir," growled the captain. "I'd rather have a set-to with one of the tigers here."

"Tigers!" cried Brace; "there are no tigers in the New World."

"They call 'em tigers here, sir, though they've got spots instead of stripes. Jaggers I suppose is the proper name. Fierce beasts they are too. But poisonous snakes—ugh! They give me the creeps. But there, these things always get away from you if they can."

"Let us change the subject," said Sir Humphrey; "I am quite satisfied with your men's judgment, Captain Banes, and I daresay we shall become very good friends."

"Of course, sir," said the bluff man addressed. "I'll answer for them, as I told them I'd answer for you two gents. By the way, I hear the Yankee chap wants to charter a vessel for some such a voyage as you gentlemen mean to make."

"Yes," said Sir Humphrey; and the brothers related their interviews of the morning.

"Want'll have to be his master," said the captain, who had listened, smiling grimly during the narration. "I don't see myself going on such a trip with him. I took a dislike to that chap as soon as I saw him. Well, I wish him luck. Then if it's all the same to you, gentlemen, I'll have your stores on board a bit late in the afternoon when the sun's getting lower, and— Well, now! look at that. Think he heard what I said?"

"I hope not," said Sir Humphrey quietly. "It's as well not to excite people's dislike by making remarks about their appearance before them."

"Right, sir," said the captain. "That's one for me."

"I beg your pardon, Captain Banes," cried Sir Humphrey earnestly. "I did not mean to—"

"It's all right, sir; I deserved it," said the captain bluffly, "and I hope now he didn't hear. Poor beggar! It is his nature to. Now, gentlemen, what do you say to coming and having a look over your cabin and berths? All being well, they'll be your quarters for many a long month to come."

"By all means," they cried, and started for the brig at once.

Chapter Four
Aboard the "Jason"

"Sits like a duck, don't she, gentlemen?" said the captain proudly, as they approached the riverside. "I don't say but what you may find faster boats, but I do say you won't find a better-built or better-proportioned brig afloat. Look at her."

The captain had good cause to be proud of his vessel, and he showed his pride by having her in particularly trim order, while his crew of a dozen men were smart, good-looking young fellows, as trim as their vessel, and very different from the ordinary run of merchant seamen, being quite the stamp of the smart, active, healthy-looking Jacks of Her Majesty's Fleet.

Everything was smartly done, beginning with the manning and rowing ashore of the captain's boat, while as the little party ran alongside and stepped on deck the crew were gathered together ready to salute the brothers with a cheer.

"Why, captain," said Sir Humphrey, after a sharp glance of satisfaction around him, "you surprise me. The 'Jason' looks more like a yacht than a merchant brig."

"No, no, no, no, no, sir," said the captain, in a remonstrant tone; "as clean and smart, p'raps; but there isn't the show. Look here, though," he continued, nodding to one of the brothers and taking the other by the edge of his coat, "things happen rum sometimes, don't they?"

"Certainly," said Sir Humphrey, smiling at the skipper's mysterious way of taking them into his confidence. "With regard to what? Has anything happened rum, as you call it?"

"To be sure it has," said the skipper, screwing up his eyes. "You want a boat suitable for going up rivers, don't you?"

"Certainly," said Sir Humphrey, "and I seem to have found her."

"You have, sir, and no mistake, accidentally, spontaneous-like, as you might say. Do you know, I planned the rigging-out of that boat so that she might go up big rivers in South America?"

"Indeed?" said Sir Humphrey, looking at the speaker curiously.

"Ah, you think I'm blowing, sir, as the Yankees call it—bragging."

"I have no right to doubt your word, captain," said Sir Humphrey stiffly.

"Thankye, sir," said the captain; "but you do," he added sharply, turning upon Brace.

"That I don't," said the latter quietly. "I don't know much about you, captain, but you look too much of the straightforward Englishman to boast."

The captain's eyes closed quite up now— well, not quite, for a sharp flash came from out of the narrow slits as their owner chuckled softly and clapped his young passenger heartily upon the shoulder.

"And thank you, youngster," he cried. "You and me's going to be good friends, I see. No, my lad, there's no brag in my make. I've got plenty of faults, including a bad temper; but sham was left out when I was made. But about the 'Jason': I did contrive her for river work."

"So much the better," said Sir Humphrey. "She draws little water, I suppose?"

"Bit too much, sir; but I didn't mean that. I was alluding to her rig."

"Indeed!" said Sir Humphrey.

"Why, you ought to have had her schooner-rigged," said Brace sharply.

"Nay, I oughtn't," said the Skipper, screwing up his features more tightly. "Schooner wouldn't do so well for these river waters. A brig's best."

"Why?" said Sir Humphrey.

"Square sails up aloft come in handiest. I've seen the Hightalians who do the fruit trade up the big rivers that run north from the Plate—La Plata, you call it. They sail up for months to go and buy oranges to bring down for Europe and the States. They use brigs with spars so long you'd think they'd topple their boats over. Do you know why?"

Brace shook his head.

"Then I'll tell you, my lad. They sail up and up, and the banks close in till at last they're going up what looks like a great canal with the forest trees right down to the water's edge, shutting them quite in."

"That is just the sort of place we want to sail up, eh, Free?" said Brace.

"Exactly," replied his brother.

"Plenty of 'em up where you're going," said the skipper, "and you'll be able to sit on deck and fish and shoot without going ashore. But a schooner of the regular sort would be no use there."

"Why?" asked Brace.

"Because a schooner would be becalmed. Her big fore and aft sails would have all the wind shut out from them by the trees. With a brig like this all you have to do is to run up a couple of topgallant spars like those you see tucked under the bulwarks there, long thin tapering fellows like fishing-rods, and hoist a couple of square sails high up on them, and you catch the wind, and on you go."

"Yes, I see," said Brace. "Then those long thin masts are ready for such an emergency."

"That's right, squire," said the captain, smiling; "only I don't call that an emergency, only a matter of plain sailing. It makes one ready to go straight on, for I don't know anything more wherriting to a sailor than having a nice breeze blowing overhead and not coming down low enough to fill his sails. I've been like that before now in one of these rivers, but I don't think I shall be again. Of course one must expect a stoppage now and then in the dry times when the water falls and leaves the river shallow. There's no fighting against that, and no seamanship will teach a skipper how to find the deep channels in a river where the banks and shoals are always shifting. But come and look at the quarters below. You won't find any polished wood and gilding, squire," he continued, turning to Brace, with a dry smile.

"Do you suppose I expected any?" said Brace shortly.

"Well, no, I suppose not. But there is some polish, because the lads put that on with elbow-grease. No stuffing neither on the seats."

"Of course not," said Brace. "We did not try to find a fancy yacht."

"That's right," said the captain; "but anyhow, when a man's tired, a wooden seat is a bit hard, so I've got some horsehair cushions to go on the lids of the lockers. I like 'em myself. Now then, gentlemen, can you make shift here?"

"Yes, and a very good shift too," said Sir Humphrey as he and his brother stood looking round the fairly roomy cabin, whose fittings were of Quakerish simplicity, but scrupulously clean.

"As clean as on board a man-o'-war," said Brace.

"To be sure," said the skipper drily. "Why not?—Then you think it will do, gentlemen?"

"Excellently," said Sir Humphrey.

"That's right, gentlemen. There are your berths in there. That's mine, and those two belong to my mates," he continued, pointing out the different divisions in the stern of the brig. "I've got a good cook too, for I like decent eating and drinking. He can't make what you call side dishes and French kickshaws. But he can make turtle-soup when we catch a turtle, and I'll back him against any cook in the British Navy to make a good cup of coffee."

"That will do," said Brace.

"Frizzle a rasher o' bacon."

"So will that."

"And make bread cakes."

"Why, Brace, we shall be in clover," said Sir Humphrey, laughing.

"But he has his faults, sir," said the captain solemnly.

"All cooks have," said Sir Humphrey, smiling. "What is his worst?"

"His plum-duff isn't fit to give a pig."

"Is it like the one of which the passenger complained?" said Brace, laughing.

"Eh? I dunno," said the skipper, staring. "I don't know that I ever heard of that one. What sort of a pudding was that?"

"It must have been worse than your cook's, for the passenger said he did not mind putting up with flies for currants, but when it came to cockroaches for raisins he felt bound to strike."

The skipper screwed his face up till there were so many wrinkles that there did not seem to be room for another.

"No," he said, "my cook's plum-duff was never so bad as that, squire; but there's no knowing what may happen. If it ever does get so bad you and me'll drop him overboard. Now then, gentlemen, like to see the men's quarters?"

"Oh, no, captain," said Sir Humphrey; "we're quite satisfied."

"You take the rest from the sample you've seen?"

"Certainly," replied Sir Humphrey.

"Then the next thing is to get your traps on board, sir—later on, as I said."

"Exactly. We'll go back ashore, and you can look at them, and then I suppose we may leave it to you."

"Yes, gentlemen; I'll give orders to my first mate, and he'll have 'em brought aboard and stored in a compartment below that I've got partitioned off with bulkheads. There's a hatch in the deck, and a way in as well from the cabins, so that you can get to the stores when you like."

"What about the ammunition?"

"There's a place below communicating with the compartment by a trap, sir. Come and see."

The captain led the way into the dark store-like place, which proved to be eminently satisfactory, cut off as it was from the brig's hold. Soon afterwards the brothers went ashore, congratulating themselves upon how capitally matters had turned out; and the first face they saw upon landing was that of the American, who was seated under a tree smoking an enormously long cigar and making the fumes of the tobacco hang round beneath the wide brim of his white Panama hat.

"Keeps the flies off," he said, nodding to Brace. "Try one?"

"Thanks, no," said Brace, as he had a whiff of the strong, rank tobacco. "I'd rather have the flies."

"So would I, Brace," said Sir Humphrey angrily, as they went into the hotel; "and the smoke too, rather than that man's company. Bah! how he does annoy me with his inquisitive ways!"

Chapter Five
Luggage Aboard

Inquisitive ways indeed, for as the evening drew near there was the American still smoking as he sat in a deck chair watching the crew of the "Jason" busily getting the packages belonging to the brothers on board.

Brace had made up his mind to see the luggage and stores placed on board the brig, which had now been warped alongside one of the wharves; but, on going out from the hotel and catching sight of the American, he went back and joined his brother, who was having a long final chat with Captain Banes.

Consequently, so to speak, the American had a clear course, and he sat in the deck chair he had borrowed, smoking cigar after cigar, as if, like a steamer, he could not get on with the simplest thing without sending up vapour into the hot air.

But he did not sit in silence, for his tongue ran on, and he found something to say to the second mate, who was superintending the getting on board of what he called the passengers' "traps," and something else to every man of the busy crew, who, in consequence of a hint given by Captain Banes to his first officer, carefully took everything on board themselves, without invoking any of the black or coolie labour to be obtained upon the wharf.

"He's a rum one, my lads," said the second mate to the men. "Let him talk: it pleases him, and it don't do you any harm."

"All right, sir," said one of the sailors: "I don't mind. He's pretty free with the terbacker."

"What?" said the mate, putting his hand in his pocket and fingering one of half a dozen cigars lying loose therein: "has he given you some?"

"Yes, sir, a lot: says it's real Virginny."

"Humph!" ejaculated the mate. "Must be pretty well off.—Mind those chests, my lad. Those are ammunition."

The men went on unloading a rough truck piled up with chests, portmanteaux, and cases of various kinds, before attacking a second truck-load, while the American sat lolling back in his chair, smoking away, his eyes twinkling as he scanned each package in turn and watched for every opportunity to have a word with the busy mate, never letting a chance go by.

"Why, lufftenant," he said, "why don't you smoke and make your miserable life happy?"

"Because I'm at work," said the mate bluffly.

"My skipper don't stand smoking when we're busy."

"Don't he now? Bit of a tyrant, I suppose," said the American.

"Humph!" ejaculated the mate gruffly.

"I like him, though," said the American: "seems to know the ropes."

"Oh, yes, he knows the ropes," said the mate. "Easy there with that chest."

"Easy it is, sir."

"Now, I wonder what's in that case," said the American. "It's marked with two X's and a cross and SpG and OG. Now, what would that be, lufftenant?"

"Dunno," replied the mate. "Rareohs for meddlers, I should say, sir."

"Should you now?" said the American drily. "I shouldn't. Yes, I like your skipper, and I should have liked to have a voyage with him."

"Pity you didn't, sir," said the mate.

"Yes, that's jest how I feel; but I was too late. They're taking a deal of luggage with 'em, ain't they?"

"Yes," said the mate, as the men had the empty truck wheeled out of the way and attacked the next. "A pretty tidy lot, and it's heavy too."

"Seems to be," said the American. "Fine lot o' gun tackle, ammunition, and suchlike. Wish I'd been going too."

"Wish you had, sir," said the mate, fingering the presentation cigars, and then to himself: "What a whopping fib! I wouldn't sail in the same craft with such a nuisance."

"I'd tell my men not to let that case of cartridges down if I was you, lufftenant," said the American, as the men raised a heavy chest.

"What case of cartridges?" said the mate, turning sharply. "Humph I didn't know that was ammunition."

"Looks like it," said the would-be passenger drily.

"'Tarn't branded," said the mate. "Oh, yes, it is. But what fool marked it there at the bottom instead of the top?"

"I reckon that is the top," said the American, taking his cigar from his lips to send forth a great puff of smoke.

The loading and unloading went on, the heavy packages being swung on board by means of a crane, the lighter being carried over a gangway on the sailors' backs; and as fast as they reached the brig's decks they were lowered through an open hatch.

As the packages were taken off the truck, the American's eyes twinkled, and he had something to say about each.

"Strange deal of baggage," he said, when nearly all was on board. "Must say it's a big lot for two passengers."

"More than you've got, sir?" said the mate.

"Twice as much, lufftenant. But hullo, what have you got there—barrel o' brandy?"

"No," said the mate roughly; "it isn't juicy: it's dry."

"That's queer, lufftenant, but so it is: there's holes in the top. What do they mean?"

"I haven't been inside, sir," said the mate roughly.

"Ain't you though? Well, I s'pose not. Ain't anything alive, though, is it?"

"Alive? Pooh! Ventilation holes to keep the things from fermenting. I dessay it's something in the eating line."

"Be nice too, I dessay," said the American. "Wish I was going. I should like to have had some of that. Anyhow, mister, I think I'd be careful with that hogshead in case your men might let it go down. It'd be a pity to spoil it by letting it slip 'twixt the wharf and the ship."

"We'll take care of that, sir," said the mate, as the chains were hitched to the barrel and it rose slowly from the stones of the wharf, swinging slowly in a half-circle, and was lowered through the deck of the brig.

"There we are," said the mate, with a laugh, as he turned to the American.

"Yes, there you are, lufftenant. Bit heavy, wasn't it?"

"Oh, no, nothing much.—Now, my lads, look alive!"

There was a chorus of: "Ay, ay, sir!" and a few minutes later the contents of the last truck were reposing in the partitioned-off space in the brig's hold.

Then, and then only, the second mate turned to the American, and, taking out one of the cigars presented to him, bit off the end.

"Now," he said, "work done, play begins. I'll trouble you for a light."

"A light? Oh, certainly, lufftenant," replied the American, handing his match-box. "You'll like those cigars. They're good ones."

"I'm sure of that," said the mate.

"Stop ashore, and have a bit of dinner with me up at the hotel."

"You're very good," said the mate; "but I must get back on board. There's a lot to do. I expect we shall drop down the river to-night."

"Eh? Soon as that?"

"Yes. The skipper is off to sea."

"Oh, but you might find time for that. A man must eat. Ask the boss to give you leave."

"Humph! I hardly like to ask him, as the time for sailing is so near; but well, there, I will."

"That's right. Come and dine at the hotel just for a pleasant chat. Wish I'd been coming with you on your voyage."

"I begin to wish you were," said the mate, smiling. "You'd have found me handy when you wanted to ask questions."

The American looked at the speaker keenly, and then smiled.

"I understand," he said. "So you think I ask a lot?"

"Well, yes," said the mate, laughing. "You are pretty good at it."

"I suppose so. Way I've got. Pick up knowledge that how. Seems to me the way to learn. Hullo! What are they doing with your ship?"

"Warping her out again so as to be ready for dropping down when we start."

"Is that better than going off from the wharf?"

"Yes, a dear; but excuse me: there's the skipper yonder. I'll go and tell him I want to be off for a few hours."

"You do," said the American, "and you'll find me here when you come back."

"If the skipper knows where I want to go," thought the mate, "he'll say no directly, for he hates that Yankee, so I won't say anything about him. Not a bad sort of fellow when you come to know him; but of all the inquisitive Paul Prys I ever met he's about the worst. Never mind: he has asked me to dinner, and I'll go."

The next minute the mate was face to face with Captain Banes.

"Ah, Lynton," cried the skipper, "there you are, then. Got the gentlemen's tackle and things on board?"

"Yes, sir, all on board."

"That's right. We shall drop down the river about one; so see that all's right."

"All is right, sir, and I want you to spare me for three or four hours."

"Spare you to-night?"

"Yes. I want to dine with a friend."

The skipper raised his eyebrows and stared.

"Want to dine with a friend? Why—oh, well, I'm not going to imitate that Yankee and ask questions about what doesn't concern me. I was going to ask you to join us in the cabin, to meet the gentlemen; but that will do another time. Yes, of course, Lynton, and I wish you a pleasant evening; but no nonsense: I sail at the time I told you."

"And if I'm not back you'll sail without me?"

"That's right."

"No fear, sir," said the mate.

"I know there isn't, my lad, or I should have said no. I'll tell Dellow to send a boat ashore for you at ten."

The skipper walked off leaving the mate looking after him and frowning.

"He needn't have been so nasty about it. But he wouldn't sail without me if I were not back."

The mate did not stir till he had seen Captain Banes on board. Then and then only he went in search of the American, but did not find him, and after a certain amount of search and enquiry he was walking along with overcast brow, thinking that there was some cause for the skipper's dislike to his host in prospective, and that the American was a bit of an impostor, when he came suddenly upon Sir Humphrey and his brother, followed by one of the men from the hotel carrying a portmanteau, and on their way to the brig.

"Wonder whether they'll know me again?" thought the mate; but the next moment he ceased to wonder, for he received a friendly nod from both as he passed them and went on to the hotel to enquire whether anything was known about the American gentleman there.

"Mr Franklyn Briscoe?" was the answer. "Oh, yes, he's coming in here to stay now those two gentlemen are gone. He has ordered a dinner for himself and a friend."

"Oh, here you are then," came from behind him the next moment. "I've been looking for you everywhere."

"So have I for you," said Lynton, rather surlily.

"Oh, I see. I am sorry. You see, I had to find a place where they would give us some dinner. Here, come into my room. This is the place. It won't be a New York nor a London dinner, but it's the best I can do here, and it won't spoil our chat."

"Of course not," replied Lynton, "and I came for that more than for the eating and drinking."

"That's right," said the American bluffly. "There, come on: this is my room now those Englishmen are gone."

The mate followed his host, and after a certain amount of patient waiting the dinner was brought in, and he found the American friendly in the extreme, so that the time passed quickly, and the hour of departure was close at hand with the guest wishing that he had asked the captain to make the hour eleven instead of ten for the boat to be sent ashore from the brig, which was once more swinging from the buoy in mid-stream.

Chapter Six
The First Night on the Brig

"The night is pleasanter out here on the river, captain," said Sir Humphrey, as he sat with his brother on the deck in company with the captain and the first mate.

"Yes, sir, one can breathe," said the gentleman addressed, "and I can always breathe better out at sea than I can in a river. Well, have you thought of anything else you want from the shore, for time's getting on?"

"No; I have been quite prepared for days," replied Sir Humphrey. "What about you, Brace?"

"Oh, I'm ready," was the reply: "as ready as Captain Banes."

"But I'm not, my lad," said the captain. "I can't sail without my second officer. By the way, Dellow, did you give orders for the boat to go ashore for Lynton at ten o'clock town time?"

"I?" said the first officer staring in the dim light cast by the swinging lanthorn under which they sat talking. "No. Do you want one sent?"

"Of course," said the captain tartly. "I told you to send one."

"I beg pardon, sir," replied the first officer. "When?"

"Tut, tut, tut!" cried the captain angrily, as he glanced at his watch. "When I came aboard: and it's now half an hour later. How came you to forget?"

"Well, really, sir—" began the first mate warmly. "Tut, tut, tut! bless my heart!" cried the captain. "Really, Dellow, I beg your pardon. It quite slipped my memory."

"Indeed, sir," said the first officer stiffly. "It did not slip mine."

"No. How absurd. I forgot all about Lynton. Send a boat ashore at once to fetch him off to the brig. He must be waiting."

"No, sir, he's not waiting, or he would have hailed," said the first officer, as he strolled off to give the orders, while the two passengers, being tired after a very busy day, bade the captain "good night," and went below.

"You won't sit up to see us start, then?" said the skipper.

"No, for there will be nothing particular to see," replied Sir Humphrey. "I'll keep my admiration till we are well out at sea."

"And that will be at breakfast-time to-morrow morning, gentlemen. I should not mind turning in for good myself. As it is, I'm just going down to snatch a couple of hours before Dellow comes and rouses me up."

As Brace Leigh and his brother closed the door of their cabin the former saw the captain in the act of lying down upon one of the lockers, and as, about half an hour after, Brace lay awake listening to the strange sounds of the night which came through the open window, he distinctly heard the plash of oars, and soon afterwards the rubbing of a boat against the brig's side, followed by sips on deck, then upon the stairs.

After that there was a rustling sound as of someone passing into a cabin and closing the door, while after a little pacing about all was still on deck, and then a cloud of darkness seemed to come suddenly over the young man's brain, one which did not pass away for many hours, and not even then till his brother took him by the shoulder and shook him.

"Come, Brace, lad, wake up. Going to sleep all day?"

"No, no," cried the young man, springing out of his berth. "Why, the sun's up!"

"Yes, long enough ago. I've been sleeping as soundly as you, and the cook has been to say that breakfast will soon be ready."

"How stupid! I meant to have been on deck at daybreak. Where are we—out at sea?"

"No; as far as I can make out we are not above a mile or two below the town, and at anchor."

"Why's that?" said Brace, who was dressing hurriedly.

"I don't know, unless the skipper is repenting of his bargain. I was afraid he was too easy over everything."

"Oh, don't say that," cried Brace, in a disappointed tone.

The brothers were not long before they stepped on deck, to find all hands looking anxious and strange of aspect, as they stood watching the captain and first officer.

"Good morning, captain," said Sir Humphrey warmly. "Why, I thought we were to be out at sea by now."

"It's a bad morning, gentlemen," said the captain, frowning, "and I don't see how we are to start."

"What!" said Sir Humphrey, frowning and speaking angrily.

"Ah, I thought you'd take it that way, sir," said the skipper, scowling; "but you're wrong. I'm not going back on what I said."

"Then what does this mean?"

"It means, sir, that I've lost Jem Lynton, my second mate."

"Lost him?" said Brace quickly. "Why, he stopped ashore to spend the evening with somebody."

"That's right, squire."

"You mean he hasn't come back," said Brace contemptuously.

"No, I don't, sir," said the captain; "because he did come back."

"But you said you had lost him," cried Brace.

"That's right, sir: so I have," the captain answered. "He was to be fetched back from the shore, as you heard last night."

"Yes, I heard you tell Mr Dellow to send the boat for him," said Brace. "Well?"

"Boat was sent, sir, and the men say they brought him aboard. That's right, isn't it, Dellow?" and the captain turned round to his first officer.

"Quite," said the first mate, who looked very much disturbed, and kept on wiping his dewy forehead with the back of his hand.

"Tell 'em," said the captain. "Speak out."

"Tom Jinks was with the boat, gen'lemen," said the first mate slowly; "and he says Mr Lynton come down a bit rolly, as if he'd had too much dinner. He'd got his collar turned up and his straw hat rammed down over his eyes. Never said a single word, on'y grunted as he got into the boat, and give another grunt as he got out and up the side. Then he went below directly, and they've seen no more of him!"

"Tell 'em you didn't either," said the captain.

"No, I didn't neither," said the mate.

"To make it short, gentlemen," said the captain, "Dick Dellow here went on deck about one to cast off and go downstream in the moonlight, and sent the boy to rouse me up; and when I come on deck Dick says: 'Jem Lynton don't show his nose yet.' I didn't say anything then, for I was too busy thinking, being a bit sour and gruff about Jem, and with having to get up in the middle of the night; and then I was too busy over getting off with a bit o' sail on just for steering. Then I felt better and ready to excuse the poor chap, for I said, half-laughing like, to Dick Dellow here: 'Jem aren't used to going out to dinners. Let him sleep it off. He'll have a bad headache in the morning, and then I'll bully him. He won't want to go to any more dinners just before leaving port, setting a bad example to the men.'"

"Then, to make it shorter still," said Brace, "the second mate did not come back?"

"Didn't I tell you he did come back, sir?" said the mate huskily.

"Yes, but—" began Brace.

"You don't mean to say—" began Sir Humphrey.

"Yes, gentlemen, that's what I do mean to say," growled the captain. "He came aboard right enough, and went below. Nobody saw him come up again, and there's his bed all tumbled like. But he must have come up again and fallen overboard, for he isn't here now; and as soon as we found it out I give the order to drop anchor, and here we are."

"But how did you happen to find it out?" said Sir Humphrey.

"Tell him, Dick," said the captain.

The first mate shrugged his shoulders, and said gloomily:

"It was like this, gen'lemen. The skipper said one thing, but I says to myself another. 'Jem Lynton's no business to go off ashore the night we're going to sail,' I says, 'and I shan't go on doing his work and leaving him sleeping below there like a pig.' So I waited till the skipper was busy forward talking to the look-out, and then I slips down below to get hold of poor old Jem by the hind leg and drop him on the floor."

"Yes?" said Brace, for the mate stopped.

"Well, sir, I goes to the side of his berth, holds out my right hand—nay, I won't swear it was my right hand, because it might have been my left; but whichever it was, it stood out quite stiff, and me with it, for there was no Jem Lynton there: only the blanket pulled out like, and half of it on the floor."

"One moment," said Sir Humphrey. "The second mate slept in your cabin?"

"Yes, sir. I see what you mean. Did I see him? Yes, I did, fast asleep and snoring, with his back to me."

"And when you went down again he was not there?"

"That's it, gentlemen," said the captain, breaking in; "and he's not aboard now. There's only one way o' looking at it: the poor fellow must have been took bad in the night, got up and gone on deck, and fell overboard."

"Horrible!" exclaimed Brace.

"That's right, sir. Soon as Richard Dellow here found it out he come up to me on deck and give me a horrid turn. 'Poor Jem's drowned,' he says, 'for he aren't down below.'"

"But have you thoroughly searched the vessel?" cried Brace.

"Searched, squire?" replied the captain. "Where is there to search? He wasn't here, and as soon as I could think a bit I let go the anchor, for we must go back to Johnstown and give notice, so that an enquiry can be made. Not that there's anything to enquire about, for it's all as plain as a pikestaff. I don't know what I could be thinking about to let him go, when he ought to have been aboard at his work; but I didn't want to be hard. There, you know all we know, gen'lemen, and as soon as the tide begins to make we must run back to port, for we can't do anything more till that bit o' business is settled."

Sir Humphrey and his brother were silent, for there seemed to be nothing to say in face of such a terrible catastrophe; and, as if moved by a mutual desire to separate, while the brothers walked forward towards where the crew were gathered together watching them, the captain and mate went aft, the former shaking his head sadly, the latter looking terribly depressed and out of heart.

Chapter Seven
The Missing Man

"This is a terrible business, Brace," said Sir Humphrey.

"Yes; it quite puts a damper upon our plans."

"Seems like a suggestion of unknown horrors of a similar kind which will dog our footsteps all through."

"Don't say that, Free," said Brace earnestly. "I know it is terrible; but it might have happened under any circumstances. You talk as if it was to do away with our expedition."

"I'm afraid it will as far as Captain Banes is concerned, my lad. He is sure to back out of it now."

"I'm afraid so too," said Brace sadly; "but only for a few days."

"I don't know, my boy: sailors are very superstitious and fond of looking upon things as omens. It is very sad, for that second mate was a smart, intelligent fellow, and I looked forward to his taking an interest in our work and being our companion in many a pleasant trip."

"Oh, it's horrible," said Brace bitterly. "So well and strong only yesterday when seeing to our cases and luggage, and now—"

"Dead," said Sir Humphrey sadly, "and—"

"Boat ahoy!" shouted one of the men, drawing attention to a canoe paddled by a black, coming down with the tide in mid-stream, and only a few hundred yards above where the brig swung from her chain cable, which dipped down from her bows into the muddy water.

At the hail a second man; a white, with a coloured handkerchief tied about his head, rose up in the stern of the fragile vessel, snatched off the handkerchief to wave it above his head, and nearly capsized the canoe, only saving it by dropping down at once.

"Ugh!" yelled one of the crew, a big bronzed fellow of six- or seven-and-twenty, and, turning sharply round, he upset one of his mates as he made for the forecastle hatch, but was hindered from going below by the brothers, who were standing between him and the opening.

"What is it, Tommy, mate?" shouted one of the men.

"Look, look!" groaned the scared sailor. "His ghost—his ghost!"

In an instant the rest of the men took fright and shrank away from the bows, to hang together in a scared-looking group, the first man, addressed as Tommy, holding one hand to his mouth as if to check his chattering teeth.

"Stand by there with a rope," came from the boat; but not a man stirred, and just then the captain and mate came trotting up from aft.

"Here, what's the matter, my lads?" cried the former.

"Master Lynton's ghost, sir," stammered the trembling sailors.

"Mr Lynton's grandmother!" roared the captain, snatching up a coil of rope and flinging it to the bareheaded man in the boat, who caught it deftly as it opened out in rings. "Here, what do you mean by that cock-and-bull story, Dick Dellow?"

"Cock-and-bull?" stuttered the mate, scratching his head.

"Yes, cock-and-bull," roared the captain. "Can't you see he's there, all alive, oh! in that canoe? Here, you, Tom Jinks, lay hold of this rope, and don't stand making faces there like a jibbering idiot. Catch hold."

"No, no," faltered the great sailor; "it's his—"

"Catch hold!" roared the captain; "if any man here says ghost to me, law or no law, I'll rope's-end him."

The big sailor's hands trembled as he took the rope, but before he had given it a pull one occupant of the canoe came scrambling on board with the other end of the rope in his hand, while the canoe, now lightened of half its load, glided astern, with the black paddling hard.

"There's going to be a row," whispered Brace merrily to his brother, as they stood there, feeling as though a great weight had been removed from their breasts. He was quite right, for before the supposed drowned man had taken a couple of steps the captain was at him.

"Here, you, sir," he roared, "do you want to have sunstroke? Where's your hat?"

"I dunno," was the reply.

"Here," shouted the captain, who was in a towering passion, "where's that Tom Jinks?"

"Here he is, sir; here he is, sir," cried half a dozen voices, and the men opened out to give him a full view of the trembling sailor.

"Now, sir, what call had you to tell us that you had brought Mr Lynton aboard last night?"

"So we did—didn't we, mate?"

This to another of the sailors, who was staring hard at the new-comer.

"Oh, yes, we fetched him off in the little boat," said the man addressed.

"No, you didn't," said the second mate sourly.

"Well!" exclaimed Tom Jinks, who began to see now that it was real flesh and blood before him. "Why, we did, and you was—well, I ain't going to say what. Wasn't he, mate?"

"Oh, yes, that's a true word," said the other man.

"You don't know what you're talking about," said the second mate indignantly; "and if either of you says that I was on I'll knock you down."

"No, you won't, James Lynton," said the captain warmly. "You don't handle either of my men. Look here, did you come aboard last night in the boat?"

"No, of course not."

"Then who did?" cried the captain. "The men must have brought somebody."

"Oh, yes," said Tom Jinks, "we brought him aboard."

"I say you didn't," cried Lynton. "I went to sleep, I s'pose, after dinner, and I didn't wake up again till this morning."

"Then you ought to be ashamed of yourself, James Lynton," said the captain indignantly.

"I ham," cried the second mate boldly: "right down, and no mistake."

"A warning to you not to go out eating and drinking more than is good for you," said the captain.

"I didn't," replied the mate. "I took just what was good for me, and no more."

"It seems like it," said the captain sarcastically. "Instead of coming aboard in your own ship's boat according to the terms of your leave, you come back in a dug-out after your vessel's sailed, and without a hat."

"Yes, I know," said the mate testily; "but didn't I tell you I felt ashamed of myself? Eh? what say?"

"Is this here yours?" said the first mate, who had suddenly gone below to the cabin, and returned with a straw hat in his hand.

"Yes, that's mine. How did you get it?"

"You came aboard in it last night."

"I didn't," cried the second mate, who looked staggered.

"Oh, yes, you did, sir," cried Tom Jinks. "Didn't he, mate?"

"That's so," said the man addressed.

"But I tell you I didn't. I went to sleep after dinner, and didn't wake till this morning, and found the brig had sailed."

"Of course she had—to her time," said the captain angrily. "He don't know what he's talking about, gentlemen," he continued, turning to the brothers. "I'm very sorry, but I'm not going to have any more time wasted. Now then, my lads, capstan bars, and bring that anchor up with a run. You, James Lynton," he went on, as the men ran to obey their orders, "I'm ashamed of your goings-on. What have you been about? Walking in your sleep, I suppose."

"I dunno," said the second mate, scratching one ear. "I can only recollect Mr Franklyn Briscoe saying—"

"Mr Who?" roared the captain.

"That American gentleman who wanted to come with us."

"You don't mean to say you've been with that inquisitive chap, do you, sir?"

"Yes. What harm was there in that?"

"What harm? Look at you this morning."

"Oh, well, I don't know how it was," said the mate.

"Then I'll tell you how it was, sir. It was my second officer making an excuse to go ashore, and getting into bad company. But never no more, James Lynton: never no more. You don't deceive me twice like this."

"It was all an accident," grumbled the delinquent.

"Yes, of course, and a nice state we were in, believing that after you came aboard you fell over the side and were drowned."

"You didn't think that, did you?" cried Lynton.

"Didn't think it? Why, of course we did, sir. Didn't I come to an anchor as soon as I found you were not aboard?"

"I don't know," said Lynton, looking from one to the other.

"Then you know now, sir. Pretending to me that you were going to a dinner—*eating*."

"So I was," cried the mate.

"Not you, sir. Going somewhere drinking."

"That I wasn't. Mr Franklyn Briscoe came and asked me to go and have a bit of dinner with him."

"What! that American?" cried the captain.

"Yes."

"Then that makes worse of it."

"There, I don't know: bad or worse," said the mate. "All I know is that I went to sleep after dinner, and when I woke up he was gone and I couldn't find my hat."

The first mate exchanged glances with the captain, who spoke out at once.

"Then how did your hat come on board, sir?"

"I don't know, I tell you, captain," cried Lynton. "All I know is that as soon as I woke up I went half-mad, and ran down to the river, to find you'd sailed without me; and then I got that black fellow to paddle me down after you in his canoe."

"And a deal of good that would have been if I hadn't anchored," growled the captain. "There, sir, get to your duties, and let's have no more of it."

"But I want to clear my character, captain, before the crew and these two gentlemen."

"You hold your tongue, my lad, or you'll be making worse of it."

"But there's some mystery about it," said the mate warmly. "Yes, I can see you nodding and winking, Dellow, and making signs to the men. Here you, Tom Jinks, you said I came on board last night?"

"Yes, me and my mate here rowed you aboard; didn't we, mate?"

"Ay, ay, lad," was the reply, and their questioner banged his right fist down into his left palm as if to get rid of some of his rage.

"There," he cried, "have it your own way, all of you; but you don't catch me going ashore to dine with a gentleman again."

"No," said the captain sharply, "I shan't. Now then, look alive there."

The anchor was soon after swinging from the bows, the sails filled, and the brig began to glide down with the stream, and by the time the cabin breakfast was at an end the banks of the muddy river were growing distant, and various signs pointed to the fact that they were approaching the open sea. That evening, with a gentle breeze from the north sending them swiftly along, the low coast-line looked dim and distant across the muddy waters, the mighty rivers discolouring the sea far away from land, and, glass in hand, Brace was seated in a deck chair trying to make out some salient point of the South American coast.

Then all at once something dark eclipsed the picture formed by the glass, and Brace Leigh lowered it suddenly from his eye to try and make out what it was. He found that it was the second mate's head.

Chapter Eight
Something Startling

"Evening, sir," said Lynton. "Growing too dark to see much with a glass, isn't it?"

"Yes; I was just going to shut it up and put it in the case," replied Brace. "I say, don't you go and sham dead to upset us all again."

"There you go!" cried the mate angrily. "I did think it was going to drop now. Nobody seems to believe my word."

"Don't say nobody, for I will," said Brace quietly. "I was only joking you a bit. But tell me: that coast-line I could see before it grew so dark was all forest, I suppose?"

"A lot of it," replied the mate, with a sigh or relief; "great thick dense forest with dwarfish trees growing out of the mud, and if you could see now, you'd find all the leaves sparkling with fireflies up the creeks and streams."

"Then the sooner we reach our river and begin to sail up, the better I shall like it. How soon it grows dark out here!"

"It does in these latitudes," replied the mate.

"But I say, Mr Leigh, don't you go thinking that I went ashore carrying on and drinking, because I didn't."

"I promise you I will not."

"Thankye," said the mate, as he stood looking along the darkened deck, with the lanthorns now swinging aloft. Beneath a rough awning the captain had made the men rig up over the cabin, that gentleman was seated chatting with Sir Humphrey, while the first mate stood by them, listening to their conversation, and occasionally putting in a word.

Three or four folding-chairs had been placed aft for the benefit of the passengers, one of which Brace had marked down for his own use, and he was thinking of fetching it along to where they stood, as he talked to the second and fastened the strap of his binocular case.

"Ah," said the mate, "you'll find that little glass handy when you begin shooting for picking out the birds and serpents and things, and—"

He took off his straw hat to wipe his forehead, for the air was hot, moist, and sultry. He did not, however, apply his handkerchief, but stood with it in his right hand, his straw hat in his left, gazing down at it.

"Puzzles me," he said, changing the subject suddenly.

"What: how to find the birds and reptiles among the leaves of the great trees?"

"No, no," said the mate impatiently. "I mean, how it was this straw hat of mine came on board."

Then, in a hoarse whisper: "Mr Leigh, sir: look—look there!"

He stretched out his hand with the hat in it, using it to point towards the spot where one folding-chair stood, dimly seen, close up to the starboard bulwark.

"Well, I see it," said Brace. "It does not seem any the worse for coming on board without you."

"But I can't make it out," whispered the man, in a strange way. "I hung it up in the American gent's room—the one you had, sir—and the last I remember is seeing him sitting opposite to me across the table; and now look there. See him?"

"No," said Brace; "I can see no him. What do you mean?"

"The American," whispered Lynton, catching the young man by the arm. "There, can't you see him sitting in the dark yonder?"

"No," said Brace quietly. "I say, Mr Lynton, you'll be better when you've had a good night's rest. You talk as if you could see a ghost."

"That's it, sir; that's it," whispered the man wildly. "Come away—come away."

"Nonsense, man. There's nothing over yonder, only—"

Brace stopped short in blank astonishment, for the nearest lanthorn turned round a little as the brig heeled over, and there, faintly seen, and looking strangely transparent, the seated figure of the inquisitive American seemed to loom out of the shadow.

But the startled fancy that it might be anything supernatural passed away in an instant, and he felt ready to laugh at the superstitious sailor, as he saw a glowing spot of light about on a level with the figure's lips, and directly after smelt the peculiar odour of tobacco as it was wafted to him by the warm night air.

"Come away," whispered the mate, gripping Brace's arm with painful force.

"Nonsense," said Brace firmly. "That's how your hat came on board."

"Ugh!" ejaculated the mate, and he sent the straw hat he held whirring away from him with all his might.

He meant to have sent it overboard, but straw hats have boomerang-like ways of behaving peculiar to themselves, as most wearers know to their cost; and the one in question, instead of rising and skimming like a swallow over the bulwark and dropping into the sea, performed a peculiar evolution, turned in the direction of the group under the awning, dived down, rose again, just touching Sir Humphrey's ear, missing the first mate, and striking the captain with its saw-like revolving edge just below the chin.

"Here, hullo!" roared the latter gentleman; "what are you about?"

"Guess it warn't a bad throw, though, in the dark," said a familiar voice, which made the captain spring to his feet with a cry of astonishment; and the next moment the group from beneath the awning were gathered about the imperturbable smoker seated in the folding-chair.

"That you?" shouted the captain, and the personage addressed took his cigar slowly from his lips and emitted a great puff of vapour.

"Yes, skipper," he said coolly; "it's me," and he replaced his cigar.

"What in the name of all that's wonderful are you doing here?"

"Doing, skipper?" said the American quietly. "Smoking. Precious hot, ain't it?"

"Hot, sir?" roared the captain; "it's nothing to what it's going to be. How dare you? Why, you're a stowaway!"

"Am I, skipper? Well, do you know," said the American, in the most imperturbable way, "I thought I was a lump of human fat melting slowly away and running out on to your deck."

"How did you get here?"

"How did I get here? Why, two of your men brought me aboard last night in your boat."

"Well, of all the impudence!"

"Now, now, now, skipper, don't get in a wax. Just act like a man, and order me a drink, half water, half lime-juice, for my throat feels as if it had been sanded with hot sand."

"I'll order you over the side, and set you ashore at the nearest point of land."

"Not you, skipper. It would be like committing murder, and raise up international difficulties."

"I don't care, sir; I'll do it. You've got the wrong man to deal with if you think you're going to play any of your Yankee tricks with David Banes. Here, Dellow, heave-to and man the big boat."

"Good ten miles to the shore," said the first mate in a low remonstrant tone of voice.

"I don't care if it's twenty. I said I wouldn't take him as a passenger, and I won't."

"Ten miles for your chaps to pull in the dark, and ten miles back," said the American coolly: "that's twenty, and say another ten miles as allowance for currents, which run strong, I've heard say. That's thirty miles. Say, skipper, hadn't you better take it coolly and make the best of it?"

"No, sir, I had not."

"But I have made up my mind to sail with you, skipper, for I reckon I shall like this trip."

"And I reckon you will not," said the captain grimly. "You're very sharp, sir, but you've cut yourself this time, and you're going to be rowed ashore as soon as it's light."

"Hah, that's better, skipper. Your lads couldn't do it in the dark, and they'd never find the brig again."

"That's right," said the captain. "I'm not going to run any risks, for the sake of my men; but ashore you go as soon as it's light."

"And what about for the sake of me? I have heard that some of the natives about here are the old Caribs."

"Yes, sir, regular old-fashioned savages; and you won't find any hotels, nor captains to worry with questions."

"I've heard too that they're cannibals, skipper. S'pose they eat me?"

"So much the better for them and the worse for you. But that's your look-out, not mine."

"Well, you are a hard nut, skipper," said the American, leaning back and smoking away.

"I am, sir: too hard for you to crack. You're not the first loafing, cheating stowaway I've had to deal with."

"Cheating, eh?" said the American, turning his face to Sir Humphrey and Brace in turn. "Hark at him! I don't want to cheat. I'll pay my share of all expenses."

"No, you won't, sir, for I won't have your money. This brig's let to these two gentlemen for as long as they like. You've played me a dirty trick after being told that I was engaged, and you've got to go ashore. I see through your tricks now. You inveigled my second mate ashore to dinner with you."

"Asked him, and treated him like a gentleman," said the American.

"You stole his straw hat."

"Nay, nay, only borrowed it, skipper."

"Stole his hat, sir."

"Say took, and I won't argue, skipper: I was obliged to."

"Left him asleep, and stole aboard in the ship's boat."

"Yes, that's right," said the American. "I thought you were going to say I stole the boat. That's right. The men wouldn't have rowed me aboard if it hadn't been for the mate's hat."

"And for aught you cared I might have sailed and left that poor fellow behind—eh, Lynton?"

"That seems about the size of it," said the second mate.

"Gammon!" cried the American good-humouredly. "You're too good a seaman, Captain Banes, to go off and leave one of your officers ashore."

"That's oil," said the captain sharply; "but I'm not going to be greased, sir. You're going ashore: if only for playing me and my second officer such a dirty trick."

"Say smart, not dirty, skipper."

"Dirty, sir, dirty."

"Only business, skipper. I'd made up my mind to come, and it seemed to me the only way."

"Ah, you were very clever; but it won't do sir. You're going ashore."

"But what about that cool drink, skipper?"

"And as soon as it's light," said the captain, ignoring the request. "Mr Dellow."

"Ay, ay, sir."

"Set the course a few miles nearer shore. No fear of a squall off here."

"Well, I dunno, sir," said the mate. "I don't think I'd run in too close. The water's shallow, and there's often very heavy seas closer in."

"Be bad for an open boat, skipper," said the American.

"Very, sir," said Captain Banes. "I daresay you'll get pretty wet before you're set ashore."

"That's bad, skipper; but I wasn't thinking of myself, but about my traps."

"Your traps?"

"Yes, I've got a lot of tackle that won't bear wetting. Dessay there's a ton altogether aboard."

"What!" roared the captain. "You've no goods aboard?"

"Oh, haven't I? Guns, ammunition, provisions, and stores of all sorts."

"How did they get here? Bring 'em in your pocket?"

"Nonsense. Your second mate brought 'em aboard."

"What? Here, Lynton, speak out. Have you been in collusion with this fellow, and brought his baggage aboard?"

"Not a bag, sir," cried the mate indignantly.

"Oh, come, I like that!" said the American, laughing. "Didn't I come and sit by you and smoke and see it all done?"

"No!" cried the second mate angrily.

"Well, you Englishmen can tell crackers when you like. What about that big cask with the holes in?"

"That cask? Was that yours?"

"Of course it was, and all the rest of the things on that truck," said the American coolly. "You don't suppose I should have come and sat there to see anybody else's tackle taken on board, do you?"

"Well," broke in Brace, laughing, "judging by what I've seen of you, sir, I should say you would."

The American turned upon him in the midst of the laugh which arose, and said smilingly:

"All right, sir, have your joke; but when I ask questions or hang around to see what's going on I do it for a reason. I wanted to go on this voyage in this ship, sir: that's why I was so inquisitive; and here I am."

"Yes," said the captain hotly, "for the present. And so you tricked my second officer and men into bringing your baggage on board, did you?"

"Schemed it, skipper, schemed it," said the American coolly.

"Exactly. Very clever of you, my fine fellow; but look here: suppose I make you forfeit your baggage when I set you ashore?"

"Law won't let you, skipper."

"I'm the law on board my ship," cried the captain angrily. "Suppose I refuse to stop my vessel to get your baggage out of the hold, and that precious cask?"

"Good, that's right, skipper—precious cask," said the American coolly.

"Precious or not precious, I shall set you ashore, and continue my voyage, and whether it lasts one month or twelve, you may wait for your baggage till I come back, and you may look for me wherever I am."

"You can't do it, skipper," said the American smoking away quietly.

"Oh, can't I, sir?" cried the captain. "You'll see."

"No, I shan't, skipper. It would be murder, I tell you, to set me ashore, and double murder to sail away with my luggage."

"Bah!" cried the captain.

"You see, there's that cask. What about it?"

"Hang your cask! I'll have it thrown overboard."

"Oh, I say, you mustn't do that," cried the American, with some slight display of energy; "the water would get in through those holes bored in the top, and spoil the contents."

"What's that to me, sir?" cried the captain.

"Murder number three, because I have warned you not to do it in the presence of witnesses."

"Murder!" cried the captain, looking startled. "Why, what's in it?"

"Only my servant."

"What!" came in a chorus.

"My boy—my servant," said the American coolly; "and he ought to be let out now, or he'll be smothered. I found it very hot down there, sitting among the boxes and chests. I dunno how he finds it, shut up in a cask."

"I say, gentlemen," said the captain, with a gasp; "is this fellow an escaped lunatic—is he mad?"

"Not I," said the American, answering for himself; "I was, though, down there when I got in."

"Hah! broke in," cried the captain sharply.

"That I didn't. I found the door open when I left the berth where I lay down when I first came aboard. Pretty sort of a thick-headed chap it was who stowed that cask. Made me mad as a bull in fly-time. There were the holes to guide him to keep this side upwards, but he put the poor fellow upside down. Nice job I had to turn him right in the dark, and all wedged in among casks. I hope he ain't dead, because it would be awkward for you, skipper."

"Look here, sir," cried Sir Humphrey angrily, while Brace stood fuming; "do you mean to tell me in plain English that you did such a barbarous, criminal act as to shut up a man or boy in a cask to bring him aboard this brig?"

"Barbarous! criminal! Nonsense, sir. He liked the fun of it, and I made him as comfortable as I could. Plenty of air-holes, cushion and a pillow to sit on and rest his head. Plenty to eat too, and a bottle of water to drink. I told him he'd better go to sleep as much as he could, and he said he would. He must have been asleep when I came up a bit ago, for I couldn't make him hear."

"Captain Banes," cried Brace excitedly, "give orders for the hatches to be taken off at once."

"Just what I'm going to do, squire," said the captain. "Here, Dellow, see to it. But I call you all to witness that I wash my hands of this business. If the man's dead I'm going to sail back to port and hand this man over to the authorities."

"We'll settle that afterwards, Captain Banes," said Sir Humphrey stiffly.

"Right, sir; I'll lose no time," said the captain, and all present stood looking on while, under the first mate's orders, the hatches were opened, more lanthorns lit, and a couple of men sent below with a rope running through a block.

"Make it fast, my lads, and be sharp," cried the mate, as he leaned over the opening in the deck, swinging a lanthorn so that the sailors could see to hitch the rope about the cask. "Ready?"

"One moment, sir," came from below. Then:

"Haul away."

"Keep him right side upwards, you sir," said the American coolly.

"Right side upwards, sir!" growled the captain fiercely. "You deserve to be headed up in the cask yourself and thrown overboard."

As he spoke, the big cask appeared above the combings of the hatchway, was swung clear of the opening, and lowered again, to come down with a bump upon the deck.

"Here, quick," cried the captain. "Bring an axe and knock off those top hoops."

"Nay, nay!" cried the American coolly.

"Don't interfere, sir," said Sir Humphrey; "it is to get the head out."

"I know," said the American; "but one of those borings is a round keyhole. He'll open the head from inside if he's awake: and if he don't I can."

"If he's awake!" said Brace bitterly.

"P'raps he isn't, for he's a oner to sleep. Stand aside, skipper."

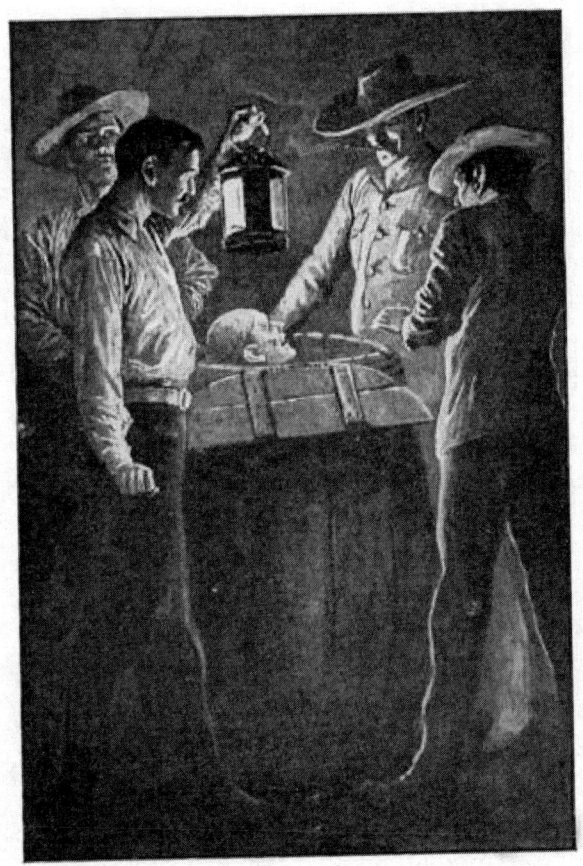

"'Well, Dan, how goes it?' said the American."

The captain turned upon the man fiercely, but it had not the slightest effect upon him, for he kept his cigar in his mouth and smoked away, as he drew out a key like that used for the boot of a coach, thrust it into one of the holes in the head, gave it a turn, and the head of the cask opened outward in two pieces which turned upon hinges; while as the first mate thrust forward the lanthorn he held, it was nearly knocked out of his hand by the skull-cap-covered head which shot up, sending a thrill of relief through the circle of lookers-on.

"Well, Dan, how goes it?" said the American.

The fresh arrival, who seemed to be a thin diminutive-looking fellow of any age, whose perfectly smooth face looked peculiarly yellow, planted his hands one on either side of the cask, sank down, and then sprang up again, cleverly passed his legs over the side and landed himself—as if shot out by a spring—upon the deck, where he stood shrinking from the light, yawned long and widely, and then said slowly:

"Oh, all right, boss. Bit hot and sleepy. What's o'clock?"

"Time you and your precious master were over the side," cried the captain angrily.

The man or boy, whichever he was, turned in the direction of the voice, blinking quickly in the faint rays of the lanthorn light as if even they dazzled him, and went on:

"Who's him, boss?"

"That, Dan? That's the captain."

Brace burst into a hearty fit of laughter, in which his brother joined, and after a brief pause this was taken up by the two mates and followed by the men who were looking on.

"Ho!" cried the captain angrily: "it's a capital joke. Very funny, no doubt; but it strikes me somebody's going to laugh on the wrong side of his mouth. Just wait till it's daylight."

"Oh, it's all right, skipper. You can't set us ashore now," said the American, laughing.

"Can't I? Oh! we shall see about that, my fine fellow. If you think I'm going on this voyage with a couple of lunatics on board you're preciously mistaken. I'd sooner sail to Egypt with a cargo of black cats."

"Hark at him," said the American merrily to Sir Humphrey and his brother. "He likes his joke."

"Joke, sir?" cried the captain. "You'll find this no joke, Mr Yankee Doodle."

"Go along with you, captain. Yankee Doodle knows John Bull better than he knows himself. You're not going to make me believe you'll set me and my man ashore and leave us in a savage place to die of starvation and ague."

"You soon will believe it, though, sir," said the captain; but in spite of his annoyance he could not thoroughly infuse his tones with sincerity.

"You're only blowing, skipper, when you might be taking pity on that poor chap of mine who's been shut up in the barrel all these hours without giving a single squeak; and all because he'd risk anything so as to go with his master. That's true, isn't it, Dan?"

"Yes, that's right, boss," replied the little fellow, who kept passing his tongue over his lips.

"Hungry, Dan?"

"No, boss. Thirsty. Horrid."

"Did you finish your bottle of water?"

"No, boss; I couldn't get the cork in proper, and when I knocked it over while I was asleep the cork came out and all the water ran away."

"Not amongst my cartridges, I hope, Dan?"

"I dunno, boss. I never see where it run to in the dark. Only know it didn't run where I wanted it to go. I *am* thirsty."

The second mate handed him a pannikin which he had fetched from the cask lashed amidships, and the American's servant took it and began to drink with avidity.

"Here, you, Lynton," cried the captain: "who ordered you to do that?"

"Common humanity, sir," said Brace quickly.

"Then it was like his uncommon impudence to order my officers about, squire," said the captain gruffly, but without so much of his former fierceness.

"Hah!" ejaculated the drinker, as he drained the tin; "never knowed water was so good before. Thank-ye, mister. Ketch hold."

The second mate took the tin, and to the astonishment of all, the uncasked servant threw himself flat upon his chest and stretched himself out as much as he could, took a few strokes as if swimming, and then turned quickly over upon his back, went through similar evolutions, grunted, and stretched again.

"What's the matter, Dan?" said his master quietly.

"Taking some of the creases out, boss. That barrel warn't big enough for a chap my size, and I feel quite curly. There's a crick in my neck, one of my legs is bent and t'other's quite screwed."

"Oh, you'll be better soon," said the first mate.

"Yes, I'm coming right again," replied the man.

"Wait till you've had a trot or two up and down Captain Banes's deck. You'll let him, won't you, skipper?"

"Urrrr!" growled the captain.

"Oh, come, skipper, ain't it time you left off being so waxy? You can't set me ashore, you know; so say no more about it. I'll pay handsomely for the trip."

"Don't talk to me," growled the captain. "That gentleman has chartered the brig, and it's his for as long as he likes. I can't make any bargains with you or anyone else."

"Ah, now you're talking sense, skipper. That's speaking like a man. Well, Sir Humphrey Leigh, let's hear what you've got to say to me."

"I say that you have taken an unwarrantable liberty, and—"

"Hold hard, sir, hold hard. Let's settle that one thing first. Well, yes, I suppose it was; but here was I with all my plans made: arms, ammunition, stores, everything, man included—he is a man, you know, though he's such a dried-up little chap. How old are you, Dan?"

"Thirty last birthday, boss," said the little fellow promptly.

"There, sir. Well, that's how I was. Red-hot too to get up one of these big rivers to explore and collect everything that came in my way, but no vessel to be had. Felt as if I must get back home when I heard about you and the skipper here; and then I tried my best to get you to let me go shares in the expedition, and you wouldn't. You know you wouldn't."

"Naturally," said Sir Humphrey.

"We won't argue about that, sir. That's how I was. Amurricans when they've got a thing to do don't turn back. It goes against their grain. Go ahead's our motto. I started to do an expedition up a South American river, and I'd got to do it—somehow: straightforward if I could; if I couldn't— back way. That's how it was with me, and here I am. It was artful, dodgy, and not square; but I couldn't help it. There, I speak plain, and I want you now as an English gentleman to help me with the skipper here. You see, I'm a naturalist, ready for any amount of hard work, a reg'lar enthoosiast of travelling and collecting, and I'll pay my share of all expenses. That's fair, isn't it?"

"Oh, yes, that's fair," said Sir Humphrey; "but we don't want you."

"Not just now, sir; but you may. You don't know what holes you may get into up the river. Come, sir, I throw myself on your mercy. You're captain of the expedition, and I'll serve under you. Don't send me adrift now."

"Well, of all the enterprising, pushing men I ever encountered—" began Sir Humphrey.

"Yes, that's it: enterprising. I am enterprising, ready to do anything to carry out the objects I have in view. Come, sir, I promise you that you shan't regret it."

Sir Humphrey frowned as he looked the American and his man over, and then turned to his brother, who shrugged his shoulders and smiled.

"What do you think about this?" said Sir Humphrey.

"Don't ask me, Free," replied the young man. "I have a strong leaning towards mercy."

"But we don't like this man well enough to make him our companion."

"No, but he may improve," said Brace.

"He may get worse," said Sir Humphrey shortly.

"I hope not," said Brace. "You see, we're started, and it would be horrible to go back. We can't set him ashore."

"Impossible!" said Sir Humphrey decisively.

"Very well then, we must take him."

"It seems as if there is no alternative," said Sir Humphrey, frowning. "We cannot allow the captain to set him ashore."

"He wouldn't want stopping," said Brace, laughing gently.

"You think he would not do it, Brace?"

"I'm sure he wouldn't," replied the young man. "He barks and makes a noise, but he wouldn't bite like that."

"Well, then, we must make the best of it, Brace, for I certainly will not turn back."

"Then you'll take him?"

"I shall give way to the extent of asking Captain Banes to let him go with us."

"Don't," said Brace, in a low voice, as he glanced at the American and saw that he was watching him closely.

"What! not ask him?" said Sir Humphrey. "Why, just now you were in favour of doing so."

"So I am now, Free," said Brace, drawing his brother to the side, so that they could be alone; "but I want you to take it entirely upon yourself. You've chartered the brig; and it is yours. Captain Banes is, so to speak, under your orders, you being head of this expedition."

"Quite right, Brace," replied Sir Humphrey, nodding his head, and looking satisfied with his brother's decision.

"I should act at once as if I were fully in command, and make a stern bargain with this American naturalist that if he comes with us it is, as he proposed, completely under your orders."

"Exactly," said Sir Humphrey, and the brothers walked back to where their would-be ally stood waiting patiently, and Captain Banes was giving vent to his annoyance by growling at both mates in turn, and then at the men for not being smarter over getting up the cask.

"Captain Banes," said Sir Humphrey.

"Sir to you," growled the captain.

"My brother and I have been discussing this business, and we come to the conclusion that we cannot under any circumstances return to port."

"O' course not," said the captain, nodding approval.

"But on the other hand we cannot be guilty of so inhuman an act as to set this gentleman and his servant ashore upon a wild coast, at the risk of his life."

"Hear, hear!" cried the American, and the captain grunted.

"But, as he has chosen to take the risk and is prepared for an inland expedition, we decide that he is quite at liberty to join ours and go with us, on the condition that he follows out my orders as to what is done."

"Of course—of course," cried the American. "Hear, Mr Skipper?"

"Oh, yes, I hear," said the captain.

"Then that is settled," said Sir Humphrey. "Mr Briscoe, I trust that in the future we shall be better friends."

"No fear of that, sir," said the American quietly. "Sir Humphrey, you're a gentleman. Mr Brace, you're another. It's going to be acts now, not words. I only say thankye, and I want you and your plucky young brother to believe me when I say you shan't repent your bargain a bit."

"I believe I shall not, sir," said Sir Humphrey gravely.

"As for you, Captain Banes," continued the new member of the expedition, "I'm going to show you that I'm not such a ruffian as you think. And now, gentlemen, as I haven't had a wink of sleep for two nights, I'm going to ask the skipper to let me have a berth and to give orders for my man here to be furnished with a bunk. I've kept it up, gentlemen, as long as I could, but now I'm dead-beat. I've been asleep in my legs for long enough. Now it has crept up from my waist to my chest, and it's attacking my head. In another ten minutes I shall be insensible, and when I shall wake again is more than I know, so I'll say at once: Thank you all—all round, and good night."

A little difficulty arose as to a berth; but this was soon solved by the second mate giving up his in favour of a mattress upon the cabin floor, and the brothers were left alone with the captain, who preserved an ominous silence, till Brace spoke half-laughingly:

"You don't like the new arrangement, captain?"

There was a grunt. Then:

"Put that and that together, squire, would you if you were in command of this brig?"

"Certainly not," said Brace quickly; "but I shouldn't have put the poor fellows ashore."

The captain mumbled a little, and by the light of the swinging lanthorn Brace caught a gleam of white teeth, and knew that he was laughing.

"That was what he'd call bunkum, and we call bounce, squire. Of course I shouldn't have put him ashore. But I felt as if I meant to when I said it."

"Then you are not so very much dissatisfied, captain?" said Sir Humphrey.

"Yes, I am, sir, for I don't like to be bested. No man does, especially by one of these clever 'Merican chaps. For they are clever, there's no getting over that."

"I don't like that either," said Sir Humphrey; "but it's evident that this man is an enthusiast in travel and natural history."

"Oh, yes, sir; but why don't he go and enthoose in somebody else's vessel? I'm afraid you've been cutting us out an awkward job to get on with that customer."

"I hope not," said Sir Humphrey. "He promises very fairly."

"Yes, sir, but will he perform? You see, if he was an Englishman he might, but I never knew an American yet who liked to play second fiddle in anything. But there, sir, you're chief, and I don't see how, short of going back again to set him ashore, you could have done anything else."

"Thank you, captain," said Sir Humphrey. "I did what I thought was best under the circumstances."

"You did, sir. Squire here—Mr Brace—thought I was going to turn rusty, I suppose."

"I did," said Brace.

"Yes, but I wasn't. I blaze up a bit when I'm put out, gentlemen, but I soon settle down into a steady warm glow, and keep within the bars."

"Then there's an end of an awkward episode, captain," said Sir Humphrey. "I was afraid at one time that we were going to have a tragedy."

"So was I, sir," said the captain sharply. "It's a mercy that ugly-looking yellow monkey of a chap was not smothered in that cask. My word! he must be a plucky fellow!"

"Or too stupid to have grasped the danger," said Brace.

The captain nodded.

"Well, you gentlemen," he said, "I'm going to stop on deck till we're a few miles farther off the shore; so I shall keep Mr Dellow company till it's Lynton's watch, and then I shall turn in. Good night, gentlemen, good night."

"Good night," said the brothers in a breath.

"If you hear it come on to blow before morning, you needn't be surprised, for I think we're going to have a bit of wind. Young Uncle Sam was right about sending a boat ashore with him. She'd never have made the shore, nor the brig again."

Brace looked sharply round, trying to pierce the darkness, but in vain.

Chapter Nine
The Mighty River

Before morning the "Jason" was pitching and tossing in a heavy sea which had risen very suddenly, and for the next week, whenever the brothers cared to face the rain, wind, and spray, they found Captain Banes on deck looking very grim and anxious and evidently in no humour for entering into conversation.

The officers and crew too looked worn and harassed with hard work and the buffeting they had received; but it was evident that they took it all as a matter of course, and were perfectly confident about the ability of the brig to weather a far worse storm.

It was quite bad enough, and prolonged till the pitching of the vessel became very wearisome; but there was one thing which always met the eyes of the brothers when they went on deck, and that was the figure of Briscoe tucked up in the best shelter he could find, beneath bulwark or behind deckhouse, clad in glistening black waterproof; and smoking a big cigar.

He always saw the brothers as soon as they appeared on deck, and if they nodded to him he was quick to respond, but he never forced his company upon them; and it was so too in the cabin, for he was quiet and unobtrusive, speaking readily when spoken to, but only to subside at once when the conversation flagged.

"What has become of his inquisitive organ, Brace?"

"That's what I was thinking: he seems quite a different man."

The storm was over at last, and one morning, as the brig was running due west under a full press of sail, it suddenly struck Brace that the water over the side was not so clear as it had been an hour before when he was leaning over the bulwark gazing down into the crystalline depths, trying to make out fish, and wondering how it was that, though there must be millions upon millions in the ocean through which they were sailing, he could not see one.

"We must be getting into water that has been churned up by the storm," thought Brace; but just then the second mate came up and he referred to him.

"Water not so clear?" he said. "No wonder; we're right off the mouths of the Amazon now."

"So far south?"

"Yes, and running right in. Before long the water, instead of being like this—a bit thick—will be quite muddy, and this time to-morrow we shall be bidding good-bye to the sea, I suppose, for some time to come."

Lynton's words were quite right, for the next day, after a most satisfactory run, Brace stood gazing over the bows of the brig at the thick muddy water that was churned up, and finding it hard to believe that he was sailing up the mouth of a river; for, look which way he would, nothing was to be seen but water, while when he tried his glass it was with no better success.

But at last the land was to be made out on the starboard bow, or rather what was said to be land, a long, low, hazy something on the distant horizon.

A couple of days later there was land plain enough on both sides of the brig, and they commenced a long, dismal progress up stream, of a monotonous kind that was wearisome in the extreme.

As time went on, though, there was a change, and that was followed by plenty of variety in the shape of huge trees, with all their branches and leaves tolerably fresh, floating seaward, just as they had fallen from the bank after the mighty stream had undermined them. In one case there were land birds flitting about the few boughs that appeared above the water, but generally they were gulls snatching at the small fish attracted by the floating object.

Once there was a great matted-together patch of earth fully thirty yards long and half as wide, a veritable island with bushes still in their places, floating steadily seaward, and helping to explain the muddiness of the water and the shallowness of the ocean far out and to right and left of where the great river debouched.

Several consultations took place between the captain and Sir Humphrey as to the course to be taken, and the latter politely asked Briscoe to join in the discussion and give his opinion.

"No," he said; "I shan't say anything. I've only one idea about it, and that is to sail up one of the big rivers that run out of this, one that has not been explored before, so as to get amongst what's new."

"Well, that's what we want, isn't it, Free?" said Brace.

"Exactly."

"Then I needn't interfere in any way, gentlemen," said Briscoe. "I only say choose your river, and let's get to work: only pick one that has banks to it where we can land and do something."

"Then you don't want us to go as far as we can up one of the explored rivers?" said the captain, smiling.

"Certainly not," cried Brace.

"I understand, gentlemen. Give me time, and I'll take you to just the place you want. I know the river, but I never heard its name. It runs, as far as I could make out, due nor'-west: that is, as far as I went up. After that it went no one knows where."

"That's the place," cried Brace. "Is it very big?"

"Tidy, squire," said the captain. "It's very deep, and there's plenty of room for the brig; and, what's better, the current's sluggish, so that we can make our way."

"What about the forest? Is it far back from the waterside?"

"Hangs over it, so that one can send a boat ashore every night with a cable to make fast to one of the great trees, and save letting down and getting up the anchor."

"But about the river itself: can you take the brig up far—no rocks, shoals, or waterfalls?"

"Nothing of the kind, sir," said the captain. "It's all deep, muddy, sluggish water running through a great forest, and I should say it carries off the drainage of hundreds of miles of country. It must come from the mountains right away yonder, and sometimes there must be tremendous rains to flood the stream, for I remember seeing marks of sand and weeds and dry slime thirty or forty feet up some of the trunks, and I should say that at times the whole country's flooded and we shall have to look out to keep from grounding right away from the river's course."

"You will take care of that," said Sir Humphrey, smiling.

"I shall try, sir," said the captain grimly, "for I don't think you'd like to wake up some morning and find the brig in the middle of a forest, waiting till the next flood-time came."

A week later, after being baffled again and again by adverse winds, Brace and his brother stood upon the deck of the brig one evening just as the wind dropped, as if simultaneously with the descent of the sun like a huge globe of orange fire behind a bank of trees a hundred yards to their left. The river, smooth and glassy, glowed in reflection from the ruddy sky, the sails flapped, and, no longer answering to her helm, the vessel was beginning slowly to yield to the sluggish current, when there was a rattling sound as the chain cable ran through the hawse-hole, and directly after the anchor took hold in the muddy bottom, the way on the brig was checked, and she swung in mid-stream with her bowsprit pointing out the direction of her future course—a long open waterway between two rapidly-darkening banks of trees whose boughs drooped over and dipped their muddied tips in the stream.

"Will this do, squire?" said the captain.

"Gloriously," said Brace; "but I thought you meant to make fast every night to one of the trees."

"By-and-by, my lad, by-and-by, when there's a handy tree. This would be bad landing for a boat—all one tangle of jungle, and hard to get through. You wanted to get where it was wild: hear that?"

"Yes," said Brace excitedly, as he heard a long-drawn cry from out of the forest, one which was answered from a distance, while the last cry was replied to faintly from still farther away. "What's that—a jaguar?"

"Monkey," said the captain drily, "and that grunting just beginning and rising into a regular boom isn't made by the pumas, for I don't think there'd be any in these great forest-lands."

"What then?" said Brace, in a low voice, as if awe-stricken by the peculiar sounds.

"Frogs, my lad, frogs."

Quaaak! A peculiarly loud and strident hollow echoing cry, which was startling in its suddenness and resembled nothing so much as a badly-blown note upon a giant trombone.

"What's that?"

"That?" said the captain, thrusting his hat on one side so as to leave ample room for scratching one ear. "That? Oh, that's a noise I only remember hearing once before, and nobody could ever tell me what it was. There's a lot of queer noises to be heard in the forest of a night, and it always struck me that there are all kinds of wild beasts there such as have never been heard of before and never seen."

"I dessay," said a voice behind them which made them both start round and stare at the speaker, who had been leaning over the bulwark unobserved.

"What's that?" said the captain sharply.

"I said I dessay," replied Briscoe; "but that thing isn't one of them."

"What is it then?" said the captain shortly.

"One of those great long-legged crane things that begin work about this time, fishing in the swamps for frogs."

"You think the noise was made by a crane?"

"Sure of it, mister," was the reply. "I've sat up before now at the edge of a swamp to shoot them for specimens, and there's several kinds of that sort of bird make a row like that."

"Humph!" ejaculated the captain gruffly. "You seem to know. Perhaps, then, you'll tell us what made that noise?"

He held up his hand, and all listened to a peculiar whirring sound which began at a distance, came closer and closer till it seemed to pass from under the trees, swing round the ship, and slowly die away again.

"Ah, that!" said Briscoe quietly. "Sounds like someone letting off a firework with a bang at the end gone damp. No, I don't know what that is. Yes, I do," he added hastily. "That's a big bird too."

"Crane?" said the captain, with an incredulous snort.

"No, sir," said the American: "different thing altogether. It's a night bird that flies round catching beetles and moths—bird something like our 'Whip-poor-Wills' or 'Chuck-Will's-widows.'"

"Bah!" said the captain.

"Yes, that's right," cried Brace: "a bird something like our English night-hawk that sits in the dark parts of the woods and makes a whirring sound; only it isn't half so loud as this."

"Well," said the captain grudgingly, "perhaps you're right. I'm not good at birds. I know a gull or a goose or turkey or chicken. I give in."

The strange whirring sound as of machinery came and went again; but the maker was invisible, and attention was taken from it directly by a loud splash just astern.

"Fish!" cried Brace.

"Yes, that's fish," said the captain. "No mistake about that, and you may as well get your tackle to work, squire, for these rivers swarm with 'em, and some of them are good eating. Bit of fish would be a pleasant change if you can supply the cook."

"But it's too dark for fishing," said Brace.

"Better chance of catching something," said the captain. "But that isn't fish; that's something fishing."

There was no need for the captain to draw attention to the fact, for those near him were straining their eyes towards the shore, from which a strange beating and splashing sound arose, but apparently from beyond the black bank of trees formed by the edge of the forest.

"There must be a lake on the other side of the bank," said Brace eagerly.

"No," replied the captain; "only one of the creeks that run inland among the trees. Come, do you know what that is?"

"It sounds like an alligator splashing about in shallow water," replied Brace.

"You've hit it first time, squire. It's a big one lashing about with its tail to stun the fish so that they float up ready for his meal. That's right, isn't it, Mr Briscoe?"

"Quite," said the American. "I've seen them doing it in the Mississippi swamps; but they were only small ones, five or six feet long. This one sounds as if it were a thumper."

"Yes," said Sir Humphrey, "I suppose there are monsters in these waters. Ah!" he continued, as the splashing grew louder; "that sounds like a warning to us not to think of bathing while we are up the river."

"Bathing!" cried the captain. "I should think not. You can't do it here, sir, for, besides alligators and different kinds of pike, these waters swarm with small fish that are always savagely hungry. The big ones are plentiful enough, but the little ones go in shoals and are as ready to attack as the others, and they have teeth like lancets, so take care."

The splashing ceased, and this seemed to be the signal for fresh sounds to arise both up and down the river and from the forest depths on either bank, till the night seemed to be alive with a strange chorus, which, as Brace and his companions listened, culminated in a tremendous crash, followed by a dead silence.

"Whatever is that?" whispered Brace.

"Big tree tumbled," said Briscoe carelessly.

"But there is no wind—there was no lightning."

"No," said the American, "but it had to tumble some time. You often hear that in the woods: they go on growing and growing for hundreds of years, and then they stop from old age and overgrowth, and begin to rot and rot, till all at once, night or day, the top's too heavy for the bottom, and down they come. We'll go and have a look at that one in the morning."

Chapter Ten
In the Black Forest

There was a fascination about that night scene which kept Brace and his brother on deck for hours trying to pierce the black darkness, and whenever they made up their minds that it was time to go down to their berths something was sure to happen in the mysterious forest depths or near at hand in the river.

One time it was a piercing cry as of someone in agony; at another a sneering, chuckling laugh taken up in a chorus as if by a mocking party of strange watchers, who, accustomed to the darkness, could see everything going on aboard the brig; whisperings; sounds of crawling creatures passing over sticky mud and wallowing impatiently in their efforts to get along; peculiar angry barkings uttered by the alligators; and a dreadful rustling in the trees, which Brace felt certain must be caused by huge serpents winding in and out amongst the branches.

He suggested this to the captains who uttered a grunt.

"Very likely," he said. "They do creep about in that way after the monkeys. 'Tis their nature to. This is the sort of country for those gentlemen, both the dry ones and the wet ones."

"I don't understand you," said Brace. "Oh, you mean the boas and the anacondas."

"That's right, squire, and I daresay we shall see some tidy big ones. Yes, that sounds like one working about. Ah! he struck at it and missed, I should say. Bit disappointing, for snakes like their suppers as well as other people, and I'm going down to have mine. Are you coming?"

"No," said Brace decisively; "I'm going to stay up here and listen."

Sir Humphrey and Briscoe elected to do the same, and for another hour they listened, and watched the display made by the fireflies; while every now and then, as the muddy water trickled and seemed to whisper against the sides of the brig, the listeners were startled by some strange splash close by, which sounded to them as if the river swarmed with huge creatures which kept on swimming around and beneath the vessel, partly attracted by curiosity as to the new visitor to their habitat, partly resenting its presence by splashing and beating the surface as they rose or dived.

"It's all very interesting," said Briscoe at last, "and I could stop here all night watching and listening; but we must have sleep, or we shall be no good to-morrow, so I'll say good night, gentlemen. If anything happens, my gun and rifle are both loaded, and I'll come on deck directly."

"That's right," said Brace sharply. "But what can happen?"

"Who can say?" replied the American. "We know we're in a wild country, perhaps the very first of all people who have come so far into the forest, and we don't know what enemies may come. I'm pretty sure of two: stinging insects and fever; but there's no telling what may come out of the dark jungles. We're pretty safe from wild beasts, but for aught we know we may have been watched by savages ever since the morning. Savages generally have canoes, bows, spears, and clubs. I don't say it's likely, but some of them might come creeping aboard in the night, and if I was captain I should arm the watch. Ugh! what's that?" he cried, in a horrified tone.

"Barrel of my rifle, Mr Briscoe," said Lynton quietly, from out of the darkness.

"Why did you do that?" said the American sharply.

"Only to show you that the watch is armed, sir; and if there is anything unpleasant in the night we shan't be long in letting you know."

Another hour passed before Sir Humphrey and his brother went below, and then their first act was to thrust cartridges into their guns and rifles, and to lay them with their ammunition-belts ready to hand; but even after that precaution sleep was slow in coming to Brace's pillow, for he lay listening to the rush, gurgle, and splash of the river till the strange sounds grew confused and died out, all but a peculiar rustling that seemed to be made by a huge serpent creeping among the branches of the trees: and this puzzled the listener, for it was impossible that trees and a huge reptile could be out in the middle of the great muddy river.

Then it seemed that the anchor which held them fast out in mid-stream must have dragged and the brig have been carried by an eddy close in shore, to run aground, so that the masts were tangled with the overhanging boughs.

Thoughts came fast after this, but more and more confused, till they were so mixed that the listener could pick out nothing clear from what had become a mental tangle in which he grew so weary that nothing seemed to matter in the least, and he did not trouble about anything more till a voice said:

"Come, Brace, isn't it time you roused up?"

The reply was a dull thump on the floor caused by the young man rolling out of his berth, to find his brother half-dressed, and that the troubles of the night had been merely dreams, for a glance out of the cabin window showed that the brig's stern was in mid-stream, with the muddy water turned to ruddy gold by the rising sun, in whose rays the current flashed and looked glorious beyond the power of words to paint. The banks of trees which dipped their boughs right into the stream, instead of looking mysteriously black, were also glowing with colour, and in several parts full of moving life, as birds of brilliant hues flitted from bough to bough, and an excited company of active monkeys swung themselves here and there in their eagerness to get a view of the strange object which had invaded their forest home.

It was settled at once over breakfast that a boat should be manned directly after the meal, so that a landing might be effected on one or the other shore, the forest promising endless attractions for the naturalists.

"All right, gentlemen," said Captain Banes; "the boat shall be ready, for there isn't a breath of air this morning."

"Why do you speak like that?" said Sir Humphrey, noting the captain's manner. "What has the wind to do with it?"

"Only that if there was a breeze I should advise you to take advantage of it and go on up the river, for you'll do no good here except by shooting from the boat."

"Oh, but we must land and go up country a bit," cried Brace.

"It isn't to be done, squire," said the captain. "Take your glass when you go on deck, and you'll see that the forest is all one tangle, through which you'd have to cut your way, unless you can find a creek and pole the boat along among the trees."

"There must be a creek in yonder," said Briscoe, "where we heard that great alligator splashing."

"Well, try, gentlemen," said the captain, smiling; "there's nothing done without: only don't go and overdo it, for you'll find it terribly hot and steamy under the trees."

"I'll see to that," said Sir Humphrey quietly; and soon after, well provided with arms and ammunition, the party stepped into the boat, the men dropped their oars into the water with a splash, and in an instant there was a tremendous eddy and a little wave arose, showing the course made by some startled inhabitant of the river—fish or reptile, probably the latter, disturbed from where it had lain in the shadow of the brig.

"Might have had a shot if the water had been clear," said Brace excitedly. "I've got ball in one barrel."

"Good plan," said Briscoe, "for you never know what you may see next. I'd keep an eye upward amongst the low boughs of the trees. Use yours, too, Dan."

Brace was already carrying out that plan, attracted as he was by the sight of parrots and the glimpses of green and scarlet he kept seeing—brilliant tints that evidently formed part of the gorgeous livery worn by the macaws which made a home high up amongst the top branches of the huge trees.

Brace glanced back at the brig swinging in midstream by her chain, with her square sails hanging motionless in the hot air; and then as the men dipped their oars gently, the boat glided close in towards the overhanging boughs, which displayed every tint of rich tropical green.

One was literally covered from the water's edge to its summit with a gorgeous sheet of brilliant scarlet blossoms, over which flitted butterfly and beetle, a very living museum of the most beautiful insects the travellers had ever seen.

"It does not seem as if we need go any farther, Brace," said Sir Humphrey.

"So I was thinking," said the former. "Look at those lovely humming-birds. Why, they're not so big by a long way as the butterflies."

"I was looking," said Sir Humphrey, "and longing for a tiny gun loaded with dry sand or water, to bring some of them down. Look at the bright blue steely gleams of their forked tails."

"No, no," whispered Brace, as if afraid to speak aloud lest the glorious vision of colour should pass away; "I meant those tiny fellows all blue and emerald-green there, with the tufts of snowy-white down above their legs. Oh, what a pity!"

The last words were said as the blaze of blossom and flitting colour passed away, for as the boat glided on they passed in amongst the veil of drooping leaves and twigs which brushed over their heads and shoulders, and were at once in a soft twilight, looking up into a wilderness of trunks and boughs, where for some moments after the sudden change all looked strangely obscure and dense.

But there was plenty to see there as the men laid in their oars and one in the bows thrust out the hook to take hold of a branch here and there and drag the boat along towards a more open part, which soon took the form of a vegetable tunnel, proving to be an arched-in muddy creek, amongst whose overhanging cover something was in motion, but what it was did not become evident for a few minutes in the gloom.

"Is it a great serpent?" said Brace huskily.

"No," said Briscoe quickly. "A party of monkeys playing at follow-my-leader. Look, there they go, close after one another. It looks just like some great reptile, but you can see now. They're afraid of the boat."

He had hardly spoken when the latter quivered from the effects of a sudden concussion.

"Take care," said Sir Humphrey. "You've run upon a sunken trunk."

"No, sir," said the man in the bows, as he held on to a tree with the boat-hook; "that wasn't our doing. It was one of they alligators gave us a slap with his tail. Look at the water. There he goes."

The man was right enough, for the water was eddying violently from the passage of something beneath, and proof was given directly after, by the appearance of a dark gnarled something a few inches above the surface, this something curving over and being in the act of disappearing, when, carried away by the excitement of the moment, Brace raised his double gun, took a quick aim, and fired, with the result that there was a tremendous splash, the appearance of a flattened tail for a moment, and amidst a discordant screaming from overhead, the occupants of the boat had a glimpse of what seemed to be a writhing hank of enormously thick chocolate and tawny-yellow cable, which seemed to have been thrown from above, to fall with another splash into the water some twenty yards in front of where the boat lay. Then there was a momentary gleam of colour as the object writhed and twined, and then the muddy water rose and fell and washed among the trunks which rose straight from the surface, while for a few moments no one spoke, but every eye was directed at the spot where the water quivered as if something was in motion beneath.

"I fired at the alligator," said Brace, turning to his brother with a half-startled look.

"Yes, and scared that big snake," said Briscoe. "He was having a nap tied up in a knot on some big branch. I've seen 'em sometimes hanging over the side in thick folds. You tumbled him over with the startling. Warning to him to take a turn round the branch with his tail."

"Be ready to fire," said Brace hurriedly. "It is sure to come up again to try and creep into a tree."

"No," said Briscoe quietly. "He won't show himself again for hours."

"Nonsense," said Brace impatiently; "it would be drowned."

Briscoe smiled good-humouredly.

"Drowned?" he said. "Just about as much as an eel would. Nice place this for a bathe, what with the alligators and the anacondas. Not much chance for a man if one of those brutes took hold of him. Pull him under in a moment."

"Do you think one of those creatures would attack in the water?" said Sir Humphrey.

"I've seen one drag a pig down," said Briscoe. "They're as much at home in the water as out, and they can swim as easily as a water-snake."

"Then there's nothing to prevent that thing from thrusting out its head and seizing one of us," said Brace.

" The man with the boat-hook went on drawing the

"Nothing at all," replied Briscoe, and then he smiled as he saw the men exchanging glances and Dan taking out a keen bowie-knife. "But he won't. He'll lie down below there among the roots for hours, I daresay. If he did come up of course we should give him a shot."

"Ugh!" said Brace, shuddering. "But what are we going to do?"

"Push on up the creek," said his brother. "We may come to an open part. Go on, my lads."

The man with the boat-hook went on catching the boughs and drawing the boat along, and twice over a splash and the following movement of the water amongst the mossy, muddy tree-trunks told of the presence of some loathsome reptile; but the men sat fast, gazing stolidly to right and left in search of danger, and more than once Brace gave a glance at his double gun as if to see that it was cocked and ready.

The sensation was not pleasant, and it attacked everyone in the boat. The American might be right, they thought, and the serpent remain startled and quiescent down in the depths of the muddy water, but still they felt the possibility of that terrible head darting out at a victim, and a low sigh of relief rose again and again as the distance from where the serpent fell increased.

It was plain enough now that they were in a winding creek whose sides were dense with trunks and branches forming an impenetrable barrier had there been the slightest inclination to land; but all thought of this passed away almost from the beginning. In fact, it was perfectly clear that the only way to penetrate the forest was to go up some waterway such as the one they were in, and this they followed slowly for a few hundred yards, the man with the boat-hook cleverly guiding the vessel in and out amongst the many obstacles, till the place grew darker and darker through the density of the foliage overhead.

The creek was for the most part painfully still—painfully, for the weird gloom raised up the idea that thousands of eyes were watching their movements, and that at any moment some terrible attack might be made.

That they were surrounded by living creatures they had ample proof given them by strange rustlings among the branches overhead, and sometimes by a sudden hasty rush which, as Briscoe said, might be anything.

"What do you mean by anything?" said Brace, in a low voice.

"Snake, monkey, big bird, or cat; but, you see, everything is afraid of us and scuffling away as hard as it can, even in the water. Look at that."

"Yes, I see," said Brace, "another alligator."

For the American had drawn his attention to a wave raised up by something rushing past the bows of the boat.

"Well, I don't know about that," said Briscoe; "I rather fancy that was one of those gar-fish—alligator gars, they call 'em in the States. They're great pikey fish with tremendous teeth."

"But not big like that?"

"Oh, but they're big enough and precious fierce and strong. I shouldn't wonder at all if that was one of the brutes."

"What's that?" asked Sir Humphrey, a couple of hours later, for the man with the boat-hook turned and spoke.

"Don't see as I can get any farther, sir; the boat's about wedged in here, and there don't seem any way of getting on without we had a saw."

"Is there no room to right or left?" said Brace. "It seems a pity to go back yet."

"P'raps you'd take a look, gen'lemen," said the sailor.

Brace was in the act of laying down his gun when his brother, who was before him, stood up, and then uttered a sharp ejaculation, close upon a dull twanging sound from somewhere forward among the trees.

"What is it, Free?" cried Brace excitedly.

"An arrow," said Sir Humphrey sharply. "Here, quick, Brace; it may be poisoned. You, Mr Briscoe, keep a good look-out for—"

The rest of his speech was stopped by the sharp report of the American's gun, who fired as he half-knelt in the stern of the boat, aiming just above the men's heads.

The next moment he and his man fired again, and as the report died out the occupants of the boat could hear a splashing sound as of paddles some little distance in advance.

Chapter Eleven
Grim Danger

Brace felt an icy chill run through him, and for a few moments he was paralysed.

Not longer, for directly after a thrill of excitement set every nerve throbbing.

Laying down his gun, he snatched his knife from its sheath, thrust the point inside the sleeve of his brother's flannel shirt, ripped it to the shoulder, and laid bare the great white biceps muscle, in which the head of an arrow was embedded, so nearly passing through that as Brace placed his hand beneath the arm he could feel the point of the missile.

"Don't hesitate," whispered Sir Humphrey. "Poisoned or not poisoned, that arrow must be extracted. Will you cut down to it or shall I let Briscoe?"

"I'll do it," said Brace, through his set teeth; "but I can't help hurting you, Free: I must do that."

"Go on. Act," said his brother firmly. "*I'm* not a child. Cut boldly."

Brace placed the point of the knife close to the shaft of the arrow, his hand trembling so that he could not keep the point still. Then he was as firm as a rock, for the thought came to him that he must be doing wrong to make so terrible a cut, and he knew that he risked dividing some important vessel.

The knife fell into the bottom of the boat with a loud jangling sound, for the right idea had come, and Brace played the surgeon as if he had been trained to the profession.

Keeping his left hand beneath his brother's arm just clear of the raised skin where the point of the arrow pressed, he seized the shaft firmly, gave a sudden thrust, and forced the arrow-head right through, keeping up the pressure till both barbs were well clear, and with them four or five inches of the thin bamboo.

"Now, one of you," he cried to Dan, "pick up my knife and cut through the arrow."

The man grasped the idea, and with one cut divided the shaft, while in less time than it takes to tell it Brace pulled with his left hand, and the part of the shaft in the wound was drawn right through, while the blood began to flow.

The next moment Brace's lips were applied to the wound, first on one side and then on the other, making it bleed more freely; and this he supplemented by holding his brother's arm over the side and bathing and pressing the wound.

"It may be a false alarm, lad," said Sir Humphrey, speaking slowly and calmly; "but it is as well to take the precaution."

"Yes, of course," said Brace huskily, and his heart sank low and the chill of dread increased, for as he sucked the wound where the arrow had entered he was conscious of a strange pungent acid taste, which clung to his lips and caused a stinging sensation at the tip of his tongue.

He scooped up a little water in the hollow of his hand and then snatched it away, flinging the water over his brother's face, for he was conscious of a sharp pricking sensation as if he had scarified the skin against a thorn.

But he plunged his hand into the water again and raised it quickly to his mouth to wash away the bitter taste before applying his lips once more to the wounded arm.

This time the water reached his mouth, but he felt a repetition of the pricking in his fingers, and to his astonishment two tiny silvery fish fell into the bottom of the boat, while he found that two of his fingers were red.

But he had no time to think of self, and he worked hard bathing and encouraging the bleeding from both orifices of the wound and applying his lips to them again and again.

Sir Humphrey was sitting motionless in the bottom of the boat with his back against the side, bearing the pain he suffered patiently, and lighting bravely to master the mental agony which attacked him with suggestions of all the horrors that attend a poisoned wound.

Meanwhile Briscoe had not been idle. The keen inquisitiveness of his nature was now shown in a very different way, for his eyes were searching the depths of the forest as he peered through the gloom among the dimly-seen trunks again, and he fired twice in the direction from which the splashing of paddles had been heard.

He never turned his head nor shifted his eyes for a moment from that point, reloading by touch alone, while after he had fired the first shot he took upon himself to give orders to the sailors in a stern, firm voice.

"Get back to the brig as fast as you can, my lads."

It was not until he had assured himself of the fact that their enemy was in retreat that he turned for a moment to where Brace was busy with his amateur surgery.

"That's right," he said; "I shouldn't bandage it up yet. Let it bleed, in case the arrow was smeared with anything nasty. It's hardly likely that it was, though."

As he spoke he picked up the barbed head, glanced at it, and then slipped it into his pocket in the most indifferent way.

"I wouldn't fidget about that," he said to Sir Humphrey. "Most of the things we hear are old women's tales. Here, hold my gun," he added sharply to his man.

He thrust an arm round Sir Humphrey, just as his eyes were closing and he glided slowly along the side of the boat.

The next moment he too leaned over to scoop up some water and trickle it over the fainting man's face.

"Bah!" he ejaculated, "how sharp they are!" For a little silvery fish, which in company with a shoal had darted at his finger, fell with a pat on the wounded man's breast, and lay quivering and leaping till it disappeared through the grating at the bottom of the boat.

"Does that fainting mean danger?" cried Brace excitedly.

"Oh, no. Let his head go right down, and he'll soon come to."

"But you are of opinion that the arrow was poisoned," whispered Brace, in a whisper which was expressive of painful anxiety.

"It had been smeared with some stuff by an ignorant savage; but it may not be poisonous to human beings, and even if it were you've been drawing it all away from the wound."

"Oh, make haste, men; make haste," cried Brace excitedly.

"Let 'em be, my lad," said Briscoe; "they're doing their best. Come, keep cool, for your brother's sake."

"Oh, don't talk like that," cried Brace wildly. "Look at him: he's dying and we right away in the forest like this."

"You keep cool," said the American sternly. "He isn't dying nor anything like it. Only fainting from the shock, and he'll soon come to. It won't help him for you to turn hysterical like a girl. You began right; now keep it up."

"What, shall I go on doing something to the wound?"

"No, I'd let that be now. You must have cleared it from anything that wiped off as the arrow passed in, and he's a strong, brave fellow. There, look: he's coming to."

Sir Humphrey's eyelids had begun to quiver, and at the end of a few minutes he had quite recovered consciousness.

He lay back gazing straight up at the boughs of the trees, beneath which they were passing more quickly now, for they were gliding along with the current; but twice over he let his eyes rest upon those of his brother, and he lightly pressed the young man's hand.

"It's very unlucky," he said. "So unexpected and uncalled for. I hardly expected that we should have to encounter this."

"They're a treacherous lot," said Briscoe quietly. "It's enough to make a man fire upon them at sight. Wound hurt much?"

"It feels as if a red-hot iron had been thrust through it," said Sir Humphrey.

"Glad of it," said the American, who was taking the affair in a very calm manner.

"What!" exclaimed Brace, as he turned round quickly with flashing eyes.

"Glad of it, sir. Good sign. Fine, healthy pain. Now, if it had felt numb and dull I shouldn't have liked it, for it would have sounded as if something nasty was on the arrow. There, you keep a good heart, and we'll soon have you back on board. Then you can have a few hours' sleep, and you'll be all right by night."

"I hope so," said Sir Humphrey calmly, and he closed his eyes once more, while Brace turned his upon his companion with a look full of wild anxiety, but only to receive a quiet nod and a reassuring smile in return.

"I don't think there are any more near," said Briscoe, "and I don't want to have the unpleasant feeling upon my conscience that I've killed a fellow-creature; but if any more of them send arrows in this direction, Dan and I will shoot at sight, and we're uncommonly good shots."

He had hardly uttered the last words when there was a sharp whirr as if a beetle had darted by the speaker's ear, and they could see an arrow stuck quivering in a tree the boat was just passing, while Dan immediately sent a charge of buckshot crashing among the leaves.

Old Gold: Cruise of the "Jason" Brig |

"That was a bad aim," said the American, facing sharply round, "and I can't see who sent it. Can you make out a bit of dark skin anywhere among the bushes, Dan?"

The man shook his head as he quickly reloaded his weapon, and there was a grumbling murmur in the negative.

The rustling, washing sound of the water beneath the boat as the men urged it along with all their might, everyone giving a thrust with his oar whenever he could reach a tree, was now the only thing that disturbed the silence.

But the opening out of the creek into the river seemed as far off as ever, and Brace's agony increased as he kept watching for the bright sunshine flashing from the water, but only to turn his eyes back to where his brother lay with his face looking very hard and drawn.

"Can't get a glimpse of anyone," said Briscoe; "and I don't think it's of any use to fire to scare 'em. Whoever fired that last shot must be on the land, for there's no sign of a boat. Does anyone of you hear paddling?"

"No, no. We can't hear anything moving," came in chorus.

Then Brace spoke out excitedly: "Surely we ought to be back in the river by this time! Have we missed our way?"

"Well, I don't like to say we have," replied the American; "but it does seem a very long time before we get out of this watery swamp. Hold hard a minute, my lads, and try and make out how the stream runs."

The men ceased thrusting at the tree-trunks as soon as Briscoe had given the word, and by slow degrees the boat came to a stand, and then began to float back in the opposite direction to that in which they had been forcing it.

"Why, we're going wrong," cried one of the men excitedly, springing up.

"Well, never you mind," said the American sharply. "Just you sit down and wait for orders. We'll tell you which way to go."

"But—" began the man.

"Silence, sir!" cried Briscoe sharply. "All! look out!"

An arrow stuck in the side of the boat so close to Brace that it passed through his loose flannel shirt, pinning it to the wood; and Briscoe swung himself round and fired sharply in the direction from which it had come.

The shot rattled among the leaves, and they and a few twigs came pattering down into the water, while directly after there was another report from right away to their left.

"Hah! that must have come from the brig," cried Brace.

"Right," said Briscoe. "Now then, lads, you know which way to punt her along: the creek opens out and winds about in all sorts of ways, and I daresay we could wander in a regular maze for hours; but we know which direction to make for now. You listen keenly for the next answer to my shot, Mr Brace, for I'll fire again soon: only I should like something to fire at. See that arrow?"

"Yes," said Brace, stretching out his hand to withdraw the arrow from where it had pierced the side of the boat.

"Don't do that; let it be, and draw your flannel over the feathering. Look at the slope it takes. I fancy the man who shot that must have been seated on the branch of a tree."

"It may have been shot from a distance and taken a curve."

"No," said Briscoe; "there are too many boughs for it to have come through. It was sent from pretty close, I should say; and between ourselves I hope we shan't have any more. Ah, that's right, my lads. She's moving nicely now. I only wish you were able to row."

"Same here, sir," growled the man handling the boat-hook; "and we wish you could bring down one of they savages as keeps on trying to hit the target, meaning we. This sort of thing aren't pleasant here in the dark."

The American nodded, as his eyes literally glittered in the gloomy shades, for he kept on turning them in all directions, and then with his face lighting up he took a quick aim and fired away to his right, scattering leaves and sending them pattering down; but apparently with no other effect save that there was another shot fired, and certainly from a much nearer point.

Just then the men gave a cheer, for as they urged the boat in the direction of the spot whence came the last shot, they caught sight of a bright ray of light.

Five minutes later there was a distinct lightening of the gloom, and before many more minutes had passed the boat was forced out suddenly through a curtain of drooping boughs into the dazzling light of the open river.

The "Jason" was riding at anchor quite a quarter of a mile lower down the stream, while close in shore was another of the brig's boats, standing up in whose stern the unmistakeable figure of Captain Banes was seen.

Chapter Twelve
Aboard the Brig Again

The two boats reached the anchored vessel about the same time, and Sir Humphrey, who looked ghastly, was carefully lifted on board and borne down into the cabin, where the captain examined the injured arm.

Brace watched his countenance anxiously while he was doing so, feeling, as he did, ready to cling to the first hand extended to him in his terrible difficulty, for his brother lay back now half-insensible and as if overcome by a terrible feeling of drowsiness. The young man stood silently waiting for the captain to speak.

"Now then, squire," said the captain grimly, after his long examination, "do you want to hear what I think of this?"

"Yes, yes, of course I do, captain," cried Brace excitedly.

"Then look here, squire, I'm not a doctor nor a surgeon; but a skipper who goes on long voyages all over the world gets to know something about physic as well as about broken bones and out-o'-joints, cuts, and scratches."

"Yes, of course, I know that," said Brace, who was becoming very anxious about his brother's condition, and could not understand how the captain could remain so calm and unmoved.

"Well, then, this is just the same as a cut, only it happens to be a deep one that goes right through the arm."

"Yes, yes, I know that," said Brace impatiently. "But—"

"Wait a bit, squire. You young chaps are always in such a hurry. Now, I was going to say that your brother here, being a fine healthy man who don't take liberties with his constitution, all there'd be to do would be to tie up the cut and make him a sling for his arm, keep the wound clean, and wait patiently till it had grown together again."

"But don't you see it's a wound from an arrow? Talk low, or he will hear you."

"Not he," said the captain; "he don't understand a word we're saying—poor chap! He's quite unconscious. I know what you mean about the poison, and I've seen a man once who had a poisoned arrow shot into him."

"And did he look like my brother does now?"

"Not a bit, my lad; and I fancy that if there was any poison on the arrow that went through your brother's arm, you pretty well sucked it out and washed it away."

"Then you don't think there is any danger?" asked Brace.

"That's right, squire. I don't think there's any danger. Mind, I say *think*, for I'm not a proper qualified man."

"But you can tell me your candid opinion about my brother's wound," said Brace.

"Well," replied the captain, "I'll go so far as to say that if I'd got that hole through my arm I should be very savage, I should make use of some language, and I should say I'd shoot every Indian I saw with a bow and arrows, and of course I shouldn't do it; but I don't think I should make myself uncomfortable about it any more, but just leave it to Nature to cure."

"You think that he will recover, then?" said Brace eagerly.

"I do," said the captain. "What have you got to say about it, mister?"

He turned to the American as he spoke, and Briscoe, who had been keenly watching the half-insensible patient all the time Brace and the captain had been speaking, rose up slowly.

"I'm not a doctor, skipper," he said, "and the only experience I have had in this way has been with rattlesnake bites."

"Well, that's near enough for me, sir," said the captain tartly. "I should say that the difference between the symptoms of a wound from a poisoned arrow and one caused by a poisoned tooth wouldn't be very great."

"Perhaps not," said Briscoe thoughtfully. "Well, I don't quite like this drowsiness that has come over our patient; it's 'most as if he had been given a dose of opium to soothe the pain. It is the only bad symptom I see."

"Don't say you're no doctor, sir," said Captain Banes, with a low chuckle, "because it seems to me that you are."

"Why do you think so?" said Briscoe, looking at him wonderingly.

"Because you've put your finger down on the exact spot directly."

"I do not understand you."

"Why, I mean this. What did I do, squire, when you and I were alone in the cabin when we first brought your brother aboard?"

"You gave him a part of a glass of water with some laudanum in it."

"To be sure I did, to calm down the pain; and that was what I call laudanum and Mr Briscoe here calls opium."

"Then I agree with you, Captain Banes, that there are no bad symptoms at present," said Briscoe quickly. "Let us leave him to sleep off the effect of what you have given him, and see how he looks when he wakes up."

"Eh? What is it, Dellow?" said the captain sharply, for the first mate appeared at the door of the cabin.

"We want to know what's to be done," said the mate.

"What about?" asked the captain. "What's the matter?"

"Three arrows have come aboard since you came down."

"Were you able to see who shot them?" said the captain.

"No."

"Is there any wind?"

"Not enough to fill a sail," was the mate's response.

"Humph! and it's no use to drop down lower, because I expect the Indians have canoes. Keep the men all under cover of the bulwarks, and you and Lynton can take a couple of rifles and amuse yourselves shooting any wild beasts you see on the starboard bow. But mind you all keep well under cover. You understand?"

"Oh, yes, I understand," said the mate, smiling in a peculiar way; and he went to the arms rack and took down two rifles and ammunition-belts for the second mate and himself.

"Hold hard a minute," said the captain. "Just understand this, Dellow: if they leave you alone you leave them alone. If they don't they must take the consequences."

"I understand," said the mate coolly. "How's Sir Humphrey going on, sir? Is there any danger?" This was to Brace.

"The captain and Mr Briscoe think there is nothing to be alarmed about," was the reply. "I hope they are right."

"So does everybody, sir," said the mate warmly. "He seems to be sleeping easy like."

Brace nodded.

"Well, he wouldn't be doing so if poison had got hold of him."

"Right, Dellow," said the captain, nodding his head with satisfaction. "Look here, squire, you try and make your mind a bit easy."

"I am going to," replied Brace.

"Well, then, let Sir Humphrey have a good sleep while you go on deck with Dellow here, and take your rifle with you too. You're a good shot, and ought to be able to bring some of those foreign archers to their senses."

"I came to collect natural-history specimens," said Brace warmly. "I don't want to slaughter ignorant savages."

"Then you don't believe in that Italian law?" said the captain, with a chuckle.

"Which Italian law do you mean?" said Brace, staring.

"Well, Roman-Latin then, if you like. It's all the same, isn't it—old Italian *Lex talionis*. That means, serve out the chap who has served you out, don't it?"

"Something of the kind," said Brace, smiling. "No, I don't want to take revenge on those who are perhaps innocent."

"Just as you like, sir," said the captain, rather gruffly; "though I don't see where the innocence comes in. But, setting aside taking revenge, I suppose you won't mind helping to defend the vessel if some of these fellows should come off in their canoes to attack us?"

"Why, of course not," said Brace warmly. "You know I would do my best."

"To be sure I do, squire," said the captain, smiling. "Well, then, suppose you go and help Dellow and Lynton, and I daresay Mr Briscoe will join you as well."

"Certainly, captain," said the American: "a few shots now may give the Indians a lesson, and save us from having to fire hundreds later on. Perhaps it will be the means of preventing them from molesting us again."

"But is anyone to remain with my brother?" said Brace.

"He wants no watching, my lad. He's best left alone. You can come down now and again to have a look at him."

Chapter Thirteen
A Sight of the Enemy

Brace hesitated for a few moments before making any move to go on deck. Then, seeing Briscoe go to the arms rack and return with rifle and ammunition, he followed his example and went on deck, to find the brig swinging gently by its cable and the crew all lying about on the deck to shelter themselves from the sun as well as from the Indians, two of whose arrows were just as they had fallen, sticking upright in the white boards, between the seams of which the pitch was beginning to ooze out, looking bright and sticky in the sun.

"Lie down, sir, lie down!" shouted Dan, and Briscoe dropped flat upon the deck at once, his rifle clattering against the boards; but before Brace was down, a couple of arrows came *ping, ping,* to stick in the deck, while a third pierced and hung in one of the sails, a fourth dropping with a hiss a little short of the brig and into the water.

"This is nice, Mr Brace," cried Lynton, laughing. "It's as the circus clown said, too dangerous to be safe."

"Yes," said Dellow, who was crawling towards the starboard bulwark on hands and knees, dragging two rifles after him. "Come and lay hold of one, Jem. Mind you don't shoot yourself. It's the wooden end of the rifle that you have to put up against your shoulder, and the hole in the iron barrel which you are supposed to point at the enemy."

"Is it now?" said the second mate sarcastically. "I'm much obliged and thankye for telling me. You put the bullet in at that end of the gun too, don't you, and push it through with the ramrod like a popgun, eh?"

"Yes, that's right," said Dellow, chuckling; "but hit the poor fellows soft the first time so as not to hurt 'em much. If they get saucy afterwards, why then you must hit hard."

"All right; I'll mind," said Lynton, looking at Brace and smiling; "but this ought to be stopped, for the niggers are wonderfully clever at hitting the brig. They shoot right up into the air and guess at their aim, so that the arrows seem to come down out of the sky."

"Yes," said Brace, who was now gradually beginning to take an excited interest in the encounter with the natives; "it's the way they shoot the floating turtles, so that their arrows pierce the shell instead of glancing off."

"There's another," said Dellow. "Well, I wish they'd keep to their turtles. I don't like them practising on me. What's that one like, Mr Brace? Is the point broken?"

"No," said Brace, who had crept sidewise along the deck so as to reach the last arrow that had come on board, and carefully drawn it out, to sit examining the head.

"Poisoned?" asked the mate.

"I'm afraid so," replied Brace. "Look at this stuff lying in the groove," and he pointed to what appeared to be some kind of gum, adhering to the roughly-made head.

"Ah! looks nasty," said Briscoe; "but it isn't obliged to be dangerous to human beings. You see, they use their arrows principally for small game. I don't believe, mind you, that your brother's going to be much the worse for his trouble."

"I sincerely hope not," said Brace, with a sigh.

"So does everybody, sir," said the mate. "But come: it's our turn now. Let's see if we can't stop this game before some of us are hit."

"Yes," said Briscoe, who had taken up, examined, and then smelt the arrow-head, ending by moistening a paper which he drew from his pocket and rubbing the arrow-point thereon, with the result that the paper received a brownish smear and the soft iron became clear.

After a few moments he said:

"There is no doubt about the arrows having been dipped in something, and we must not run any more risks."

Brace experienced a chilly feeling as he thought of his brother, but he made an effort to master the nervous dread by devoting himself to the task they had in hand.

"The arrows seem to come from the foot of that great tree," he said, pointing to where a giant rose high above the heads of its neighbours and sent forth huge boughs, the lowermost of which swept the surface of the river.

"I fancy they come from some twenty feet up," said Briscoe thoughtfully.

"You're right, sir," said his servant. "Look at that," and he drew his master's attention to a shaft which just at that moment rose from out of the densest part of the tree, described an arch, and fell upon the deck.

"I can't see him," cried Lynton, who was crouching in the shelter of the bulwark; "but I fancy I can make out where he is."

"Try," said the mate, and the next minute Lynton fired, his bullet cutting the leaves of the pyramid of verdure, and the report startling a flock of bright green birds, which flew screaming across to the opposite bank of the river.

"A miss," said the mate. "Now you try, sir. It's random work though."

Brace felt a shrinking sensation, but he knew that the time had come for action, and rested his rifle upon the bulwark and sent the bullet hurtling through the densest part of the tree.

"Bravo! Well done!" cried Briscoe.

"What is it?" said Brace eagerly. "I couldn't see for the smoke."

"I could," said the mate. "There was somebody there, and, hit or no, your shot startled him, for I saw something go crashing down through the boughs. I believe you've finished him, and we shall have no more arrows from there."

"Think there was only one of them then?" said Lynton.

"Oh, no, my lad; there's no knowing how many there are of the beauties, but I fancy there's one the less."

The mate had hardly spoken before another arrow stuck in the deck, its inclination showing that it had come from an entirely fresh direction. But it had hardly touched the deck with a dull rap before the American's rifle uttered its sharp crack, and the bullet sent the leaves of a tree some distance farther to the left pattering down.

"That looks as though there were some more of them about," said the mate gruffly, and he knelt in shelter, keenly watching for his opportunity of delivering a shot.

Just then the captain came on deck, and Brace hurried to meet him. He did not speak, but looked at the captain with questioning eyes.

"Sound asleep, squire," said Captain Banes, in answer to Brace's mute enquiry. "Well, how many have you brought down?" Then, without waiting for an answer, he continued: "I don't suppose there are above half a dozen of them. Just a hunting party in a canoe. Look here, Dellow, we shall have to try to scare them away before they do any more mischief."

"Well, we are scaring them," said the mate gruffly. "I believe we've brought down two."

"But they keep on shooting," said the captain, as another arrow came on board not far from the spot where they were sheltering, "and I can't say I want to have one of those things sticking into me."

"What shall we do then?" said the mate.

"Here, you," cried the captain to one of the men, "go and tell the cook to stick the poker in the galley fire."

The man went on all fours along the deck nearly as actively as a dog, and his fellows laughingly cheered him, even the captain smiling grimly before turning once more to the mate.

"Get one of those little flannel bags of powder and load the brass gun. You can point her towards where the blackguards are, and she'll go off with such a roar that it may startle them and send them paddling for their lives."

"Maybe it will," said the mate gruffly; "but I doubt it."

"Never mind your doubts, my lad. It won't cost much to try. I don't suppose they ever heard a cannon fired in their lives, and they'll think we've got the thunder to help us. We'll run a double charge in: the brass gun will stand it."

"Suppose she bursts?" said the mate rather sourly.

"Suppose?" said the captain sharply. "There, you do what I tell you. If she does burst I shall have fired her, and she'll kill me, and you'll be skipper, so you're all right."

"No, I shan't," said the mate gruffly, "for she'll kill me. I'm going to fire her myself."

"Load her then," said the captain, chuckling, "and don't go on setting a mutinous example to the men. Squire Brace looks quite startled."

The mate smiled grimly and went below, to return with a couple of little flannel bags and crawl with them to where the little signal cannon was lashed to the deck.

Brace followed, preferring to assist in the preparation of this experiment to firing in the direction of naked savages.

"Here, I shall be having all the skin rubbed off my knees," said the mate, nodding at Brace. "Nature never meant me to go along like a four-footed beast."

"It is awkward," said Brace, smiling.

"Awkward isn't the word for it," grumbled the mate. "Got your knife handy?"

Brace nodded, and drew it from his pocket, and the mate slit open one of the bags so as to pour about half its contents into the mouth of the little cannon.

"It's all very fine of the skipper to talk," he said, placing the whole cartridge now in its place, "but I'm very fond of the first mate of the 'Jason' brig, and I should be sorry to do him any mischief. I should look well, I should, if I had to go back home as a ghost to tell my wife all my bits had been eaten by the savage fish in this river. I know her ideas well, and she wouldn't like it, I can tell you. There you are; down it goes," he continued, taking the little rammer from where it was strapped to the carriage and driving the bag home on to the top of the loose charge. "Is the powder up, sir?"

"Yes," said Brace; "the touch-hole's full."

"That's right, then. Avast there; be smart with that red-hot poker."

The man who had taken it to the galley trotted away again in his dog-like fashion, disappeared, and then came into sight again directly, to shout out to the mate:

"Cook says it aren't half hot enough, sir."

"Bring the poker," roared the mate. "Told you to fetch it, didn't I? What do I want with what the cook says?"

The man darted into the galley again and reappeared directly with the poker. The other men commenced roaring with laughter when they saw him, for he limped aft like a lame dog now, one hand being occupied with the poker.

"Ahoy there!" shouted the captain; "be smart with that gun. Look out."

For just then the prow of a good-sized canoe appeared from beneath the overhanging boughs of the trees, and was paddled out quickly by four men, while two more stood in the stern fitting arrows to their bows.

"Steady!" growled the mate, as he slewed the mouth of the cannon round in the direction of the coming boat. "Now then, pass me that poker. Here, Mr Brace, you'd better get into shelter away from the pieces. That's right, my lad. Be off."

The man trotted back and settled himself down under the bulwark, and just then Brace laid hold of the poker.

"Let me fire," he said.

"What, aren't you skeart, sir?" said the mate, with a grin, as he relaxed his hold.

"Not very much," said Brace quietly; "only that the poker isn't hot enough."

"She'll do it, my lad. One moment; there's nothing except the wad inside, but I may as well sight the gun at the enemy and let 'em have the benefit of the blast."

Brace stood back from the gun for a moment or two while the mate ran his eye along the little barrel, and then as the canoe was within forty yards the latter cried:

"Now then, sir; let 'em have it."

Brace applied the end of the poker to the loose grains lying in the little rounded depression about the touch-hole of the cannon; but the cook was right: the poker was far from hot, and the end failed to ignite the powder.

"Have you a match?" said Brace, impatiently throwing the implement down.

"No," was the reply. "A match over here, someone."

Men began fumbling; but at sea men chew their tobacco instead of smoking, and no box was forthcoming. At that moment Brace tried again, for, though wanting in the power to ignite the priming at the end, the poker was fairly hot a few inches from the point, and he noted that it was making the pitch bubble in the seam it lay across.

"Sight the gun again," cried Brace hurriedly, and the mate sprang to obey his order, exposing his head and shoulders in doing so, and very nearly paying the penalty, for a couple of arrows whizzed by pretty closely.

Directly after, in response to another touch from the middle of the poker, there was a flash, a puff of white smoke, and a roar like thunder. The gun-carriage in its recoil leaped from the deck and fell with a loud bang upon its side, while the crew burst into a hearty cheer.

The effect of the shot had been beyond the captain's expectation. In their utter astonishment and dread the Indians had to a man sprung out of the canoe, overturning it in the act, and were swimming and diving their best to reach the shelter of the hanging boughs, while their frail vessel was floating bottom upward rapidly down the stream.

"Good aim, Dellow," cried the captain. "Well fired, squire."

Brace glanced at the result of the shot, and then darted to the companion-ladder, to hurry down into the cabin so as to see what the consequences of the heavy report had been there, for in the hurry and excitement of the preparations he had for the moment forgotten his brother.

To his surprise and satisfaction, however, Sir Humphrey lay back sleeping heavily, with a soft dew beading his face, and evidently perfectly free from suffering.

Brace laid his hand upon his brother's forehead, to feel that it was comparatively cool, and upon touching his wrist it was to find the pulse beating steadily and well.

The next minute he was stepping gently back, and ascended once more to the deck.

"Oh, here he is," said the captain. "Look sharp, squire, if you want a shot at the blackguards before they get into shelter."

"Not I," said Brace half-angrily. "Ah, look, look!"

There was no need for him to shout, for a wild cry drew the attention of all to one of the swimmers, who suddenly threw up his arms and then began to beat the surface wildly, but only for a second or two, before with a couple of sharp jerks he was dragged under water, while another cry from the savage nearest to the shore gave warning that his was to be a similar fate, one jerk, however, sufficing to drag him under, just as his companions reached the shelter of the trees.

"Horrid," growled the captain, as, evidently satisfied that there were no others to shoot, he stood close to the bulwark.

"What was it drew them under?" said Brace hoarsely.

"Can't say, squire," replied the captain. "Might be alligators, snakes, or a shoal of the savage fish that swarm along these rivers. Lesson to us not to try bathing."

"Could nothing be done for them? Can we launch a boat?" faltered Brace.

The captain shook his head slowly, frowning the while.

"Impossible, my lad; but we don't know that we're safe here. There may be scores more in hiding under the trees by the bank yonder; so keep down, everyone."

The order was obeyed, but no more arrows came on board, while from behind the deckhouse Brace stood with Briscoe watching the upturned canoe growing smaller and smaller in the distance, Brace expecting to see some daring swimmer appear from the shore, trying to get on board.

He said something of the kind to Lynton, who joined them just before the canoe disappeared round a curve of the river, but the latter smiled before he made a reply.

"You forget what sort of a shore it is," he said. "Those fellows could not get along through that jungle a quarter so fast as the canoe drifted with the stream, if they could get along at all. Well, it's been a bad time for them: they've lost their boat and two of their crew."

"And serve 'em right," said Dellow, who had overheard the conversation. "They should have left us alone. It isn't their fault that Sir Humphrey isn't lying below there dead and cold instead of getting better fast."

"Ah! you have seen him, then?" cried Brace anxiously.

"Been below with the skipper, sir, and there won't be much the matter by this time to-morrow if the savages leave us alone."

Chapter Fourteen
A False Alarm

"It's my opinion," said Captain Banes, "that when the sun goes down a breeze will spring up; and I mean to get as far up as I can before it is too dark to see, for the sooner we're out of this neighbourhood the better."

"Do you think there's a village of these people near?" asked Brace.

"Oh, no; there may be a few huts with the wives and children close at hand, but so far as I know there are only a few of them here and there up the rivers leading a hunting and fishing life."

But the captain's prophecy was not fulfilled. There was a little ripple on the water for a few minutes after sundown, but not enough breeze to fill out a sail, and the darkness came on with the brig swinging easily by the creaking cable, which ground and fretted in the hawse-holes.

"Now, squire," said the captain, turning to Brace, "how's it going to be? Shall we be all right here at anchor, or will those chaps who got ashore hunt up all their friends and come off in canoes when it's dark, to kill us and sack the brig?"

"I'm not experienced enough to say," replied Brace, smiling. "What do you think?"

"I think I don't know, my lad: it's as likely to be one way as the other. What do you say to dividing the crew and passengers into two watches, all well armed and ready for the worst? One watch on deck, the other below, just lying down in our clothes with a rifle for a bedfellow, ready to run up at the first call."

"I should say it would be very wise," said Brace, "and I think we had better do it."

"But there's another way, my lad: suppose we up anchor and drop down with the stream for a few miles before letting go again."

"I don't like going backward," said Brace, "and we might be getting into a worse place."

"Out of the frying-pan into the fire, eh? Right: so we'll stop here and be fried."

The division was made, and soon after dark Brace found himself keeping a sharp look-out on deck in company with Briscoe and part of the crew, the captain taking the first watch, while the first and second mates were below with half the men, ready to rush up at the first summons.

This plan was quite in accordance with Brace's wishes, for it enabled him to keep stealing down to his brother's berth, and after these visits he would return on deck better satisfied, for the patient was still sleeping heavily, and there was not a symptom visible that could cause alarm.

The captain was also of this opinion, he informed Brace, as the young man took a turn or two with him up and down the deck.

"You've nothing to fidget about, squire. That arrow was poisoned, sure enough; but what you did, and the bleeding, washed all the bad stuff away, and the wound will begin to heal up at once. There, you go and use your eyes in all directions, my lad. I want to think."

The dismissal was imperative, and after sweeping the edge of the forest and gazing for a long time up and down the river again and again with his glass, Brace stopped beside the American, who was seated on the bulwark with one arm holding on by the shrouds and his rifle across his knees, silent and watchful in the extreme.

"Seen anything?" whispered Brace.

"A few fireflies; and I've heard a splash or two: that's all," was the reply.

"Think we shall be attacked to-night?"

"Likely enough. If we are it will be by canoes dropping down from that projecting part of the bank yonder. The enemy will come upon us quietly in the darkness, and we shall only know they are here when they begin swarming over the side."

"And then?" said Brace, as he stood with his eyes fixed upon the dimly-seen point a hundred yards above, where a faint spark of light glimmered out from time to time as if a party of savages were gathered there, and were passing the time in smoking before the attack was made.

"Well, then," said Briscoe coolly, "we shall have to shoot some, and knock the rest back into their canoes or the river, I suppose."

"That sounds pleasant," said Brace.

"Yes, but we must take the rough with the smooth. One can't expect everything to go right. But don't let's meet trouble half-way. Just as likely as not we may go on for a month now and see no more of the enemy. I wonder whether this river leads up to the old golden city."

"Which old golden city are you speaking of?" asked Brace wonderingly.

"The old one the Spaniards and the early English voyagers were always seeking."

"But that was only an old fable."

"I don't know," said Briscoe thoughtfully. "They had it, I suppose, from native reports, and they never found it."

"Of course not. It *was* only a travellers' tale."

"Perhaps so, but the wealth of Mexico and of Peru did not turn out to be a travellers' tale."

"Well, no," said Brace slowly.

"And there is plenty of room out here in the mountains or beyond the forest for such a golden city."

"Oh, yes, plenty of room," said Brace.

"There is gold in the upper waters of the rivers, for I have found it. We shall find some in this, I'll be bound—some day when we've sailed up as far as we can, and then pushed on up the shallows in a boat right away towards the mountains."

"What mountains?" asked Brace.

"The unexplored mountains from which these great rivers spring."

"Unexplored?"

"Certainly. Travellers have been pretty well everywhere in other countries, but there are vast tracts here in Central South America that have never been tapped as yet by explorers. Who knows what we may find?"

"Ah, who knows? Well, we shall see."

"If only our health holds out and the winds favour us till we have sailed up into the higher regions. What would help us most are floods to give us plenty of deep water."

"Are we likely to get floods?"

"Plenty. Every storm in the mountains swells these rivers, and if the wind will blow well from the sea we can get up a tremendous distance, for we shall have plenty of deep water."

"But you want, like us, to try and collect plenty of fresh natural-history objects, don't you?"

"Of course."

"You don't dream of discovering any old golden city, as you call it?"

"Not in the least; but if we do come upon traces of any old civilisation during our voyage we shall not pass it by without examining it as far as we can. What's the matter?"

Brace had suddenly gripped his companion's arm whilst he was speaking, and in response to Briscoe's question he thrust his right hand over the side of the brig and pointed up the river.

Briscoe shaded his eyes and gazed in the indicated direction for some moments.

"I see nothing," he whispered at last.

"Look again, a little way out from the point."

There was another pause in the darkness, and then the American spoke.

"Your eyes are better than mine. Yes, I see it now. What do you make of it?"

"Three canoes following one another and coming slowly with the stream."

"Full of men?" said Briscoe.

"It is too dark to see."

"Pst! Captain!" whispered Briscoe, and that gentleman crossed to where they stood.

"See anything?"

For answer Brace pointed up stream, and after a sharp glance the captain sent one of the men below, and the whole party were upon the *qui vive*, with hardly a word being uttered, for every man was prepared for the alarm. That which had been fully expected had occurred, and, rifles in hand, officers, passengers, and crew took the places to which they had been appointed.

Brace's heart beat fast as he stood gazing at the long low shadowy objects gliding slowly nearer and nearer to the brig, thinking the while that if he were captain he would give the order at once for fire to be opened with buckshot, so that it might scatter and wound as many of the Indians as possible without causing death.

But he was not in command, and he started with surprise, for the captain's voice suddenly rang out with an order, though not the one he anticipated.

"Stand by, a couple of you," he said, "and be handy there, Mr Dellow, to let go the port anchor. I expect they'll foul the cable and send us adrift."

There was a pattering of feet upon the deck, and the next moment Captain Banes's hand was upon Brace's shoulder.

"Your eyes are a little out of focus, squire," he said quietly. "They magnify too much, and see more than there is."

"Why—what—surely—" stammered Brace.

"It's all right, my lad," said the captain quietly. "Better than seeing nothing when there's real danger coming on board."

"They deceived me, captain," said Briscoe.

"So they did me, sir, at the first squint. I thought we were in for a scrimmage, and that before long I should be cutting up sticking-plaster and putting it on. Two fine old sticks of timber those, squire, and they must have come down some fierce falls to be stripped of their boughs like that. Now, then, are they going to foul our cable and send us adrift or will they slip quietly by?"

Brace felt so annoyed and disgusted that he could find no words for the moment, and he stood there watching the two old tree-trunks coming closer and closer, till the foremost just missed the cable, and directly after touched the brig's bows with a slow, dull, heavy impact which made her jar from end to end.

"Bah!" ejaculated the lad, in his disgust, and, turning away, he left the deck, glad of the excuse of going down into the cabin to see after his brother.

But the second mate was waiting for him when he came up, ready with a bantering laugh.

"I say, sir," he whispered, "aren't you a bit too eager for a fight?"

Brace said nothing, but, mortified by his mistake, walked right aft, to stand leaning over the stern, gazing down into the black waters as they came rushing and whispering from beneath the vessel, eddying about the rudder, and suggesting wonders of the mysterious monsters that might even then be gazing up at him with glassy eyes, meditating a spring and a snatch to seize and drag him down to their lair, as he had seen the two savages snatched from life not many hours before.

"Horrible!" he muttered, half-aloud, as he shrank away with a shudder.

"What's horrible?" said the familiar voice of the American behind him; "being chaffed by the skipper? Don't be so thin-skinned."

"Oh, it wasn't that," said Brace frankly. "I was slightly annoyed for the moment, but it was only a mistake."

"Of course, and it's better to be too particular than not particular enough. We should look well if we were taken by surprise. What was horrible, then?"

"I was thinking about those two Indians being seized and dragged down as I looked over the side, and of the possibility of a huge snake making a snatch at one, and then—ugh!"

"Were you?" said Briscoe, with a faint laugh. "Why, I was leaning over the side yonder, and I turned quite nervous with fancying something of the same kind. A bit cowardly, I suppose, but it would be an awful death."

"Don't talk about it," said Brace. "If you're cowardly in that way, I am. I never thought of these rivers being infested with such horrible creatures."

"The worst being the crocodiles," said Briscoe; "but they wouldn't be out here in the swift stream. I should say that the place to beware of the serpents would be the shallow, still creeks in sunny parts of the forest, or in the pools of the swamps, where they lie half-torpid till some animal comes in to bathe or drink."

"Hadn't we better change the conversation?" said Brace, laughing. "What about the Indians? I don't feel disposed to keep watch any more."

"Why? The danger is as great as ever."

"So is that of being laughed at for my false alarm."

"Oh, you should not notice that. Let's go forward again."

As the pair walked to the bows it was to pass the men of the watch, the rest having gone quietly below again; and no one spoke or made allusion to what had taken place, so that Brace resumed his vigil in peace, till it was time for the relief to come on deck, when he descended, to find his brother sleeping so peacefully that, in spite of all efforts to the contrary, he could not finish the night by watching at Sir Humphrey's side, for his head slowly sank sidewise as he sat upon the cabin locker, and then all was blank till there was a creaking noise in the adjacent cabin—a noise which made him start to his feet and look wonderingly around.

Chapter Fifteen
From Shadow to Sunshine

Brace Leigh was half-asleep still as he looked down at his sleeping brother, and had hard work to collect his thoughts before making out that it was a brilliant sunny morning, that Dan was busily preparing the breakfast, and the brig careening over to port as the water rippled by her bows.

Then everything was plain: there had been no attack in the night, the breeze had sprung up with the sun, and the brig was gliding at a fair rate up the river.

But best all and most welcome was the appearance of Sir Humphrey when Brace descended after going on deck for a refreshing morning bath, the toilet equipment consisting of a rough towel and a bucket of water dipped out of the river by one of the men.

For as Brace went to the side of the berth to gaze anxiously in his brother's face, Sir Humphrey's eyes opened and he stared wonderingly up into those bent upon him.

"What a horrible dream!" he said slowly. "I dreamed I—Why, it was all true: I was shot with a poisoned arrow."

"Yes, Free, it's all true enough," said Brace, laying a hand upon the other's forehead, to find it burning hot.

"Yes, I remember everything now. I felt that I was going to die."

"We were afraid so too."

"But I'm not dead, Brace."

"Not a bit, old fellow. Does your arm hurt much?"

"When I move it. Then it stings. I say, that must be a good, healthy sign!"

"I should think so."

"But my head aches terribly—it is burning and throbbing."

"Aha! good morning, Sir Humphrey," cried the captain cheerily. "Come, that's better. Why, you frightened us all last night."

"I am very sorry."

"And I am very glad," said the captain. "Did I hear you say just now that your head was aching very badly?"

"Yes, terribly."

"Well, don't be uneasy about that. I gave you a strong dose of opium yesterday, and you've only just slept it off. Never mind about the head. Let your doctors see your arm."

This was carefully unbandaged, the captain displaying no mean skill.

"Swollen a bit," he said; "the bandages have been drawn too tight. A nasty hurt; but you're a healthy man, and the wound looks the same. There's no poison here."

"Do you feel sure?" asked Sir Humphrey, while Brace looked anxiously on.

"Certain, sir. Look for yourself. A bit hot and inflamed, and very tender to the touch, but quite natural. A poisoned wound would look very different from that. Here, squire, we'll give it a good bath and a new bandage and it will be quite easy. We're not going to turn back from our voyage because our leader has been hurt."

"Your words do me good, captain," said Sir Humphrey, smiling. "A man cannot help feeling just a bit nervous when he has received such a wound, can he?"

"Of course not, sir. He wouldn't be a man if he didn't. I don't suppose a marble image minds much about a chip or its head being knocked off. But I know I should."

"Should you, captain?" said Brace drily.

"Of course I—No, I shouldn't," cried the captain. "I suppose a fellow wouldn't think much without his head. But let's talk sense. I'm not a doctor, Sir Humphrey, but I've had a lot of queer jobs to tackle in my time, and only lost one patient. He was too much for me. Fell from the main-top cross-trees and broke his neck. I couldn't set that. But I did set a broken arm and a broken leg. Made 'em stronger than they were before. Then I had a chap nipped between a water-cask and the side of the hold. Broke two of his ribs. I mended him too."

"How did you manage to set the ribs?" said Brace, noting that the captain's decisive way influenced his brother.

"Made 'em set themselves, squire. I gave him as much as he could eat, and then made him draw in as much air as he could and hold it while I put a great broad bandage round him. I had a piece of canvas pierced with eye-holes, and laced it up tight about his chest with a bit o' yarn. He came right again in no time. So will you, sir. All you want for this arm is rest, plenty of cold bathing, and clean bandages. Nature will soon heal that up. How does the sponging feel?"

"Delightful!" said the patient.

"And what about your head?"

"Very bad."

"Cup of tea will soon set that right, sir; but I meant your thinking apparatus—let's have some more water, squire. There, I'll hold his arm over the basin, and you trickle it on from the spout of the can gently. That'll make the muscles contract healthily and help the swelling to go down."

"Most comforting!" said Sir Humphrey, with a sigh of relief. "But what did you mean about my thinking apparatus?"

"Not going to fancy your wound's poisoned, are you?"

"N–no," said the patient, hesitating. "I suppose I need not fidget about that?"

"Not a bit, sir," said the captain gruffly, as he went on busying himself about the wound. "I daresay there was something on the arrow-head, but squire here cleansed the wound beautifully, and you can see for yourself that this side is all right, and take our word for it that the other looks just the same. Now, squire, we'll have some of that lint on, and a light bandage to keep it clean and cool. He'll have the arm in a sling and hold it still, so that there's no fear of any more bleeding, and it will heal up again in a very short time."

Sir Humphrey unconsciously sighed again, but it was a sigh of relief and a few minutes after Dan brought him a cup of tea, of which he partook, and once more dropped asleep when everything had been done.

"Bit weak," said the captain softly. "Best thing he can do. Sleep's a fine thing, and it seems the best thing in the world when you've got the watch and your eyelids keep on sticking together and making you feel as if you must break up a couple of sticks to turn into props. Now come and have some breakfast, my lad. I want mine. Eh? what do you say? We're sailing up?"

"Yes; we're going fast."

"Ever since sunrise, my lad, and we're miles away from where we anchored, and likely to get miles more ahead by night, so that we may hope for better anchorage and better sport than we had yesterday. Hungry?"

"Well, yes," said Brace. "I feel more at ease about my brother."

"That's right," said the captain, sniffing. "I say! ham smells good. Coffee too. That skinny chap of Briscoe's makes a splendid steward. You'll feel in better heart still when you've had your breakfast. Sun's out again."

"Yes," said Brace; "I saw it was a bright morning."

"I didn't mean that: I meant your sun, squire—the one inside a man which gets clouded over sometimes, and means dumps till it comes out again and lights him up. Sun's in: a man can't eat. Sun's out: he can. See?"

"Yes," said Brace, laughing; "I think I shall have an appetite to-day."

The next minute he was proving his words; but his efforts did not bring him abreast of the captain and the others, though the captain said afterwards in confidence:

"The passengers did not play such a very bad knife and fork."

Chapter Sixteen
Rapid Progress

A favourable breeze sent the brig higher and higher up the river all that day, the captain taking advantage of the many broad reaches to spread ample canvas.

There was only one drawback to their full enjoyment, and that was the absence of the wounded man.

Brace had the satisfaction of seeing his brother asleep again and again, sinking into pleasant restful slumbers, from which he awoke sensibly refreshed and freed from fever. In fact, all cause for anxiety seemed to have disappeared, and all on board became more cheerful.

The banks of the river were for the most part densely wooded, but twice over open park-like patches were passed where the trees were grand in the extreme, having ample room to grow in the rich soil unfettered by the parasites and vines which wove their brethren of the dense jungle into an impassable wall of verdure.

No landing was attempted, the experience they had gained making the travellers disposed to wait until more open country was reached and they could feel more secure.

The captain asked Briscoe what more he could wish for.

"If you take a boat it will only be to go up a small stream and look for curiosities. You can do that as well here on board the brig without fagging the men with rowing along under the trees, where there is not a breath of air. Look yonder now: I don't suppose you'd see such a thing as that if you were rowing. The noise of the oars would make it dive and keep out of sight."

"What is it?" said Brace: "it looks like a buffalo bathing."

"Not it, sir. Look again."

"A dugong," said Briscoe, cocking and raising his double rifle.

"Dugong or manatee. Sea-cows, we call 'em. Going to shoot it, sir?"

The American hesitated.

"It seems tempting," he said; "but I don't know. It's too big for a specimen."

"And not very good to eat; at least, I don't suppose we should like it."

"I've got it now," said Brace, who had hurriedly adjusted his glass and was watching the huge creature, which kept on showing itself in a muddy bend of the river a few yards from the bank. "It looks like a monstrous seal."

"Something like a seal, squire, but I should say it was more like a walrus. It hasn't got the great tusks of the walrus, though. You can see it well, eh?"

"Capitally," replied Brace. "Not dangerous, are they?"

"Not that I ever heard of, squire. They're great stupid innocents, as far as I know. That one wouldn't wait for a boat to get anywhere near it; but if it did I daresay in its fright it might upset the craft. I fancy all they want is to be let alone. Pretty good size, eh?"

"Yes," said Brace; "I wish my brother were here to see it."

"Very tempting for a shot," said Briscoe, fingering his gun.

"Very," said the captain sarcastically. "Couldn't well miss it, sir, eh?"

"Oh, I daresay I could," said the American; "I'm very clever that way, skipper, sometimes. But there, I don't want to kill the poor thing. Would you like to shoot, Brace Leigh?"

"No," said the young man. "It seems such a stupid, inoffensive-looking beast. I should like a shot at a jaguar or a leopard, and I could not resist having a shot at one of those loathsome old alligators if I saw one."

"There you are then," said Briscoe softly, as he pointed to what seemed to be a trunk of an old tree floating along not very far away from the brig between the verdant bank of the river and the side of the vessel.

Brace looked at it hard before he fully grasped what the object was, and then cocked the left-hand barrel of his gun.

"Don't shoot," said Briscoe. "It is only waste of powder and bullet."

"I could hit the brute without any trouble," said Brace.

"I don't doubt that," said the American; "but the bullet will most likely glance off, while if it gets home the reptile will only sink."

"So I suppose; but it will be one fewer of the savage beasts."

"One out of millions," said Briscoe. "Besides, you'll scare away that water-elephant, and we may as well watch it for a bit."

"Gone—both of them," said Brace, laughing, as he lowered the hammer of his piece, for the sea-cow suddenly gave a wallow and went down with a loud splash as if it had been alarmed by the sight of something approaching, while its disturbance of the water acted upon the great alligator, which sank at once, startling another, of whose presence the watchers were not aware till they caught a glimpse of the reptile's tail as it disappeared.

Chapter Seventeen
The Enemies in the Stream

In the days which followed Captain Banes navigated his brig so skilfully that the adventurers progressed far up into what seemed to be perfectly virgin country. Before a week had passed Sir Humphrey was able to be up on deck, looking a good deal pulled down, but mending fast.

A good-sized awning had been stretched aft for his benefit, and here he sat back during the greater part of the day with a glass to his eye, watching the many changes of the river as the brig tacked to and fro in some reaches or ran blithely before the wind in others, for the river wound about and sometimes even completely reversed its course.

And now, as the distance between the shores gradually became narrower, the travellers saw the value of the long tapering spars the captain ran up, to bear each a couple of square-sails—sky-scrapers he called them. These were spread so high above the deck that they caught the breeze when the lower pieces of canvas were either quite becalmed or shivered slightly and refused to urge the vessel against the steadily-flowing stream.

The river was still a goodly stream, and its muddy waters ran deep and showed no sign of rock on either shore.

Day after day the same kind of thickly-wooded forest was seen on both shores, until it became almost monotonous.

Now and then they saw a bare trunk, high up whose jagged, splintered branches were marks—dried, muddy weeds and seeds—which still clung and showed to what a marvellous height the river must rise at times, turning the surrounding country for miles into one vast marsh.

"Fine river this, mister," said the captain one day, as they were gliding slowly on, the pressure of the wind being just sufficient to make the brig master the stream. "Plenty of water; no rocks. I think it would be a bit different if it was up yonder where you come from."

"Yes," said Briscoe, smiling. "There'd be plenty of towns on the banks, well-cultivated farms everywhere, and all kinds of plantations; and instead of crawling along like this we should be travelling up in a steamer."

"With plenty of niggers along the banks to cut down the forests for burning in the engine fires, eh?" the captain asked.

"Yes; these forests would soon be put to some purpose, captain."

"Yes," said Sir Humphrey; "it must seem strange to you to sail on for hundreds of miles through wild land and find it quite in a state of nature. How much farther do you think we shall be able to sail up here?"

The captain did not answer immediately, but smiled in a curiously grim fashion. Then he said:

"If you'll tell me how long these favourable winds will last, sir: how long we shall be without a storm in the mountains: and how long it will be before we encounter rocks and falls, perhaps I can answer you; but this is all as new to me as it is to you, and I cannot tell you anything about what's going to happen to-morrow. But I suppose it don't matter for a few weeks. You don't want to do any boat work till you get better."

"That's true," said Sir Humphrey; "and it is very pleasant sailing up between these wonderful banks of trees."

"Yes, very pleasant, sir; but it makes my crew so idle that I'm afraid they won't understand the meaning of the word work, much less be able to spell it when I want it done."

"Never mind, captain," said Brace. "Sail away: it's all so gloriously new."

So they sailed on and on through what seemed to be eternal summer.

Now and then a shot was obtained, and some beautiful bird was collected, or a loathsome reptile's career was brought to an end, the monster sinking down in the muddy water.

On one occasion a great serpent was seen hanging in folds across the bough of a tree which dipped lower towards the river with its weight.

It was Brace's charge of buckshot which tumbled it off with a tremendous splash into the river, where it writhed and lashed the water up into foam before making for the shore, swimming with ease, much to their surprise.

The spot where it landed was fairly open, and in the excitement caused by the adventure the boat, which was always kept towing behind the brig, was manned.

Brace, the American, Dan, the second mate, and four men followed to get a good opportunity for putting the reptile out of its misery when it had about half-crawled out among the bushes.

A well-placed shot in the head effected this, and the body lay heaving gently while the party landed. The question was then eagerly discussed what should be done.

"We ought to have that skin," said Brace. "It is an enormous brute. Why, judging from what we can see, it must be thirty feet long."

"Say forty," cried Briscoe, laughing. "But who's to skin it?"

The question was received in dead silence, everyone gazing down at the slowly-heaving monster, about ten feet of the fore part of its body lying where it had crawled, and it was easy enough to believe that another twenty or thirty feet of the creature lay out of sight in the muddy water.

"I wouldn't do that job for a crown," whispered one of the men to another, and a chorus of grunts followed.

"Well," said Lynton, "who is going to volunteer? Mr Brace wants that skin taken off. We must have a rope round the beggar's neck, throw one end over one of the branches of a tree, and then we can haul him up higher and higher as we peel him down from the head."

"And suppose he begins to twissen himself up in a knot and lash out with his tail?" growled one of the men.

"Bah!" cried Lynton. "Here, a couple of you row back to the brig and get a coil of rope. I'll skin the brute myself if someone will help me to do the job."

"I'll volunteer, Mr Lynton," cried Brace; while Dan smiled and took off his coat before rolling up his shirt-sleeves.

"Will you, sir?" cried the mate; "then we'll soon do the job; but it's a bit nasty and slimy, you know, and I expect it will make us smell of snake for some days."

"Never mind," said Brace. "I'd do anything rather than lose that skin."

There was a low growling among the men as they laid their heads together before pushing off to the ship.

"Now then," cried the mate, "what is it? Why don't you be off?"

"It's all right, sir," said the man who had first protested; "we can't stand by and let you and Mr Brace do the job by yourselves. We four'll help Dan peel the beggar as soon as they've fetched the rope from the brig."

The boat pushed off, and the matter was discussed, the American suggesting that the best plan would be to make an incision just below where the skull was joined to the vertebrae, dislocate these so as to put a stop to all writing, get a noose round the neck, and then it would be easy to divide the skin from throat to tail, and draw it off.

"Oh, yes, sir," said one of the men, just as the boat reached the side of the brig; "we'll soon manage that."

"I say, Mr Briscoe," said Brace, "I suppose the ants won't be long in picking the reptile's bones quite clean."

"Oh, no; they and the flies would soon finish anything that was left in the way of flesh, but I was thinking of dragging the body afterwards into the river. It's a five-and-twenty footer, though, without doubt."

"Yes," said Brace, "but I hope they're not going to be long with that rope. I say, any fear of Indians about here?"

"Hi! look out!" cried one of the sailors, calling to Brace and the others from where they were dividing the thick growth and peering about trying to see what was beyond.

Three guns sent forth a clicking sound on the instant, as those who bore them turned to face the expected danger.

Brace's nerves quivered with excitement as he listened for the whizz of the arrows he expected to hear rush by.

"Give him another shot in the head, sir," cried one of the men; "he's trying to wriggle himself back into the water."

Brace raised his gun to fire a charge into the serpent's head again, for sure enough the monster was gliding slowly back through the undergrowth into the stream.

But the men did not wait for him to fire. Following Dan's example and setting aside all their horror and repugnance as they saw the reptile gliding back slowly into the river, they acted as if moved by the same set of muscles, and threw themselves upon the long lithe creature.

"Now then, lads, take a good grip of him," cried Dan, "and we'll run him up the bank as far as we can. Ugh!"

His mates backed him up well, seizing the serpent just behind the wounded head with powerful hands; but just as they had taken a firm hold and were about to put their plan into action, a tremendous thrill seemed to run from tail to head of the reptile as an eddy whirled up the water, and they let go and sprang away.

"Ah, catch hold again," cried Brace, dropping his gun and darting at the serpent, but before he could reach it the movement had become quicker, and they had the mortification of seeing their prize pass steadily backward under the bushes, and in spite of the renewed efforts of the men the half-crushed head reached the water, gliding down out of sight, and staining the surface with blood.

"Yah!" yelled the man nearest to the water, and he flung himself back against his mates, who could not for a moment tell what had terrified him.

On approaching the water's edge where it flowed along dark and deep beneath the pendent boughs they heard a wallow and a splash, and the lookers-on had a startled glance at a great horny, muddied head and a pair of tooth-serrated gaping jaws, which rose above the surface and were plunged again into the bloodstained water, to disappear, but to be followed by a great gnarled-bark back and a long tail which lashed the water before it passed out of sight.

Before another word could be uttered the water beneath the boughs seemed to boil up in eddies as if it were being churned from below, and during a brief space the horrified lookers-on had a glimpse or two of the slowly twining and writhing body of the serpent, as it rose to the surface from time to time, while over and under enemies were dragging at it from all directions.

"Well, if that isn't a rum un, I'm a Dutchman," cried the second mate, as they watched the tremendous struggle going on. It gradually receded farther from the bank and the combatants were carried down stream by the current. "I never saw anything like that but once before."

"Well, I never saw it once," said the American; while Brace was silent, standing peering through the dipping boughs so as not to lose an atom of what was going on. "Where was yours?"

"At home in our river," said the mate. "I was lying on my chest with my hand over the side of the camp-shedding, as we called the boards put to keep up the river-bank by the weir. I was looking down through the clear water at a shoal of little perch playing about, waiting for anything that might be swept over the weir, when a big earth-worm came down and the perch all went for it together, some at the head, some at the tail, or the middle, or anywhere they could get hold, and it was just like this till they all went out of sight as this has done. For it's gone now, hasn't it?"

"Yes, quite out of sight," said Brace, drawing a deep, sighing breath. "Why, the river seems to be alive with alligators."

"Hungry ones too," said Lynton, "and they've got a fine big full-flavoured worm for breakfast. Fancy their laying hold of his tail and pulling him away from us like that!"

"Say, Jemmy," said one of the sailors, speaking to another who was standing near him, "if at any time I'm ashore and want to come aboard, you'll have to send the boat, for I'm blessed if I'm going to try a swim."

"That's a downright fine specimen gone, Mr Brace," said Briscoe drily; "and I'm real sorry we lost him. What do you say about its length? I think we might make it fifty feet?"

"Do you think it was fifty feet long?" cried Brace, laughing.

"Well, yes, and I call that a pretty modest estimate, when we might easily have made it a hundred feet."

Dan opened his mouth, showed his teeth, and laughed with a sound like a watchman's rattle that had lain in the water.

Chapter Eighteen
The Brig Jibs

Another fortnight's sailing brought the travellers abreast of a river which flowed slowly and sluggishly into the stream they had ascended, just when its waters had begun to grow clearer and more shallow. It had become more rapid too in its course, and everything suggested that they were gradually gaining higher ground. In addition, in spite of the favourable breezes they enjoyed, the brig could now hardly stem the current.

The consequence was that at the captain's suggestion the more sluggish waters of the confluent river were entered, and the fresh course slowly pursued ever northward and westward for weeks, till it became plain that much further progress could not be made in the brig itself.

The banks had closed in so that every night the vessel could have been moored to some large tree; but one night's experience of this proved to be sufficient for the travellers, too many of the occupants of the forest giant finding their way on board and interfering with their comfort, and as the vessel swung in the stream boughs of neighbouring trees entangled themselves with the rigging.

"It's all right by a wharf," said the captain, "or in a dock; but it won't do here."

And in future they always anchored in midstream just before darkness fell.

And now, hour by hour, they had warning that their further progress with the brig would soon come to an end.

"And it's my belief, gentlemen, that it will be before night," said the captain one morning when they were all seated together beneath the awning chatting. "If you keep quite still, you can hear the stopper."

"Stopper? What do you mean?" asked Sir Humphrey, in a surprised tone. He was once more pretty well his old self.

"Well, bar, then. There, you can hear it quite plain now."

"Do you mean that low murmur?" said Brace, who was listening intently. "I thought it was the wind."

"No, sir, it's the water," said the captain. "That's either a fall or else some rapids. I've been noticing lots of little signs of a change lately, and if it wasn't for this steady wind we shouldn't be moving at all. See how clear the water is?"

"Yes, I've noticed that it has been gradually becoming clearer," said Brace. "But do you notice that the wind is dropping?"

"Yes, we are leaving it behind, and it strikes me that if you like to try about here or a little higher up you'll get some sport."

"Then we'll try," said Brace, "when we anchor for the night."

As the morning progressed, the wind rose higher and the river widened. It was as if the opening out gave play to the breeze, and a good ten miles were run before sundry warnings of shallowing water made the captain give orders for reducing the sail; but, in spite of this, as the brig rounded a curve which disclosed to the delighted vision of the travellers a glorious landscape of open park-like country backed by mountains, with the sparkling waters of a furious rapid running from side to side where the river contracted again after opening out like a lake, there was a soft grinding sensation, and the way of the vessel was slowly checked, while the next minute it was fully grasped that they were fast on a sandbank, with the open forest on one side only a hundred yards or so away, and on the other fully a mile.

"We've done it now, squire," said the captain, turning to Brace and mopping his face with a handkerchief he took out of the crown of his straw hat.

"Done it?"

"Yes; here we are, wrecked and set fast in the bed of the river."

"But I suppose we shall only remain here for an hour or two."

"Or for a year or two, or altogether, my lad. Maybe we shall never be able to get the brig off again; but we must hope for the best. It's just as if we were set in the ice up yonder in the Arctic regions, eh?"

"This place is not very Arctic," said Brace, laughing.

"No, my lad, not very," said the captain, as Sir Humphrey came up. "We seem to be in for it now, sir."

"Yes, but I suppose we are not stuck very fast. You'll send out an anchor and haul upon it with the capstan."

"Wouldn't be any good, sir. We're fast in the sand upon an upright keel, and until the water rises after a storm here we stick."

"But you talked about throwing over some of the ballast to lighten the vessel if a case like this occurred," said Brace.

"Yes, squire, that would do perhaps; but what then? Go back?"

"Go back!" cried Brace; "certainly not. We want to go forward."

"Then you'll have to go another way," said the captain decisively, "for the brig has done her work."

"But you'll be able to get her off in a short time?"

"I daresay I can, but look yonder at that cloud," said the captain, and he pointed towards where, faintly seen, a rainbow spanned the river above a rolling white cloud.

"What does that mean, captain—a shower?" Brace asked.

"Yes," said the captain, "a heavy one, squire, falling over the rocks in hundreds of tons a minute. There's our limit. That's a cloud of spray from some grand falls which I daresay run right across the river. I shouldn't wonder if the country rises now in steps right away to the mountains. If we could get up that fall, maybe we could go on sailing for a hundred miles before we came to another; but it is not possible to get the brig up, and, between ourselves, I think we've done wonders to get her up here so far."

"But suppose we content ourselves with getting so far as this, and, when we have got the brig off, turn her round and go back to the main stream and sail up there?" asked Sir Humphrey.

"Which, sir?" said the captain, smiling; "the Amazons seem to be all main streams, winding over thousands of miles of country, as far as we can make out; but if we go back it's a chance if we get up so far as we here."

Sir Humphrey merely nodded in reply to the captain's remarks, and then they all rose and walked away in different directions, each of them evidently trying to think of a means of getting over the difficulty which confronted them.

Chapter Nineteen
Discussing Plans

The next time the party were assembled was over the midday meal, when the conversation naturally turned to the question of continuing their voyage or going back.

Brace broke out with the exclamation: "We must not be beaten by a little difficulty such as this!" but his brother checked him by laying a hand upon his arm and turning to Briscoe.

"What were you going to say?" he asked the American.

"Firstly, gentlemen, that I don't want to interfere. Go where you like and how you like: it's all interesting to me; but you won't mind hearing my opinion?"

"Certainly not," said Sir Humphrey. "What do you think?"

"That we have arrived in a thoroughly wild country which most likely no one has ever reached before."

"Yes," said Sir Humphrey.

"So how would it be to make this headquarters and ask Captain Banes to rig out the biggest boat with sail and some canvas and a light pole to set up from end to end of a night to cover her in, and then row and sail up wherever we could as long as our provisions lasted? Fresh water we shouldn't have to carry; we could bring down something with our guns, or hook up something with fishing-lines; and I daresay we might get up hundreds of miles, for we should be sure to come upon side streams. That's only my idea, gentlemen. If you think differently I'm quite contented. I'm ready to keep to the bargain I have made. To me this is a regular naturalist's paradise."

"I quite agree with you, Mr Briscoe," said Sir Humphrey warmly, "and now that my weakness and the lack of spirit brought about by the effect of my wound are passing away I am getting more contented with the cruise every hour."

"Yes, sir, you alter every day," said the American, smiling.

"What do you think of the plan, captain?" said Sir Humphrey.

"Splendid, sir," was the reply. "I like it tremendously, and I was going to propose something of the kind myself. You see, you'll never want for help. My lads will be just like a set of schoolboys going out for a holiday. The only ones who will grumble will be those who have to stop aboard the brig. I'm like Mr Briscoe: ready to go where you like, and how you like: you two gents have only to say the word; and I don't think you'll better that plan."

"What do you say, Brace?" said his brother, turning to him.

"Well, at first I didn't like the idea at all: it sounded so much like being beaten and having to make a fresh start; but I think now that it's just what we as good as planned to do when we set off. When shall we start?"

"It seems to me," said Sir Humphrey, smiling, "that Briscoe's motion is carried unanimously. As to starting, we might take a boat and begin exploring at once, making day excursions. The longer ones would depend upon how soon Captain Banes could get the longboat ready."

"By to-morrow morning would do for me, sir," said the captain bluffly.

"But you would not be able to fix up the boat in such a short time."

"There's really nothing to do, sir. There's a hole in the thwart fore and aft for a short upright to carry the spar the length of the boat, and we'd make that do for mast as well. Dellow could soon cut us up a bit of canvas that would do for sail and extra cover to rig up o' nights. You'd better have the stern covered in with a regular awning. We'll be ready for you by daylight, gentlemen."

"That will be capital. Can you let us have one of the other boats, so that we can row up towards the falls at once?" said Brace.

"You can sail, squire, and save the men's arms in the hot sun. Plenty of wind for that."

"Capital," said Brace. "You might come with us, Free."

"No," said his brother; "I had better wait a few days longer before I begin."

"What will you occupy yourself with whilst we are away?" asked Brace.

"Oh, I shall find something to do. I'll stop and help Captain Banes, and see to the stores for tomorrow's expedition."

"Do you feel strong enough?" said Brace anxiously.

"I am getting stronger every day. There, take the guns with you and try and knock over a few ducks. I've noticed several fly up the river since we've been here."

"All right," said Brace. "We'll try to get some for the cook."

"And I say, squire," cried the captain, "when I was a boy, whenever I got a chance I was off fishing, and I learned from experience that the best place, and where the fish gathered most to feed upon what came down a river, was just where the water fell below a weir."

"Yes," said Brace; "I should think that would be the best place for fishing."

"Well, then, as the old saying goes, 'A nod's as good as a wink to a blind horse.' You don't want me to tell you that you're going to sail to a great natural weir of rock, up to which the fish from hundreds and hundreds of miles of big river swim in great shoals to feed."

"You mean that we should take some tackle with us?"

"That's right, and, by Jingo, the very thought of it makes me want to come with you and have a try."

"Come, then," cried Brace, "and have a good day's sport with us."

"Nay, nay, nay, my lad: duty first, pleasure after. I've got to put out anchors and see to the provisioning of that boat."

"Let Mr Dellow do it. He'll be able to see to that all right."

"No," said the captain shortly. "You go and try. Another time I should like to go with you and be a boy again."

"Well, you know your own business best; so we must put off the pleasure of having you with us till another day," said Brace.

"Yes," the captain replied; "but I warn you to take care, my lad. No going overboard. I wouldn't give much for your chance of getting out of the water again."

"But there are not likely to be any alligators or crocodiles there."

"I dunno," said the captain. "I shouldn't like to risk it. There's likely to be plenty of all kinds of dangerous fish or reptiles up yonder, and size don't count. A thousand of the little tiny sticklebacks of fish in these rivers are more dangerous than one big fellow ten foot long."

A quarter of an hour after the meal was finished, Lynton, Dan, and four of the sailors, with their faces full of sunshine, had taken their seats in a boat which had been lowered, while the men left on board looked down at them as if through clouds.

"I hope you will be careful, my lad," said Sir Humphrey.

"You may trust me, Free; I shall not do anything rash," said Brace, laughing.

"I shall look forward to a pleasant evening over your specimens, Briscoe," said Sir Humphrey, speaking more warmly to the American than had been his custom.

"I hope I shan't disappoint you, sir," was the reply.

"Got all your guns and ammunition, squire?" cried the captain.

"Yes, quite right."

"And fishing-tackle and bait and everything else you will need?"

"Yes; I believe we have taken everything aboard," was the reply.

"I'll tell the cook to have a good fire made up in the galley for roasting the ducks you are going to shoot and the frying-pan ready for the fish you are going to catch."

"All right," cried Brace merrily. "Ready, Mr Lynton?"

"Ay, ay, sir."

"Then push off."

The man holding on with the boat-hook gave a good thrust, and the boat glided away from the brig's side with the swift stream, which rolled over the sandbank, caught the boat, and whirled her away. But the little mast was already up forward and the rudder hooked on, so that when the lug-sail had been hoisted and had bellied out, the boat, answering quickly to a touch of the tiller, glided through the water, soon recovering the ground she had lost, and, careening over, swept by the motionless brig, whose sails were now furled.

"Hah!" cried Brace, as they began to race before the breeze, "this is the sort of river I like. Look, Briscoe, how clear it is. You can see the bottom now and then."

"And the fish," said the American. "Brace Leigh, I begin to think we're going to have plenty of sport up here."

Chapter Twenty
Brace Leigh's Sport

"So we're to think of the pot and pan as well as of our specimens," said Briscoe, loading both barrels of his gun.

"I fancy we shall have plenty of chances for doing both," said Brace, following suit. "How well the boat sails! Why, we have got quite a long distance from the brig already."

"Yes, and we're stemming a pretty good current too," said Lynton, who was steering with one hand and taking out a stout fishing-line from the boat's locker with the other. "But wouldn't you like to have a turn with a spoon-bait as we are going along? I don't know what fish we're going to catch, but I expect there'll be plenty of gar pike or something of that kind."

"Well, you begin," said Brace. "I'll have a turn later on. I want to try for a duck or something else eatable, and to have a look at the country round about as well. I say, aren't we carrying too much sail?"

"Not a bit," said Lynton. "Look, I can ease off in a moment. See?"

"Yes," said Brace, as, with a touch at the tiller, the boat grew more level instead of careening over as she ran; "that's right."

The boat glided smoothly along now on an even keel, and they all enjoyed the magnificent scenery as they passed near the bank, with the forest running right down to the brink of the stream and occasionally opening out into avenues of gigantic trees.

Lynton was busying himself with the tackle as they sailed on, when Brace turned to him and said:

"You don't expect to catch anything with that great drag-hook, do you?"

And he laughed at the large triangle hanging beneath a huge spoon, and furnished with a double arrangement of swivels.

"Indeed, but I do," was the reply. "Here, catch hold of the tiller, my lad. Steady. A little slower now."

"Shall we take in a reef, sir?" said Dan, who was holding the sheet.

"Oh, no, that will do, only take care you don't capsize us."

He then turned to Brace once more and continued the conversation about the fishing-tackle.

"Yes, Mr Brace," he said, "that spoon will spin splendidly, and I don't expect the fish here have been educated so far as to know what a fish-hook is. They've a lot to learn before they grow shy of an artificial bait. Think that lead will be heavy enough?"

"Yes, quite enough to scare away a shark. What nonsense! I should put on something small and light. We're not at sea."

"I know that, sir; but just you wait a bit and see. Ease off that sheet a little more, Dan," cried Lynton. "That's better. I say, we're opening up into quite a lake."

"The scenery is glorious," said Brace. "Look, there's plenty of dense forest too beyond that open part we are passing."

"Yes, and there's the waterfall," cried Briscoe. "It's grand."

Brace nodded and sat with parted lips, gazing at the grand display of falling water which was now almost directly ahead.

The whole river, which was very nearly half a mile wide at this spot, tumbled over a ridge of rocks which barred its passage, and dropped in places fully fifty feet with a dull murmuring roar which now began to be plainly heard.

"Are you looking at the falls, Lynton?" cried Brace.

"Not yet. I'm too busy just now. I want to get the line out first. There she goes, and good luck to her."

He dropped the great spoon and its armature of hooks over the side, and Brace glanced after it, to see it for a few moments as the line was allowed to run, the silvered unfishlike piece of metal beginning to spin and, as it receded farther from the boat, to assume a wonderfully lifelike resemblance to a good-sized roach swimming pretty fast.

It disappeared in a very few moments in the disturbed water, but soon after it rose to the surface again and began to make leaps and darts of a yard or two in length.

"I thought so," said Lynton drily. "That weight isn't heavy enough for the rate at which we're travelling."

"Let out more line," said Brace, "and it may sink lower then."

Old Gold: Cruise of the "Jason" Brig | 129

The mate nodded, and drew about a dozen more yards from the open winder.

"That ought to do it," he said. "I'll give the line a twist round that thole-pin, and then we shall hear it rattle if there's a bite and—here—hi! Bless my soul!"

Whizz! whoop! bang!

The thole-pin had darted overboard, the winder was snatched from Lynton's hand and struck violently against the steersman's leg.

Then both he and the mate made a dart at it to stop it, but came heavily in contact as they stooped. The tiller flew wide, and the boat careened over so dangerously that, if the man who held the sheet had not hastily let go so that the sail went flying, the mate would have gone over the side, and would soon have been left behind, as the boat was now going along at a considerable speed.

It was only a matter of a moment or two, and then the tiller was steadied, the sheet hauled home, and the boat glided swiftly on once more.

"I say," cried Briscoe, as Dan sat grinning with delight, "what's it all about?"

"About?" cried Lynton angrily; "why, my bait was taken by either a shark or an alligator. There's a hundred yards of new line gone. What's to be done now?"

"You'd better rig up another, I should say," said the American drily, "and hold on and give out when the fish runs."

"It's a rum un," muttered the mate. "I say, my lad, just keep your head out of my way next time. Are you aware that it's just about as hard as a cocoanut?"

"Never mind, Lynton," cried Brace. "Get out another line as soon as you can, while the fish are biting so freely."

"I don't know about that. The old man will kick up a row about that line being lost. It was his, and he'll want to know how it came about that I lost it."

"Never mind: we brought plenty with us. Look sharp."

Chapter Twenty One
A River Monster

The boat's way was checked, and every eye was now fixed upon the second mate as he prepared and threw out another artificial bait. At the same moment the sail was allowed to fill, and the boat glided on once more.

"They don't get this line," said Lynton confidently, "for I'll hold it all the time. Let her go, Dan: take a pull on that sheet."

The boat answered to the drag as if she had been a spirited horse resenting a touch at the curb rein, and away they went, with the water surging up towards the gunwale as she careened over.

They had sailed on for a few minutes when a loud cry came from the mate.

"Ahoy there! Oh, murder!" he yelled. "Throw her up in the wind, or I shall have my arms dragged out of their sockets."

For just when least expected there was a tremendous jerk as some fish or reptile snatched at the flying bait, and Lynton was scarcely able to keep his hold of the line.

"Let him run," cried Brace. "Give him plenty of line."

For the moment the mate was too much taken by surprise to act, but, recovering himself while one of the men snatched up and loosened more line from the winder, he let out yard after yard of the stout cord, and, the boat's way being checked, it became possible to do something in the way of playing the seizer of the bait.

"It pulls like a whale," panted the mate, as he endeavoured to control the line.

"Never mind," said Briscoe; "give him time, and you'll tire him out."

"If he don't tire me out. I say, it's a monster. It must be a big 'gator."

"Never mind what it is," cried Brace excitedly: "catch him."

"It's all very fine to talk," growled the mate, "but he'll have the skin off my hands if I stick to him, for it seems as if instead of me catching him he's caught me, and I expect he'll have me in the water soon."

Briscoe, who was as excited as anyone, burst into a hearty laugh at this, and, laying down his gun, took up the short-handled gaff-hook which lay beneath the thwarts.

"That won't be any good for this fellow," cried Lynton; "it's a great shark, I believe. Take the boathook."

"No, no; it's too blunt," said Brace. "Look here, Lynton: you go on playing him."

"Play! Do you call this play? My arms are being racked."

"He must be getting exhausted now. He can't keep on at that very much longer."

"Well, if he doesn't soon give way, I shall have to do so."

"Wait a minute or two and then get the brute to the surface, and I'll put a charge of big shot through him."

"No, no; he'll break away if you do that," cried the mate. "I want to get him aboard if I can manage it. I say: the tackle isn't too big and coarse, is it, Mr Brace?"

"I didn't expect you were going to hook a thing like this at the first attempt. Give him some more line."

"There's on'y 'bout a fathom more of it left, sir," cried the man who was casting the line off from the winder.

"Let out half and then get a hold too, my lad," said Lynton.

"Ay, ay, sir," answered the man.

"This is rather too much of a good thing," said the mate. "Here, let the boat go with him; it'll ease the strain."

"Why, he has been towing us for the last five minutes," said Briscoe.

"Hi! hullo!" cried Brace. "Oh, what luck! Gone!"

The men groaned, for the line, which had up till then been quite tense and kept on cutting through the water as the prisoner darted here and there in its wild efforts to escape, suddenly became slack, and, with an angry ejaculation, Lynton began to haul slowly in.

"I knew it; I knew it," he said: "that tackle wasn't half strong enough."

"But what bad luck!" cried Brace. "Never mind. Stick on another hook, Lynton. I say, that must have been an alligator. There couldn't be fish that size out here."

"Pulled like a sea-cow," said Briscoe.

"Cow! Went through the water like a steam launch," said Lynton.

"Well, whatever it was, it has gone now, and we must hope for better luck next time," said Brace.

They rested for a few minutes in silence; then Lynton turned to Brace and said:

"Just put your hand in the locker over there, Mr Brace, and get out the largest spoon you can find. I'm afraid it won't be big enough, and I expect this beggar has got the swivels. I say, though, this is something like fishing. When we get back I'll rig up some tackle with the lead-line. Let the boat go again."

The sail was allowed to fill, the boat careened over and began to glide away again before the wind, when suddenly the line tightened once more, and the mate yelled to the steersman and the sailor holding the sheet.

"Ease her!" he roared; "the beggar only turned and came towards the boat. I've got him still, and he's as lively as ever."

There was silence then, and for the next few minutes the battle went on, the fish or reptile towing the boat this way and that way in some of its fierce rushes.

In spite of the hard work Lynton manfully refused to surrender the line, but let it run or hauled it in according to the necessities of the moment, till there was a cheer, started by Brace, for the captive's strength was plainly failing, and at the end of another five minutes it ceased its struggles, and yielded sullenly to the steady drag.

Lynton pulled the line slowly in, whilst all the others watched with eager expectation for the first appearance of his captive.

"It must be a monster," said Brace hoarsely. "Be careful now, Lynton. It would be horrible if the line were to break, and we were to lose him after all our efforts."

"Monster? I believe he's as long as the boat; but he's pumped out now. I say, the water must be tremendously deep here. He must have dived right down to the bottom. It's a 'gator: there's no doubt about that."

"We shall soon see," replied Briscoe, who stood ready with the gaff-hook. "I shall have to trust to this."

"Yes. Drive it right into his throat, and haul him in over the side at once."

"Right. I say: he's coming now. See him?" said Briscoe eagerly.

"Quite plainly," said Brace. "The water's beautifully clear, but it's running so fast that everything below seems to be all of a quiver and it is not possible to make out the shape of anything."

"Haul slowly and steadily," said Briscoe. "I wish this thing had a stronger handle."

"It would only break if it had, with such a big fish," said Lynton, as he kept on hauling and letting the heavily-strained line fall between his legs. "Do you see him now?"

"Yes, quite plainly."

"'Gator, isn't it?"

"No: a long, thin fish."

"Not a snake?"

"No, no: a fish. It looks five feet long at the least."

"Must be ten," panted Lynton, with a groan, as he continued hauling on the line. "It feels as heavy as so much lead."

"Now then, be careful," cried Brace, cocking his double gun.

"No, no: don't shoot," cried Lynton, as he slowly hauled.

"Shan't fire unless he breaks away," said Brace between his teeth.

In the exciting moments which followed, and amidst a deep silence, only broken by the flapping of the sail and the rattle of the water against the boat's bows, Briscoe gently passed the gaff-hook over the side, thrust it down into the water, and waited till the fish should come within reach.

It only took four hand-over-hand hauls on the part of the mate, and those who gazed excitedly on could plainly see a huge head, with gaping jaws full of glistening teeth, upon its side as if completely spent, offering its white throat to the sharp hook waiting to be driven in.

Another steady draw, and the fish did not move a fin. Then one bold firm snatch, and the hook was holding well in the flesh, and in another moment Briscoe, as he threw himself back on to a thwart, would have had the fish over the side and in the bottom of the boat.

But at the first touch of the steel the monster curved itself round till its tail touched its head, and then, with a mighty effort, went off like a spring released by a trigger; there was a tremendous splash, deluging everyone with water, and the fish leaped a couple of yards off the hook, to descend with another splash.

As it divided the water, *bang, bang,* two sharp reports rang out from Brace's gun, one charge tearing through the back of the fish, which beat the surface for a few moments and then dived down, discolouring the clear water with blood.

In another few seconds the stream was alive with fish of all sizes, making the river boil as they gathered up every scrap, and greedily drank in the blood, while it was evident that the wounded monster was being savagely attacked and devoured alive by an ever-increasing shoal.

"Look: just look!" cried Lynton.

The words were unnecessary, for everyone's eyes seemed to be starting with the use that was being made of them.

Almost as Lynton spoke the whirling water was broken by the great fish springing right out, followed by at least a score of pursuers, apparently half its size and less, ready to dash at it as it struck the water again and disappeared.

"Seems to have gone this time," said the American quietly.

"Yes, and taken another spoon-bait and hook belonging to the captain," said the second mate ruefully, as he looked at the broken end of the line he held in his hand.

"Yes, and he nearly took the gaff-hook as well," said Briscoe.

"I say, Mr Briscoe, why didn't you hold him? You had him fast."

"Why didn't you hold him with the line?" said the American drily.

"Can't you see? It broke." And Lynton held out the end.

"And can't you see? What sort of hook do you call this?"

As he spoke Briscoe held out the gaff, which was nearly straightened out.

"I guess," he continued, "that you people ought to make this sort of tools of hard steel and not of soft iron."

They examined the hook, and even though it was made of soft iron the strength exerted to straighten it out as had been done must have been enormous.

"Well, anyhow, our fish has gone," said Lynton ruefully.

"And if we're not going to have any better luck than this," said Brace, laughing, "the cook will not have much use for his frying-pan. There, let's run up to the falls, and perhaps we may do something with our guns."

"Just so," said Briscoe; "only mind how you shoot, for if anything should happen to fall into the water, the fish'll have it before we know where we are. This seems to me," he added drily, "rather a fishy place."

Chapter Twenty Two
Towards the Falls

The fishing-line was laid to dry, the sail was bellied out, and the boat ran swiftly on again before the brisk breeze.

Lynton, who now steered, kept the little vessel close in shore so that a good view might be had of the beauties of the lovely surrounding country, for here tree and shrub had room to grow and assume their natural shape without being deformed by crowding neighbours or strangled by the twining monsters struggling upward so as to be able to expand their blossoms in the full sunshine.

In a short distance, though, the forest grew thicker, and the great trees crowded down closer to the water's edge.

Brace and his naturalist companion had withdrawn their gaze from the silvery sheen of the descending fall a mile ahead, to gloat over the beautifully-coloured birds, insects, and flowers which revelled in myriads in the light, heat, and moisture of the glorious bank of the stream.

Fresh beauties rose to the view at every glide of the boat, and Brace felt that what they ought to do was to check its way and stop to drink in the glories of the scene.

Chance after chance offered itself, but neither of the gun-bearers felt disposed to shoot, and their pieces rested in the hollows of their arms till suddenly, as they passed round a point, they came upon a scene in a nook some fifty yards away which made each seize and cock his weapon.

There, right down by the edge of the water, squatted a curious and most uncouth-looking form totally unclothed save by its natural hairy growth, and apparently quite unconscious of their approach as it bent over and lapped the water it raised in its shaggy hand.

But the clicking of the gun-locks aroused it to its danger, and, springing upright, it stood peering at them for some moments from beneath a pair of great hairy overhanging brows, before giving vent to a hoarse, long-continued yell.

The result of this was soon perceived, for three more such figures suddenly bounded from amongst a clump of bushes and made for the dense forest close at hand.

The first seen stretched itself up a little higher for the moment, until it looked like a big savage man, and it stood still glaring at the strangers fiercely and displaying its teeth.

Directly afterwards it uttered another deep-toned yell, and its human aspect was gone, for it went down on all-fours and seemed to turn itself into a rear-guard for the other three till they disappeared amongst the undergrowth.

The first seen then again raised itself to gaze over the bushes at the boat, and, after uttering a hoarse half-bark, half-human cry, it plunged in after the rest and was gone.

"Here, why didn't one of you have a shot?" cried Lynton.

"What at?" said Brace quietly.

"Those monkeys. It was an old man and his wife and two youngsters. Why didn't you fire? You had a good chance."

"That was why I didn't fire at them. I didn't want to hit the old man nor his wife nor youngsters. I couldn't bring myself to do it."

"That's just how I felt," said Briscoe. "Hang me if I could make out whether it was a wild man or an ape."

"It's my opinion that it was the former," said Brace, gazing back at the little embayment they had just passed.

The next few minutes were passed in silence which was at length broken by Brace.

"Look, there he is again," he said; "he's watching us from behind those bushes. Couldn't be a wild man, though, could it?"

"Of course not," said Lynton: "whoever saw a wild Indian go off on all-fours? It was a great monkey."

"But there are no great monkeys in this part of the world," said Brace. "One has to go to West Africa and Borneo for them. What do you say, Mr Briscoe?"

"The naturalists all say that there are no big apes in South America; but some travellers tell a different tale, and the Indians report that there are great half-human creatures that they are afraid of roaming about in the woods."

"I suppose that must mean that there are some species of apes on this continent, but that no specimens have been captured," said Brace.

"I'm going to make a note of what we've seen to-day," said Briscoe, "for that chap was as big as an orang-outang, and quite as ugly."

"Yes," said Brace. "It looks as if we had made a discovery. I don't see why there shouldn't be big ones in these vast forests."

"Nor I," said Briscoe thoughtfully. "There's plenty of room, and people are too ready to say that nothing more remains to be discovered. Why, only the other day they wouldn't believe in the existence of the gorilla."

"Look here," said Brace; "don't you think we ought to go back and endeavour to catch one of those young ones?"

"Perhaps," said the American drily; "but it will mean a fight, and we should have to kill the old one first."

"Do you think he would make a fight of it?" asked Brace.

"I am certain of it," said Briscoe. "Suppose we put it off for a day or two and think about it. There is plenty of time, and we are certain to get another chance."

"Go on, then," said Brace. "Let's prospect up to the falls, cross over, and try on the other side for the ducks and fish we have got to take back for the cook."

Lynton chuckled and sent the boat gliding swiftly along for the next few minutes, opening out again and again lovely vistas of river, forest, and verdant shore, all of which invited landing and promised endless collecting excursions. But the present was looked upon as a tour of inspection, and all eyes scanned the shore and every creek that was passed in search of Indians, a lively recollection of the first boat expedition begetting plenty of caution.

And all the while they sailed on and on towards the grand falls, which rapidly grew in size as they were approached, the water thundering down and the face of the cataract being obscured by the cloud of mist which rose slowly till it was wafted away to fade in the glorious sunshine.

Chapter Twenty Three
A Great Danger

So rapt were all the party in the awe-inspiring scene and in the beauty of the falls—which were broken up by island-like rocks peering out grey and green right across, so that as the adventurers drew nearer it was to gaze at the beauties of at least a dozen falls instead of one, as they had expected—that they did not notice how the wind was dropping as they advanced, nor yet the change that had taken place in the river current.

It was Brace who first marked the alteration whilst he was noticing the numbers of fish leaping and darting away in front of the boat as she glided on.

"We ought almost to stop and fish here," observed Briscoe. "We might have better luck with a smaller bait."

"Perhaps we had better try," said Brace; "but I say, Mr Lynton, look here: what do you make of this?"

"Make of what?" said the mate.

"We are not sailing nearly so fast as we were a short time ago."

"Oh, I don't know: we're making much about the same way."

"But the boat does not rush through the water as she did."

"That's right," said Briscoe. "A bit ago she nearly dipped gunwale under several times."

"I noticed that," said Brace, "and that's the reason I called attention to the smooth way we are now progressing. There's just the same amount of wind blowing."

"Yes; I say, Lynton, this isn't right," said Briscoe, in a sharp tone of voice.

"What isn't right?" said the mate testily. "We're making splendid way. The boat's sailing along beautifully."

"Yes, too beautifully," said Briscoe. "Can't you see what Mr Brace here means?"

"No; I can't see anything wrong," answered Lynton, in a grumbling tone.

"Look then," cried Brace, excitedly now; "you had better put her about at once and make for the other side."

"What for?"

"Can't you see?" cried Brace. "We were sailing against the stream a bit ago; but we're sailing with it now."

"Nonsense; that can't be," said the mate contemptuously.

"But we are," cried Brace warmly. "Look and see."

"Yes, that's right enough, sir," cried Dan sharply. "The current's setting dead for the falls, and we're being sucked sharply towards the broken water underneath them."

"Ay, true for you, mate," cried one of the sailors; "and if we get there we shall be swamped before we know where we are."

Lynton started up in the boat and stood in a stooping position holding on by the gunwale with his unoccupied hand, as he peered over the side to look at the direction of the current and then gazed up the river at the falls.

The others saw him change countenance, but he did not say a word. He gave ample proof, though, that he fully realised the danger they were incurring, for he bore hard down upon the tiller till the boat glided round, the sail filled on the other side, and they began to sail slowly in a direction parallel with the falls.

"She don't make much way, sir," said Dan, in a grumbling tone hardly above a whisper, the words being meant for Brace's ear, but the mate evidently heard what was said.

"I don't quite understand this," said he. "I never noticed any change, but the current's setting now right for the falls."

"Don't you see why that is?" Briscoe asked the question sharply.

"No. Do you?"

"Yes. I'm a bit used to cataracts. There's thousands of tons falling yonder and going down ever so deep. That makes the surface water set towards the falls, and while there's a deep current rushing down the river there's a surface current now setting upward, and it'll take us right up to the falling water as sure as we sit here if something isn't done, and that quickly."

"I don't quite see that," said Lynton obstinately, as if he did not like being taught by the American.

"Never mind about understanding it," said Briscoe sharply. "We'll work it out afterwards. You must act now."

"I am acting," said Lynton. "We're sailing right away."

"But the current's taking us up, Lynton," said Brace quickly.

"Well, I can't set more sail, nor make any more wind, can I? We seem to be getting more into shelter here."

"But you can order the men to get out the oars," cried Brace.

"Or else drop the grapnel and try to come to an anchor," said Briscoe.

"Ah, yes," cried Lynton; "we'd better do that. Perhaps the wind will rise a bit more soon. Over with that grapnel, my lads," he shouted to the men forward.

The sailors had been listening to every word, and quick as thought the little four-fluked boat anchor was tossed over the bows, and the line ran out to the extreme limit.

Brace watched anxiously for the iron to catch in the bottom and check their way. But he looked in vain.

"That's no good," said the American sharply. "Bound to say you'd want a rope ten times as long as that one up here, and if you had it no gimcrack of a grapnel like that would take hold of the smooth rock bottom."

"Well, what else can I do? We seem to be helpless," said Lynton.

Briscoe replied, in a most determined voice:

"Order out the oars, sir, if you don't want the boat to be swamped and your bones to be picked by these fiends of fish."

The men did not wait for orders from their officer, but seized the oars, and the next minute they were pulling with a long, steady, vigorous stroke in the direction the mate steered; but from where Brace sat aft he could see that they were still gliding gradually upward.

It was only too plain to him that this was the case, for he could mark their position by fixing his eyes upon a rock on the farther shore and see that they were first abreast of it and soon after leaving it behind them.

"We've got our work cut out here, Mr Lynton," said the American sternly. "I should change course again, sir, and make a tack in the other direction." Then, turning to the sailors, he said:

"Stick to your oars, my lads, and pull a steady stroke. No flurry. Be cool."

"Look here, sir: are you in command of this boat or am I?" cried the second mate, losing his temper in his excitement.

"Neither of us, I reckon," said the American coolly. "Strikes me no human being is in command of her now. She's going where the current takes her."

"Well, I don't want you interfering and giving orders to the men," answered the mate.

"Suppose we take our orders from Mr Brace here." Briscoe turned to Brace. "What do you say, sir—do you think my advice is good?"

"Yes, Lynton, it is good," said Brace firmly. "Do as Mr Briscoe says."

"All right, sir; I'll take my orders from you as I would from your brother; but I'm not going to be hustled about over my work by a Yankee who came aboard as a stowaway."

"That will do, Mr Lynton," said Brace haughtily. "I'd be willing to take my orders from any man if I felt that they were right, as I know these are, and you do too if you will only be a little reasonable and think."

"I don't want any thinking, sir," said Lynton frankly. "Yes, it's right enough. Pull, my lads, a good steady stroke, one that you can keep up for a month. Swing that sail over. That's right. Now we're off on the other tack."

He spoke out quite cheerily now, and handled the tiller so that the boat glided off in the opposite direction to that in which she had been sailing, and for the next half-hour they tacked and tacked about, sailing as close as they could to the wind, which was blowing gently right for the falls.

Their course was a series of tacks, which, if they were represented on paper, would be marked as a zigzag, and had the breeze been fresher the sailing qualities of the boat would have enabled her to easily master the current which was steadily carrying them towards the falls.

But instead of freshening, the wind, which was making the leaves quiver ashore, seemed to be growing fainter and fainter as they came nearer to the thundering falls, for it was plain enough that in spite of all their efforts the current was the stronger, and that it was only a question of time before the pulling of the men would become weaker and the boat would be drawn right on and on into the churned-up foaming water, and then—

Chapter Twenty Four
Staring at Death

It was too horrible to think of, and Brace, to keep out of his brain the mental picture of the swamped boat, the thundering water beating them down into the awful chaos, and the shudder-engendering ideas connected with the fierce fish waiting to attack and literally devour them alive, changed his position so as to kneel down in the bottom of the boat, facing the second oarsman, lay his hands upon the oar, and help every pull with a good push. Briscoe followed his example, and the strength of six was thus brought to bear upon the oars.

For a few minutes this extra effort seemed to have supplied all that was necessary, and as the men saw that they were beginning to draw a little away from the falling water they burst out simultaneously with a hearty hurrah, one that seemed to give fresh energy to the rowers. But it sounded feeble, hushed, and smothered as it were by the increasing roar of the falling water, ever growing into an overpowering, muffled thunder.

Still there was the fact that wind and muscle were stronger than the current, and the boat was steadily drawing away as they advanced in their tack towards the farther shore.

On the strength of this and to save losing ground in turning to go upon the next tack, Lynton kept on, and shouted an encouraging word or two from time to time.

"Bravo! All together! Now you have it! Well rowed, boys! Put your backs into it! You'll fetch it! British muscle and British pluck for ever! Never say die, lads! That's your style! Keep it up! Well done, Mr Brace! Well done, Mr Briscoe! Well done all! Ah–h–h!"

This last sounded like a snarl from the mate—it was uttered fiercely, and was long-drawn-out and savage in the extreme.

But he felt that he had made a mistake, and he now roared:

"Go on—go on! Don't stop to look round you. Keep on rowing for your lives, lads, and we'll do it yet!"

He was just in time, for the men's efforts had begun to slacken and something of a panic was setting in amongst them.

Everyone grasped the fact that the long reach they were now making had been a terrible error. It had brought them closer in than ever to the high mass of rocks over which the upper portion of the river was precipitated.

Somehow from the configuration of the country this high ground affected the course of the wind, or else it had suddenly dropped, for to the horror of the rowers the sail, which had fairly bellied out, began to collapse, and a minute later hung flapping against the mast, doing nothing to help the progress of the boat out of the peril in which she lay.

"Pull!" roared the mate. "Pull for your lives, my lads!"

He sprang forward, and, just retaining his hold upon the tiller with one hand, he planted his foot against the bow man's oar and kept giving a thrust in time with each stroke.

Brace's first idea was that they ought to tack at once, but he grasped the fact directly after that there was not time, for in the attempt to achieve the manoeuvre the boat would lose so much way that they would be swept irredeemably closer towards the falls; and he went on thrusting with all his might, knowing full well that the mate was right, and that their only chance was to row on parallel with the falls till they could reach the farther shore.

"Pull for your lives!" were the last words the mate shouted, and they were but faintly heard in the heavy roar, and the men pulled as they had never pulled before.

They pulled till the rough ashen oars bent and threatened to snap in two, and as Brace kept on with his regular swing and thrust his position was rendered more horrible by his being face to face with the men and forced to see their starting eyes, their strained faces, and the glint of their white set teeth, as they dragged at their oars when bidden, each man for his dear life.

But it was all in vain, and they knew it. They felt to a man that all was over. Even now they could not get their full grip of the water, for it was becoming foam charged and white with the vesicles of air rushing to the surface. But they pulled in the true Anglo-Saxon spirit, for life, of course, but with the desperate intent of pulling to the last, not to escape, but to die game.

And how soon?

Brace did not once turn his head to the right so as to see—there was no need to do so, for he was conscious of the ever-nearing presence of a glassy descending sheet dimly seen through a dense cloud of mist, which glittered and flashed, and as it rose, rolling over and over like the smoke from a slow fire, it emitted colours of the most brilliant hues—glorious refulgent colours, reflections of the sunshine, while with ever-increasing force there came that dull awful roar.

There was an appeal too now to other senses, for a dull moist watery odour rose to the lad's nostrils, and at times it suggested fish, and he shuddered slightly at the thought of how soon he might be beaten down and swept within the reach of the keen-toothed creatures.

He thought all this and more in those brief seconds, for his brain was working quickly, independently of his muscles, which never for a moment flagged in the effort to help the rowers.

How long first?

He knew there would be no fishes close up to the falls, for nothing could swim in such an air-charged mass of water, and nothing would risk itself where it would be beaten down and hurled and whirled against the rocks upon which the waters fell and eddied and played around.

Brace knew and felt that so soon as the boat was sucked a little nearer there would be a sudden glide right up to the falling water, and then in an instant they would be beaten down into the darkness right to the bottom, and then go rushing along at a terrible rate, to begin rising a little and a little more till they reached the surface half a mile or more away from where they went down, afterwards to float gently along past where the brig was anchored—

No; he felt that they would never reach the surface again; for, as soon as the rush of the water allowed, the great river would be teeming with shoals of ravenous enemies, and the friends left on board the brig would never learn the cause of the non-return of the boat's crew.

All this and more passed through his brain in those frightful minutes as the men tugged hard at the oars, and they kept on parallel with the great descending sheet of water.

Now and then, as if divided by a puff of air which did not reach them, the rolling mist opened and displayed piled-up natural piers of rock, towering above their heads and dividing the curtain of gleaming descending waters; but for the most part the falls were hidden from them by an impenetrable veil, and at last they were upon the outskirts of this mist as they rowed on.

At first Brace believed that his eyesight was dimming, and he shuddered, for the faces of his fellow-sufferers appeared to him to be strangely distorted and indistinct; but he grasped the reason, and knew now that in a few minutes more they would pass on to their death.

But no one else seemed to be affected by the surroundings. To a man, with fixed staring eyes and set teeth, the sailors dragged at their oars, waiting till their officer at the tiller should bid them cease, while his face seemed to have become set to a stony solidity which never changed, for Lynton was ready to meet the worst and, determined to help till the water beat them down, he breathed hard and thrust in the regular seaman's swing.

Suddenly Brace felt more than saw that the yard above them swung slightly, and no doubt creaked; but no sound save the deafening roar of the waters could reach to his ear, and he just glanced upward, to feel for the moment that the canvas darkened their position, and it seemed to him that the time had come, for the sail was like one of the wings of death beating over them, and a curious feeling of resignation made him calm.

He had not felt anything like fear during the last few minutes: he was only aware in a rapt dreamy way that something was about to happen—that something which was the end of everything on earth: and he felt sorry for his brother, who would take it terribly to heart that he did not return. But, directly after, his brain was intent upon the efforts he was making to help the rower in front.

Then the mist became very thick around them, and as the boat was gliding faster and still faster through the water the already moistened sail seemed to be struck a violent blow which nearly capsized the boat, as she heeled over to port and did not recover.

"We're going down," thought Brace, and he closed his eyes and threw back his head till his face was towards the sky, but only to resume his old position, for he awoke to the fact that the men seemed to be making a last desperate attempt to get out of the rushing water.

And now, as he unclosed his eyes, it was to find himself in the clear sunshine with the boat dashing at headlong speed through the water, her port gunwale only an inch or two from the surface and the wet sail bellied out in a dangerous way, while Dan was holding on by the sheet.

The roar of the water was stunning, but the sudden change in the state of affairs seemed to stun him far more, till it gradually dawned upon him that they had rowed on in their desperation till the boat had passed into a current of air, one caused by the wind striking against and being reflected from the rocks at one side of the falls, and by whose help they were gliding so rapidly into safer waters that the men suddenly ceased rowing, while Lynton uttered a yell.

"Look, look!" he shouted. "Do you see? Do you see?"

"See? How?" panted Briscoe. "I am nearly blind with staring at death."

"Yes, yes, but look, look! Mr Brace—the water, the water! We have got into an eddy, and it is setting right away from the falls."

Brace turned round and saw that Lynton's words were true. He sat staring at the water until he was recalled to a sense of what was passing around him by hearing Lynton's voice.

"Oh, catch hold, sir; catch hold of this tiller and steer. Let her go—fast as she will—so as to get away from this horrid place. Quick! quick! I can't bear it! I'm going mad!"

Brace snatched at the tiller, and only just in time, for Lynton's grasp upon it gave out, and with a lurch forward he fell upon his face, which was, however, saved from injury, for he had clasped his hands upon it, and now lay in the bottom of the boat, hysterically sobbing with emotion like a girl.

Chapter Twenty Five
Briscoe's Yellow Fever

Brace felt shocked at seeing a strong man so overcome, and carefully refrained from glancing at the American, for fear of seeing a look of contempt in his eyes.

But the weakness passed away as quickly as it had come, and Lynton sprang up, to give a sharp glance round at the surface of the broad stretch of water, and then he turned to the others, but he did not speak for a few moments.

"We're all right," he said then, in a quiet voice. "That current don't spread as far as this. Why, it was exactly like looking death right in the face, and when I'd wound myself up to meet him like a man, it was as if something went off inside me, and I ran down all at once when I found we were not to die after all."

"It was awful," said Brace, to whom the words were addressed. "I expected it to be over every instant."

After a while Briscoe said:

"I am glad we have come safely through it all. It is more than I had dared to hope for."

"That it was," said Lynton. "I don't know how you were, but I felt like a great girl. Well, it's all over, and very thankful I am. Mind shaking hands with me, Mr Briscoe?"

"Mind?" cried the American warmly, as he held out both his own to the mate. "No; why should I mind?"

"Because I turned round on you and cut up rough when we were in trouble. Thank you. I beg your pardon."

"Bah! nonsense, man. It was quite natural."

And there was a warm exchange of pressure as the two men gazed in each other's eyes.

"Perhaps you wouldn't mind either, sir?" said Lynton, turning to Brace.

"I was waiting for my turn," replied Brace heartily.

And again there was a warm pressure of hands exchanged.

"I say, both of you," said the second mate, in a low voice: "you don't think I was very cowardly over it, do you?"

"Cowardly?" cried Briscoe. "My dear fellow, I think you behaved like a hero."

"No," said Lynton, flushing. "You mean Mr Brace here."

"He means we all behaved well," said Brace laughingly; "and I think you ought to say a few words to the men."

"That's what I feel, sir; but don't you think it would come better from you?"

"Certainly not. You ought to speak. You are their officer."

"Perhaps Mr Briscoe would not object to speaking to them?"

"No; it would come best from you: so say something at once."

"All right," said Lynton, clearing his throat with a good cough, and turning to the men. "Look here, my lads.—Would you mind taking the helm for a few minutes, Mr Brace? Thankye.—Look here, my lads."

"Ay, ay, sir!" came heartily, and it seemed to put the mate out, for he coughed again, took off his straw hat, wiped his streaming brow, and made a fresh start.

"Look here, my lads," he began.

"Ay, ay, sir."

"Heave to a minute, will you?" cried the mate. "You put me out. Look here, my lads: we've just now jolly well escaped from being drowned, and—and I—we—I—here, shake hands, all of you. Brave boys!—brave boys!—brave boys!"

He repeated the last two words again and again in a husky voice, as he shook hands heartily with each of the men in turn, and then uttered a sigh of relief as he took his place at the tiller again.

"Look here, sir," he said: "I don't see that we need go on flying through the water like this. We're out of danger, and it seems to me that we've only got to keep a sharp look-out to see when the current changes and keep clear of it."

"Yes," said Brace; "I think we might slacken sail a little now. We seem to have got right out of the surface current leading to the falls."

"We'd no right to go sailing up so close to where the water comes over the rocks. That's where we were wrong in the first place," remarked the second mate.

"Yes," said Briscoe; "but it was a wonderfully interesting experience."

"That's what you call it, sir," said Lynton rather gruffly, "and I suppose you're right; but it's rather too expensive a game for me. It was experience though, and like a lesson, for I feel now as if I could navigate these waters without getting into trouble again. How do you feel about going right across now and landing?"

"I think we ought to," said Briscoe. "Why can't we go close in and then sail up as near as it seems safe before landing? After that we might shoulder our guns and see if we can climb up level with the top of the falls."

"Yes, let's try that," said Brace. "It would be most interesting."

Lynton steered the boat close in to the shore and kept her sailing along at only a few yards' distance until they arrived at a spot which looked favourable for landing.

Brace and Briscoe gave a sharp look round and then the little party landed, and, after leaving the boat-keepers with orders to fire by way of alarm if they saw any sign of Indians, Brace led off to climb a long rocky slope, which proved to be perfectly practicable for a boat to be drawn up on rollers, and soon after they were standing gazing to their right at the top of the falls, while away to their left in a smooth gliding reach there were the upper waters of the river winding away through beautiful park-like woodlands as far as the eye could see.

"Splendid!" cried Lynton. "I should just like a mile of this to rig up my house and retire from business. I say, what's he looking for?"

This was to draw Brace's attention to Briscoe, who had gone forward to descend to a little sandy nook by the water-side, where he was raking about with a stick.

"Looking for something, I suppose—to see if he can find precious stones among the pebbles perhaps. Maybe he's finding fresh-water shells. Any oysters there, Mr Briscoe?"

"Haven't found any yet," shouted Briscoe, laughing.

But Brace noticed that he stooped down once or twice and scooped up a handful of sand, to wash it about in the water and examine it very carefully before tossing it away, and then, shouldering his gun, he returned to Brace's side.

"What a lovely place this is!" he said. "Hadn't we better get back and report progress to your brother?"

"Yes, I think so," said Brace; "but what did you find?"

"Pst! Keep quiet. I don't want the men to know."

"What was it—footprints in the sand belonging to the men of your golden city?"

Briscoe looked at him sharply.

"No," he said, in a low tone so that no one else could hear, "but signs of gold itself, and we may be on the way to the legendary city after all."

"What?" cried Brace, smiling. "You don't mean to say that you are still thinking about that! I thought you had entirely forgotten it."

"To be frank, I always do think about it, for I believe in it most firmly: otherwise I should not be here."

"Nonsense! It's nothing but a myth—a legend," said Brace.

"I think not," said Briscoe gravely. "I believe it's as much a fact as the golden cities of the Mexicans and Peruvians that the Spaniards proved to be no myths."

"No: that was true enough," replied Brace thoughtfully.

"So's this. I've dreamed about it for years, and I mean to find it yet."

"Why, you surprise me. I thought it was the temple of natural history which you used as your place of worship."

"So I do, but I've got the golden city behind all that."

"Nonsense! It is, as you said just now, merely a dream."

"Perhaps."

"Where is it to be found? You did not fancy it was up the Orinoco, did you, when you planned to go up there?"

"Yes, either there or up here," said Briscoe. "Don't you understand that it must be on the banks of some river out of the bed of which the Indians could wash gold?"

"No. I should have thought it would be close to some mountain out of which the old people could dig gold."

"Then I shouldn't," said Briscoe. "The first gold-finders found it in the beds of the streams down which it had been washed. That's what I think, and I determined to come up and examine the South American rivers till I found the right one. I meant to go up the Orinoco; but the Amazons did just as well. It might be there, but it's just as likely to be here, and—"

"Let's go back and have some lunch in the boat first," said Brace, smiling at his companion's earnestness. "We can then hoist the sail and run back to the brig and tell my brother that you've broken out with the gold fever, and that there is to be no more collecting of specimens."

"No, we won't," said Briscoe drily; "for I've said what I did to you in confidence, and you won't say a word. I'm going to collect and do as you do; but there's nothing to hinder me from making a grand discovery besides, is there?"

"Oh, no," said Brace merrily; "but I don't see any reason why we should keep it a secret from my brother and the rest."

"Perhaps not, but I do. We don't want the brig's crew to go mad, do we?"

"Certainly not."

"Then don't you say a word about there being gold in this river for them to hear or the consequences might be serious."

"I shall not speak about it, for I don't think there is any."

"Perhaps not," said Briscoe drily; "but I do. For there is, and plenty of it."

"What?" cried Brace.

"That's right. Don't be surprised. By-and-by I'll show you, and open your eyes."

No more was said, and, the order being given, the men trudged back to the boat; the wind was fair, and soon after they ran back alongside of the brig and reported the possibility of getting the boat up the portage.

"That's good," said the captain. "Then I tell you what: as soon as Sir Humphrey is well enough I'll have the brig safely moored, and we'll man two boats and go right up the river."

"Then we'll go at once," said Sir Humphrey. "I shall get better much more quickly lying back in the stern-sheets of a boat than sitting about here on the deck of the brig."

"I think so too," said the captain. "What do you say then to starting to-morrow?"

"Do you think we can manage that?" asked Sir Humphrey.

"Yes; I have everything ready," said the captain.

"But suppose the brig is attacked by Indians while we are away?"

"We won't suppose anything of the kind, if you please," said the captain, "for it seems to me that we're quite out of their reach. If there had been Indians about here we should have seen some sign. Anyhow, the brig's mine, and I can do as I like with her. What I would like is to come with you on this first trip, so we'll chance leaving the brig well moored, and to-morrow off we go. I rather like a bit of shooting when there's a chance."

Chapter Twenty Six
Brace has Symptoms

Rollers were soon made by the carpenter, and the men, who were as eager as a pack of boys, worked hard over the necessary preparations, looking forward as they did to the trip as a kind of holiday excursion. Consequently, when without mishap the two boats reached the side at the foot of the falls next day, the stores were landed and carried up the slope, the boats drawn ashore and in an incredibly short space of time dragged on to the rollers, so many men harnessing themselves like a team of horses to the rope attached to the boats' keels, and cheering loudly as difficulty after difficulty was surmounted, the rollers being changed time after time till the top was at length reached.

The lowering down into the water was easily accomplished: stores were re-embarked, and then, with a brisk breeze to fill their sails, the party started upon what was to prove an adventurous voyage along the upper waters of the great river, leaving the thunder of the falls far behind.

Fish and game proved to be abundant, wood for their fire plentiful, and they bivouacked that evening under one of the forest monarchs upon the bank, partaking of the result of their shooting, Dan revelling in his task of playing cook, and grinning with delight at the praises bestowed upon him by masters and men.

To Brace's satisfaction, his brother seemed all the better for the little exertion he had gone through, and when the boats were once more sought and the fire extinguished to save them from drawing upon themselves the attentions of any Indians who might be near, Sir Humphrey was one of the first to fall asleep under the tent-like sail, the boats swinging gently in the darkness at the end of the rope secured to a huge overhanging bough.

"It's a pity not to have kept the fire going, Mr Briscoe," said Brace, as the two sat together trying to pierce the darkness as they gazed towards the shore.

"Pity for some things," replied Briscoe; "but there's for and against. It would keep the wild beasts away, but would bring the insects and reptiles to see what it means, besides rousing up the birds to come and singe their wings. I say: everybody seems to have gone to sleep."

"Except the two men of the watch in the boats' bows."

"I say!"

"Yes?" said Brace, for his companion stopped short.

"What did Sir Humphrey say to my ideas about the golden city?"

"Nothing whatever."

"Nothing?"

"Not a word, for he did not know."

"Didn't you tell him?"

"Of course not. Didn't you say that your words were in confidence?"

"Yes," said Briscoe, with a grunt, "but I didn't mean to include him. He wouldn't try to argue the case again, would he, and want to have me set ashore here?"

"Certainly not. He would say that you had a perfect right to indulge in such dreams. He would not interfere."

"Not if I was to begin prospecting?"

"Not unless you began to do anything to hinder our trip. But I say, look here: what's the meaning of this sudden interest in gold?"

Briscoe smiled.

"There's nothing sudden about it," he said. "It came on, as I told you, years ago, and I've been thinking about the golden city ever since."

"Golden clouds," said Brace derisively. "Give it up, man, and stick to the birds."

"I'll stick to them too," said Briscoe quietly. "I won't interfere with your plans."

Brace was silent for a few minutes, during which the darkness seemed to grow deeper, and the strange noises in the forest increased till it was possible for an active imagination to conjure up the approach of endless strange creatures bent upon attacking the invaders of their solitudes. But the time glided on with the water gently lapping at the sides of the boat they were in, and one moment Brace was trying hard to say something to the American, the next he was gliding up the strange river towards the overgrown crumbling walls of a city standing high upon a rocky eminence a little back from the river bank. Then all at once the swift, easy, gliding motion of the boat ceased, and though the sail was well filled out they got no nearer to the city, whose gateway stood temptingly open, while in the glowing evening sunshine crumbling wall and tower appeared to be made of deadened gold.

For a few moments Brace sat gazing hard at the buildings, feeling certain that this was the golden city of which Briscoe had spoken. Then a strange feeling of irritation came over him, and he tried to turn and order the crew to lay out their oars and pull for their lives so as to reach the goal. But somehow he could not stir to rouse up the men to row, and the boat remained strangely balanced upon the swiftly-gliding water, just as if she were straining hard at an anchor which had been thrown out astern.

Then—how the young man could not have explained—the ruddy golden city grew fainter—darker—till it died away in a dense blackness; for it was all a building-up of the imagination, in the deep sleep which had overcome the young adventurer as he leaned against the side of the boat.

Chapter Twenty Seven
A Sudden Check

Days and days passed of sailing on and on over waters which grew more and more shallow. Brilliantly-coloured birds were shot and skinned: and an ample supply of fine turkey-like fellows made the men's eyes sparkle as they thought of the rich roasts Dan would make at the evening's camping-place to supplement the toothsome fish that were hauled in, flashing gold, silver, blue, and scarlet from their scales, whenever a line was thrown out astern.

Sometimes a shot was obtained at some fierce animal or loathsome reptile, whose pursuit and capture lent excitement to the trip and fully repaid the men for their labour at the oars when the wind went down.

The change from the brig to the boat seemed to give Sir Humphrey new life, and at the end of a fortnight he was thoroughly himself again, and ready to take his turn at an oar so as to rest the men, to fish, or to land on one or the other bank of the river in search of game for the cook or specimens for their boxes of skins.

"It's glorious," cried Brace, more than once.

"Would be," said Briscoe, "if we could catch sight of the golden city."

"You'll only see it as I did," cried Brace—"in a dream; but you can read about it when we get back home, in some book of imaginary travels."

"Perhaps," said Briscoe drily; "but I have more faith than you have, my fine fellow. Just wait and see."

That afternoon a wide reach of the river was entered where the water shallowed so rapidly that all of a sudden a grating sound arose from under the foremost boat, and then came a shout from the captain to Lynton.

"Look out there," he roared. "Shove your helm down."

The second mate obeyed the order instantly; but the warning came too late, for there was a sudden check and Brace nearly went overboard, and in fact would have taken a header if Briscoe had not made a snatch at his arm.

Both boats were fast aground and refused obstinately to yield to the poling and punting toiled at by the men to get them over the sandy shoal in which they were fixed.

"Never mind, my lads," cried the captain at last: "it's getting late, and there's a capital camping-place ashore. Wade, some of you, and lighten the boats so as to run 'em in. You, Dan, and a couple more see to your fire. There don't seem to be any of those flippers in the water here. Stream's too swift for them."

The men were over the sides of the boats and into the water directly, and, thus lightened, the vessels were run close up to the bank before they grounded side by side.

"We'll lighten your boat more still, gentlemen, in the morning," said the captain, "and pole her along to find a deeper channel. It's too late now, and we're all tired. My word!" he continued, as he stood on one of the after-thwarts and looked down through the crystal-clear water at the sandy gravel; "why, this looks just the sort of place where you might wash for gold."

"Hah!" ejaculated Brace: and then to himself: "He has done it now."

The captain's loudly-spoken words had been plainly heard by all, and seemed to send a magnetic thrill through every man.

Without exception, at the word "gold" all stopped in what they were doing and stared down through the clear water at their feet with eager dilated eyes, while to Brace it appeared as if each hearer held his breath in the excitement which had chained him motionless there.

Briscoe's eyes flashed a meaning look at Brace, who glanced at him, and then he cried: "Yes; that's what I was thinking, skipper. S'pose we have a try?"

"All right, do," said the captain good-humouredly. "But never you mind, my lads: get the things ashore. You, Dellow, take a rifle and have a look-out for squalls—Injuns, I mean. Not that there's much likelihood, for there's no cover for the enemy here. Now, then; what are you all staring at? Are you struck comic? Never heard the word 'gold' before?"

The men all started as if they had been rudely awakened from sleep, and began to carry the necessaries ashore, while Brace turned to the American, who was busy at the locker, from which he was getting out a couple of the shallow galvanised-iron wash-bowls they used.

"Cast loose that shovel from under the thwart, Brace, my lad," he said. "I say, sure there are none of those little flippers about?"

"Oh, yes, I'm sure," cried Brace, laughing. "We should have known if there were before now."

"That's right," said Briscoe, stepping overboard, "for I don't feel as if I wanted bleeding."

"Are you going to try for gold?" asked Sir Humphrey.

"That was what I thought of doing," said the American, "for the place looks so likely. Gravelly sandy shallow in a great river which runs down from the mountains."

"Oh, you won't find any gold here," said Lynton, smiling.

"I don't know," said Sir Humphrey. "Try; the place looks very likely."

Chapter Twenty Eight
The Yellow Metal

The men had landed and made fast the boat, and were now gathering wood for a fire, as Brace and the American stepped to the shallowest part they could find, where the stream ran swiftly, washing the stones so that they glittered and shone in the bright sunshine.

"Suppose we try here," said Briscoe, rolling up his sleeves and making use of the shovel they had brought to scrape away some of the larger pebbles. "Now then, there, hold the bowls, or they'll be floating away."

Brace thrust them down under the water, and Briscoe placed a shovelful of gravelly sand in one, balancing it so that it was level on the bottom of the bowl.

"I say, we did not come up here to begin gold-hunting," said Brace reproachfully.

"No, of course not. Ours is a naturalists' trip, and this is testing the mineralogy of the district," said Briscoe, with a peculiar smile.

Plosh! Another shovelful of gravelly sand was raised and placed in the second bowl. Then the shovel was driven in, to stand upright.

"Now," cried Briscoe, "wash away."

"Like this?" said Brace, shaking the bowl, as he began to feel a peculiar interest in the proceedings.

"No," said the American: "like this." And, stooping down and holding his bowl just under water, he gave it a few dexterous twists which brought all the bigger stones and pieces to one side, so that he could sweep them off with his hand into the river again.

"I say, you've done this sort of thing pretty often before," cried Brace.

"Yes, a few times," said Briscoe, laughing. "Up in the north-west in cañon and gulch, with the Indians waiting for one. Come, go ahead; there are no Indians here."

"There don't seem to be," said Brace, imitating his companion's acts and washing away till nothing was left in the bottom of the two bowls but half a handful of fine sand.

"Did you find much gold up yonder?" said Brace, shaking away at his bowl.

"Lots," said Briscoe coolly.

"And made yourself rich?"

"No," said the American drily; "I made myself as poor as a rat."

"I don't understand! How was that? You found gold?"

"Oh, yes. My partners and I spent one season up there prospecting, and altogether we managed to get together a hundred thousand dollars' worth of the yellow stuff."

"That was pretty good."

"Tidy."

"Then how do you make out that you lost by it?"

"Just this way. When we got back to civilisation and totted up, allowing fairly for the time it took and the cost of travelling, and what we might have done, say at work earning eight or ten dollars a week each, we reckoned that we were out of pocket."

"Indeed?" said Brace, staring.

"Yes. Gold-hunting's gambling. One man out of five hundred—or say a thousand—makes a pile: half of them don't make wages, and the other half make themselves ill, if they don't lose their lives. So I call it gambling."

"Don't gamble then," said Sir Humphrey, who had waded to where they stood: and he looked on smiling. "Well, what fortune?"

"Nothing in mine," said Brace, "and—nothing in Briscoe's."

"Wrong," said the American: "you're new to the work, anyone can tell. There's plenty here to pay well."

"What!" cried Brace. "Why, I can't see a bit of metal."

"Look again," said Briscoe, and, dipping his shallow bowl, he gave it a clever twist to get rid of the water again and leave the fine sand spread all round and over the bottom.

He held the bowl full in the sunshine, with the last drops of water draining off.

"Now," he said, turning to Brace, "what can you see?"

"Nothing at all," said Brace.

"Nothing?"

"Well, there's a tiny speck, and something that looks just yellowish right in the middle there. But you don't call that gold?"

"Well, it isn't silver," said Briscoe, laughing, "so I do call it gold."

"Absurd!" said Brace.

"Oh, no, it isn't. That's good gold, and if properly treated the sand and gravel are rich enough to pay well."

"When I go gold-washing I shall want to be where you can find nuggets and scales in plenty," said Brace.

"Ah, so I suppose," replied Briscoe. "You wouldn't be content with a quartz reef with nothing in it visible, but which when powdered up and treated gave a couple of ounces of pure gold for every ton of rock that was broken out and crushed, would you?"

"Certainly not," replied Brace.

"Plenty make fortunes out of it, though, on such terms, and don't turn up their noses at a reef if they can get one ounce of it of a ton. This riverbed's rich, Sir Humphrey, and ready for explorers and prospectors. But let's try that sand-bank yonder, farther out."

The trio had to wade through a channel knee-deep to get to the long sand-spit, for the most part bare, but over a part of which an inch or two of clear water trickled.

Here the same process was gone through over and over again, with the result that when some shovelfuls of sand had been obtained from about two feet below the surface, the washings were rich enough to show glittering specks in the sunshine, while out of his own pan Brace picked a dozen thick scales of a rich dull yellow—the peculiar yellow of pure gold. He showed them to Briscoe, who nodded and said:

"You have struck it pretty rich."

"But how do I know that this isn't that what-you-may-call-it that's nearly all sulphur—that pretty yellow ore of iron?"

"Iron pyrites?" said the American: "by trying it with the edge of your knife."

"How?"

"Like this," said Briscoe, picking up a flat water-worn pebble and, drawing his keen sheath-knife, he took the thickest scale in Brace's pan out of the sand, to place it upon the smooth surface. "Now," he said, handing this and the knife to the young man, "try and cut that scale in two."

Brace tried, and by exercising a little pressure he cut through the yellow scale almost as easily as if it had been lead.

"There," said the young man half-contemptuously, "what does that prove?"

"That it is pure gold," replied Briscoe.

"But all is not gold that glitters," said Sir Humphrey, laughing.

"Not by a long way," said Briscoe; "but that is metal?"

"Certainly."

"It is yellow?"

"Yes," said Sir Humphrey.

"Then it is gold."

"Why isn't it iron pyrites—the salt of iron and sulphur?"

"Because if it had been it would have broken up into little bits: you could have ground it into dust."

"So you could this," said Brace.

"Impossible. You could beat it out into a thin sheet which you could blow away. That's gold, sir. I had two years' prospecting for metals and precious stones up in the Rockies, with a first-class mineralogist, and, without bragging, I think I know what I'm saying. This river's full of rich metallic gold, I'm sure of that."

"I daresay you are," said Sir Humphrey: "only if this sand-spit is ten times as rich in gold I'm not going to stay here any longer. We shall be eaten up."

"Yes," said Brace, "the little wretches! They're almost as bad as the tiny fish."

"What, these sand-flies?" said Briscoe, slapping his face and arms. "Yes, they are a pretty good nuisance. Let's get ashore towards the fire—the smoke will soon make them drift."

"Well, I've learned something about gold to-day," said Brace, as they picked their way back through the shallows to the bank of the river; "but oughtn't we to mark this place down so that it should be ready for the next gold-seekers?"

"It wants no marking down," replied Briscoe: "the place will tell its own tale to anyone hunting for it."

And he tossed the sand out of the pans, gave them a rinse, and stepped ashore.

In another hour the excellent meal prepared by Dan had been enjoyed, and the regular preparations were made for passing the night on board; but in a very short time everyone had come to the conclusion that it would be impossible to sleep in the neighbourhood of the sand-spits, on account of the myriads of tiny sandflies, whose poisonous bites were raising itching bumps and threatening to close the eyes of all who were exposed to them.

"It's getting too late to drift down the river a little way," said Lynton, "and, besides, it wouldn't be safe."

"And we should only be getting out of Scylla into Charybdis," said Sir Humphrey.

"I should like to be buried in sand up to my nose," cried Brace, whose face was getting terribly swelled.

"Strikes me," said Briscoe, "that we'd better go ashore and sleep there after making up a good smother on the fire with green stuff that will smoke well. There's plenty about."

This was agreed to unanimously after an announcement from the mate that, if they were to spend the night ashore, a proper watch would have to be set and kept.

After the necessary preparations had been made in the dry, slightly-raised clearing in the middle of which the fire had been lighted, the party covered themselves with their blankets and rejoiced in the success of the plan, for the smoke rose and in the moist night air hung low, spreading itself out in a thin layer a few feet from the ground; and beneath this canopy the weary party lay down to sleep.

Chapter Twenty Nine
The Crew down with the Golden Fit

The gold had got into Brace's head so much that, though he fell off fast asleep directly, it was only to begin dreaming of the sand and gravel beneath the swiftly-flowing shallow water, the ruddy pebbles seeming to change when he turned them over with his foot as he stood ankle-deep, for they grew yellower and glistened, till upon stooping to pick one up he saw that all he had supposed to be stones were really nuggets of gold.

He was about to stoop and pick up all he could gather, when he suddenly felt a sharp pain in his right ankle, and to his horror found that a tremendous shoal of the tiny carnivorous fish had come up the river, dimming the clear water like a cloud of silvery mud, and with a sharp cry he turned to escape to shore, and awoke.

But the pain in his ankle was no dream, for it stung sharply, and, sitting up, he drew up his foot, to find that he had been bitten by some insect.

His first thought was to rise and plunge the bitten place in the cool fresh water, and, creeping cautiously away so as not to awaken the rest, he had nearly reached the water-side when he was brought up short by a low whispering away towards where a tree stood alone.

His blood seemed to turn cold, for the thought came that a party of Indians had been attracted by the fire, and that this, their first night passed ashore, was to prove a fatal mistake.

But his common-sense soon told him that savages bent upon a night attack would never betray themselves by whispering loudly together in eager discussion, while directly after his nose became as fully aware of something being on the way as his ears.

Brace began to sniff.

That was smoke, certainly, but not the smoke of the fire, that he could smell, for it was plainly enough the familiar strong plug Cavendish tobacco which the men cut up small and rubbed finer between their horny palms before thrusting it into their pipes.

That explained all, no doubt. The flies had been attacking them in spite of the wood-smoke, and they had crept away to get under the boughs of the big tree to try what the stronger fumes of tobacco would do in the way of keeping off the noxious stinging insects.

"And no wonder," he said to himself; as he bent down to lay his hand upon his tingling ankle. "Poor fellows! They—"

Brace started upright again, and was in the act of taking a step to reach the running water, when a voice sounded louder from among the whisperers, and in the intense silence of the night he plainly heard the words:

"Not a foot furder do I go, mates, and leave that gold."

There was silence for a few moments, and then a voice said:

"You can do as you like, my lads: here I am, and here I stays till I've made my pile."

"That was Jem's voice," thought Brace; and then he listened again intently.

"What about the skipper?" said a voice.

"Skipper'll have to put up with it," said another of the men. "I like the skipper, and I haven't a word to say about the two mates. I like Mas' Dellow as well as I like Mas' Lynton, and t'other way on; but gold aren't silver, messmates, and what we might do over a shilling's a diffrun thing to what a man feels boun' to do over a pound. Here we are with the gold lying in shovelfuls among the sand o' this here river, plenty for all on us to make our fortuns, and I says it would be a sin and a shame to leave it behind to go shooting red and yaller and blue cock robins and jenny wrens to get their skins. There, that's the longest speech I ever made in my life, but it had to be done. So I says I'm your side, messmate Jemmy, and my name's gold."

There was a low murmur here, and Jem spoke again:

"Anyone else got a word to say?"

"Yes, I have," said a fresh voice. "I'm with you, Jemmy, my lad, and there's my hand on it; but there's some'at in the way."

"What's that?" growled Jem.

"What about the Yankee chap as found the gold, and Sir Humphrey and Master Brace?"

"What about 'em?" said Jem, while Brace's ears tingled.

"On'y this, messmates. They've took the 'Jason' and paid for her for as long as they like. S'pose they say we shan't stop gold-digging and tells us to go on?"

"We must tell 'em we won't leave the gold, and that they must stop and dig and wash, and go shares with us."

"Tchah! they won't. Chaps like they, who can hire brigs and skippers and crews, are chock full o' money. They'd on'y laugh at us, for they'd rather have a noo kind o' butterfly than a handful o' gold," continued the speaker. "Suppose they says we shall go on?"

"Then we tells 'em we won't, and there's an end on it."

"But the skipper won't pay us for breaking our bargain."

"Well, what's a few months' pay to men who've got their sea chesties chock full o' gold?"

"That's true enough, messmate, but s'pose they turns nasty and picks up their guns. They're wunners to shoot."

"They dursen't," said Jem scornfully. "It would be murder. Finding gold like this upsets everything else. We don't mean them no harm: all they've got to do is to jyne in and share, for not a yard further do we go, messmates, till we've got to the bottom of that gold."

"Then they'll sail without us."

"No, they won't," said Jem meaningly; "for we shall want that there brig to take us back with all our gold."

"Then there'll be a fight."

"Very well then, my lads, we must fight. Now then, it's come to this— are we going to stand together like men?"

Brace held his breath as he waited for the answer, and the time seemed long; but it was only a few moments before a murmur of assent came which told only too plainly that the thirst for gold had swept every feeling of duty or allegiance aside.

"And I've been playing the mean treacherous part of an eavesdropper," thought Brace, as he drew back softly and returned to the side of the smouldering fire, and after carefully judging the distance he made out where Briscoe was lying, and, proceeding cautiously to his side, knelt down and laid a hand upon his companion's lips.

There was a violent start, and then the American lay perfectly still, and a husky whisper arose from his lips:

"What is it?"

Brace placed his lips to Briscoe's ear and said:

"You've done it now."

"Eh? Done what?"

Brace acquainted him with all that had passed, and ended with a word or two about listening and eavesdropping.

"Listening—eavesdropping?" said Briscoe. "You did not go to listen. It was forced upon you. Why, Brace, man, it means mutiny."

"And all through your miserable craze for gold," said Brace angrily.

"Come, I like that!" replied the American. "Haven't I kept it all a secret between us two? Who was it began about the gold this evening, and made all the men prick up their ears?"

Brace was silent for a few moments.

"Yes," he said, at length; "but you jumped at the chance, and began to wash."

"I should have been a queer sort of fellow if I had not, sir. The fruit was popped into my mouth by the skipper, and of course, as it was so much to my taste, I ate it. Well, it's no use to begin shouting before we're hurt. There's one good thing over tonight's work: we've had warning, and know what to do."

"That's just what we don't know," said Brace sharply.

"Oh, yes, we do. Let's see: there's Sir Humphrey, the skipper, the two mates, and our two selves—that makes six."

"And the men are a dozen—two to one," said Brace.

"Unarmed, and in the wrong," said Briscoe; "we're armed, and in the right."

"Then you would force the men to go on—you'd fight?"

"Of course—if necessary. I'd force the men to do their duty."

"And their duty is to obey orders," said Brace quickly.

"Of course."

"Then we ought to wake and warn the others before the men come back to camp."

"To be sure, and hear what your brother and the skipper say. I'll take a look round first to make sure there's no one within hearing, for it will be another point in our favour to give the scamps a surprise by being ready for them."

"It's all right," whispered Briscoe five minutes later. "They're all whispering and plotting together yonder. Now for it. You tackle the skipper, and I'll tell your brother. Be as quiet as you can."

Brace thought that the duty of warning his brother should be his, but he said nothing, and, creeping to the captain's side, he bent over in the dark, and laid a hand upon his shoulder.

In an instant two powerful hands had him by the throat, and he had hard work not to struggle.

"Who is it?" said the captain hoarsely.

"I—Brace Leigh," said the young man, in a hoarse whisper.

"You shouldn't rouse me like that, my lad. What is it—Indians?"

Brace told him, and the captain lay back, perfectly till, gazing up at the smoke.

"Bless 'em!" he said softly. "That's trouble to-morrow morning then—not to-night. Well, have you told Dellow and Lynton?"

"No; but Mr Briscoe is telling my brother."

"Mr Briscoe, eh? Think he's siding with the men?"

"Oh, no: I'm sure he is not."

"I don't know," said the captain thoughtfully. "He jumped at that gold to-day like a baby at sugar. I've always been a bit suspicious about him, and now I see I've been right."

"What do you mean?" said Brace warmly.

"That chap's natural history has all been a cloak to screen him while he has been gold-hunting. I would bet that he came up this river with us in the hopes of finding that El Dorado place the Spaniards used to swear by."

"Quite right," said Brace drily.

"That's it, my lad; but he won't find it here. It's in quite another place."

"Indeed! Do you know?" said Brace eagerly.

"Oh, yes, I know. It's in the moon. Well, let's hear what Sir Humphrey thinks."

"Hist, captain," whispered the latter, almost at the same moment.

"Yes, sir. What do you think of it all?" asked the captain.

"It is horrible," whispered Sir Humphrey. "These men must be brought to reason."

"Don't you flurry yourself about that, sir," said the skipper grimly. "I'm going to have a few words with my two bulldogs, just to put them up to what's going on, and then we shall just keep quiet and take no notice of anything till the lads begin. Then I shall let Dellow and Lynton loose at 'em, holding myself in reserve. That will settle 'em. But if we did seem to be getting the worst of it you three gentlemen might come and lend us a hand."

"And all be ready armed," said Sir Humphrey, "as you three will be."

The captain chuckled softly.

"Armed—guns and pistols?" he said at last. "Oh, no. I daresay you gents have had the gloves on and know how to use your fists?"

"Well, yes," said Sir Humphrey; "I must confess to that. Brace is particularly smart with his."

"I'll be bound to say he is," said the captain, chuckling. "Then we are likely to have some fun to-morrow."

"You don't apprehend danger, then, skipper?" said Briscoe: "no shooting?"

"Not a bit, sir," was the reply. "We Englishmen are not so fond of using shooting-irons as you Yankees are. As to danger? Well, yes, there will be a bit for the lads if they really do begin to play the tune called mu-ti-nee. For there'll be a few eyes closed up and swelled lips. Lynton's a very hard hitter, and when I do use my fists it generally hurts. Good three years, though, since I hit a man. He was a bit of a mutineer too: an ugly mulatto chap, full of fine airs, and given to telling me he wouldn't obey orders, and before the crew. I did hit him—hard."

"Right into the middle of next week, skipper?" said Briscoe, laughing.

"No, but right overboard," said the captain, "and one of the men threw a noose about his neck and pulled it tight, bringing him alongside. There he was between drowning and hanging when I looked over the bows at him. 'Now, young fellow,' I says, 'what's it to be: obey orders or no?' 'Oh, captain, captain,' he whines, 'take me aboard.' 'Climb up by the bobstay,' I said. He wasn't long coming aboard, and I kept an eye on him, half-expecting to see him come at me with his knife; but, bless you, no: he was showing his teeth at me an hour after in a real smile, and he seemed to feel a sort of respect for me all the rest of the voyage."

"Then I hope you will be as successful with these men, captain," said Brace.

"Oh, we'll try, Mr Brace: we'll try. Well, there's nothing to mind to-night, gentlemen, so we may as well have our sleep out."

"Sleep?" said Brace. "What! with the men in a state of mutiny?"

"Pah!" ejaculated the captain. "Hallo! who's here?"

"Me—Dellow," said the first mate, in a hoarse whisper. "Lynton's here too. Is anything wrong?"

"Yes," said the captain, and the two mates were made acquainted with the trouble.

"Oh, that'll be all right, gentlemen," said the first mate quietly. "I was afraid it was Indians and poisoned arrows. You can't reason with them: you can with our lads. Lynton here is a wonderful arguer if there's any trouble there, eh?"

Lynton laughed softly, and in obedience to the captain's request all took their places again about the fire, to lie listening till the men returned, when, to Brace's great surprise, next morning at sunrise he found himself being shaken by his brother, and ready to ask whether the events of the night had been another dream.

Chapter Thirty
Frying-Pan to Fire

A good breakfast was eaten upon that eventful morning, Dan having plenty of materials for producing a capital meal, and, to judge from appearances, the men were quite ready to settle down to their tasks again, as they made no sign.

Brace had hard work to keep from casting uneasy glances at them, but he did pretty well, joining in the chat over the meal, and listening to a yarn from the captain about how he had traced out the deep channel years before in just such a shallow river as this, and how he was going to find one now.

"This'll be ten times as easy," he said, "for we only want water enough for these boats. I wanted water enough then for a big schooner, heavily laden.—What's the matter, sir?"

This was to Brace, who passed the question off.

"Nothing, nothing," he said aloud. "Go on."

"Oh, there's nothing more to tell. I found a winding channel by sounding from the schooner's boat with an eighteen-foot bamboo," said the captain loudly; and then, as Sir Humphrey was speaking to Briscoe, he bent forward to pick up a biscuit, and whispered to Brace:

"What was it, my lad?"

"Half the guns and rifles have been taken away! and I think they're hidden behind those bushes close to the boats."

"Very likely," said the captain, without moving a muscle. "All right, sir, all right. My lads have got gold dust in their eyes, and can't see right. We'll dust it out of 'em by-and-by."

The by-and-by was not long after, for the captain suddenly cried out:

"Now, my lads, lighten the cutter all you can. Jem, you and three more will man her. Like to come with me, Mr Brace?"

"Yes, I'll come," said the young man firmly, and he gazed anxiously at the men to see what was to happen next.

Nothing. No one stirred till the captain sprang to his feet.

"Did you hear me?" he roared.

For answer the crew clustered together on the shore, and there was a quick whispering, several of the men urging Jem to speak.

This he did at last, desperately, his words following one another in a hurried way.

"We've been thinking, captain, that now we've found plenty of gold we don't want to go no farther up this here river."

"Oh! have you?" cried the captain sarcastically; "*we* have? You mean you have, my lad. Well, it was very kind of you, but you see these gentlemen say that though we've found plenty of gold they would like to go a bit farther, so tumble into the boat at once, and don't you ever speak to me again like that, or maybe you'll be saying more and getting yourself into trouble."

"That's all very well, captain," said the man, after a desperate glance at his messmates; "but we think, all of us, that it won't do to leave all this gold. There's a fortune apiece for us, you and all, so we're going to—"

"Lighten that boat, I say!" roared the captain, making a rush at the man, who was, however, too quick, for he darted aside and ran back behind his fellow-mutineers.

"Bring that fellow here," shouted the captain, to the two mates, and Dellow and Lynton stepped forward at once, as if to seize the sailor and drag him to the captain's feet.

But the men stood firm, closing in round their chosen leader, backing away the while, and suddenly making a dash for the bushes close to the boats. The evolution was well performed and showed that it had been carefully thought out, for the next minute six of the men disappeared, and after stooping down came again to the front, each carrying a gun or rifle, while the other six darted behind them to arm themselves with boathooks and bamboos.

"Just you keep off, Mr Dellow, and you too, Mr Lynton, and you won't be hurt," cried Jem fiercely. "If you do come on, mind, it's your own fault if you get a charge of shot through you."

At this moment Brace made for his gun, but the captain shouted at him.

"No, no!" he roared; "we don't want anything of that kind, sir. I can bring my lads to reason without guns. Here, you sirs, throw down those tools, or it will be the worse for you. Do you hear?"

"Yes, and it'll be the worse for you, captain, it you don't keep back. Stand fast, lads. It's to make us rich men for life."

"It's to make you convicts, you dogs," roared the captain. "Now, my lads, let 'em have it."

"They're four to one, Brace," cried Sir Humphrey, through his clenched teeth. "I can't stand this. Come on."

"You might ask me to chip in," said Briscoe fiercely; "I'm coming all the same."

And the three lookers-on turned themselves into combatants and rushed to the support of the captain and his two officers, who, regardless of the weapons held by the crew, rushed at them with doubled fists.

There were shouts and yells of defiance, and directly after *thud, thud, thud,* the dull heavy sounds of well-delivered blows, for the captain was a very truthful man: he said he hit hard, and he did, while his two officers showed that they were worthy pupils; and with such an example before them in the wild excitement of the combat, the three passengers followed their fists again and again, science helping them, so that their adversaries went down or fell back struggling.

As previously intimated, the crew had six guns among them, but not a shot was fired. In fact, they were presented merely as a menace and under the vain belief that the sight of the weapons would be sufficient to make the captain's party yield at once to any arrangements the men proposed respecting the gold. Consequently, in the confusion of the attack, first one piece and then another was thrown down and trampled under foot, those who had held them taking to their natural weapons of defence, and faring very badly.

At the end of a minute, instead of the enemy being two to one, and all picked, big muscular fellows, the numbers were even, six not wounded but half-stunned sailors lying or sitting upon the earth.

One was holding his jaw, literally, and not in the metaphorical fashion of keeping silence; another was carefully rubbing his forehead as if to get rid of a lump; another had made a compress of his left hand to hold over his left eye; again another was upon all-fours like a dog, gazing ruefully at the earth and shaking his head slowly, not because he was sorry, but to rid himself of a strange dizzy sensation, while the nearest man to him was sitting down contemplating something white which lay glistening in his hand and looking wonderfully like a fine front tooth.

Just at that moment the captain shouted a warning, for the second half of the crew suddenly gave way and made a rush for the boats.

"Quick!" roared the captain; "cut them off!"

Wild with excitement now, Brace bounded forward, running faster than he had ever run before, reaching one of the men, who proved to be Jem, and planting a blow on his ear just as the fellow was stooping to raise the grapnel from where a couple of its flukes were driven firmly into the earth.

The result of this was that Jem went over side-wise just in front of another fugitive, who tripped over him and took a flying plunge, hands first, into the shallow water, sending it up in splashes which sparkled in the sunshine.

By this time Lynton was up with the rest, hitting right and left, before facing round with Brace to defend the boats, while Briscoe and Dellow came to their help, and, thus cut off; the six sailors turned off along the river bank and made for the nearest clump of trees, among which they disappeared, leaving their wounded upon the field.

"Hah!" cried the captain breathlessly, "I've 'most lost my wind. Now, gentlemen, I call that a neat job. Will you do the crowing, Mr Brace?"

"I don't think there's any need, captain," said Brace, who was examining one hand.

"Not a bit, my lad. Hullo ... hurt?"

"Only knocked the skin off my knuckles. Your men have such hard heads."

"Yes, but we've softened some of 'em," said Lynton.

"Given 'em a thoroughly good licking," cried the captain; "eh, Sir Humphrey? Better than shooting the idiots ever so much. Be a lesson to 'em," he continued, raising his voice. "You, Lynton, collect those pieces that the thieving dogs took. They dropped 'em all, didn't they?"

"Yes, sir; they've left every one of 'em," said the second mate.

"That's right. Mr Brace, just you take one of the shot guns and keep guard over these six chaps littering the deck—ground, I mean. They're prisoners, and I'm going to make slaves of them to row us up the river. I'll give 'em gold. If one of 'em tries to run after those other cowardly swabs you fire at him, sir. Pepper him well in the legs, and if that doesn't stop him, give him the other barrel upwards."

"All right," said Brace, laughing.

"I'll be ready too," said Briscoe, "in case you miss. But wouldn't it be better to put 'em in the small boat for the present, and take out the oars and sail?"

"Good idea, Mr Briscoe," said the captain. "See to it, Dellow, and make her fast to the stern of the other boat with the grapnel-line."

The first mate nodded, strode to the man who was looking at his tooth, ordered him into the lesser boat, and the man rose and went like a lamb, the rest following slowly and in a more sheepish way, as the big mate walked to them in turn and pointed meaningly ahead.

"What about the others, captain?" said Sir Humphrey.

"T'other six, sir?" replied the gentleman addressed. "Oh! they've cut and run. Let 'em go gold-washing and making their fortunes. They're off on a holiday, and as they'll have no dish-washing or other dooties to do they'll have plenty of time, and I hope they'll enjoy themselves."

"You mean to leave them behind?"

"That's about it, sir. They've gone. It isn't my doing. I didn't drive them away."

"What, skipper?" cried Briscoe, laughing. "It that wasn't driving, what was it?"

The captain's face puckered up into a peculiar grin in which the corners of his eyes participated with those of his mouth.

"Well, it wasn't a bad charge, was it?" he said. "But now then, business. Let's have all those cooking traps and things aboard again. Eh? Oh, there's your chap hard at work over them, Mr Briscoe. I missed him, and thought he'd gone off with the gang."

"What, my Dan?" cried Briscoe. "I say, skipper, did you get a crack in the fight?"

"Nary crack, sir, as you'd say," replied the captain. "Why?"

"Because your head doesn't seem clear this morning."

"I beg his pardon, then," said the captain, in a gruff voice. "Now then, all on board as soon as we can, and let's be off before we catch Mr Briscoe's complaint and want to stop and wash for gold."

The American laughed at the captain's dry remark, and joined in with the rest, working away till all that had been landed was on board the larger boat, when Brace turned to the captain.

"This is all very well," he said; "but we were aground last night, and you were speaking about searching to-day for a channel along which we could pick our way."

"That's right, sir," said the captain grimly; "but Nature's been on our side."

"I don't know what you mean," said Brace, staring at him.

"River's a foot deeper than it was last night. There's been a storm somewhere up there in the mountains."

"I see no sign of it," said Sir Humphrey. "Oh, yes, I do. Look, Brace: the water is nothing like so clear."

"That's right, sir," said the captain. "These rivers alter a deal sometimes in twenty-four hours. Have we got everything on board?"

"Ay, ay, sir," cried Lynton.

"Except the rest of the crew, captain," said Sir Humphrey.

"Oh, yes, of course, sir; but we shall ride lighter without them."

"You never mean to leave them to starve in this wilderness, captain?"

"Aren't this a matter of navigation, Sir Humphrey?" asked the captain sternly, but with a twinkle in the eye.

"Certainly not," said Sir Humphrey. "It is a question of common humanity."

"About six common men, sir," said the captain. "Well, we shall see. Anyhow, I'm going on up the river to give them a lesson; and if we come back and find them all reduced to skins and skeletons down upon their marrow-bones asking to be took aboard, why, then, perhaps, we shall see, and—what in the name of wonder's up now?"

For all at once, as the boats pushed off and the sail of the foremost was being hoisted, the six men reappeared from where they had hidden in the woods and came running towards them, shouting and making signs.

"They've caved in at once, skipper," said Briscoe laughingly. "Look here, you'd better have a court-martial and sentence them to give each other a round dozen with a rope's-end upon the bare back."

"Look, look!" shouted Brace, springing to his feet and shading his eyes, before snatching up a rifle, an example immediately followed by the rest, for there in the distance appeared the whole of the six deserters running hard in a knot, and dodging in and out among the trees as they made for the shore, while in full pursuit there was about double their number of savages apparently armed with bows and arrows, of which they made use by stopping from time to time to send a shaft in pursuit of the fugitives.

"Shall we land and go to their help?" said Brace.

"I don't think we need," said Sir Humphrey. "They seem to be holding their own in running, and I suppose now, captain, you'll have no objection to them on board?"

"Not a doubt of it, sir," said the captain drily.

"Here, Lynton, haul that boat alongside. We shall want them now, Mr Brace."

"Of course," replied the young adventurer.

"But you haven't looked down the river, sir."

"What at?" said Brace, staring; and then, panting with his excitement: "I say, there are four large canoes coming up."

"That's right, sir," said the captain gravely. "Now look the other way. See that?"

Chapter Thirty One
The Fire Grows Hotter

"I do," said Briscoe, staring. "I can see two canoes coming round the bend yonder, half a mile away."

"Two!" cried Brace excitedly; "why, there are three."

"Yes," said the captain coolly; "we're took front, back, and flank. Better put off the rope's-ending now, Mr Briscoe, eh?"

"Well, it would be better," said the American coolly, as he carefully loaded his piece. "These things are as well done privately and without a lot of lookers on. It might give these dark gentlemen a bad opinion of the whites."

"What are you going to do, captain?" said Sir Humphrey impatiently.

"There's only one course open to us, sir—and that is to fight."

"I mean what will you do about those men who are ashore?"

"Oh, they're settling that themselves, sir," said the captain, with a chuckle of satisfaction. "They've broke away like so many naughty boys who think they can manage for themselves, and as soon as they start they've got frightened and are running home for safety."

"But you'll take them on board, won't you?" said Brace.

"Certainly I shall, and make 'em fight too, sir," said the captain.

"Yes," said the American, "and they'll have to do their level best. Shall I cover them, skipper, and let the niggers have a sprinkling of buckshot to show them we are ready?"

"Yes," said the captain; "and you two gentlemen had better help. That's the first thing—to get them aboard safe."

Pieces were cocked, and their holders sat in the boats watching the flight and pursuit, Brace's heart beating violently. He glanced up and down at the novel sight of canoes where all heretofore had been so deserted, and saw at once that there was nothing to fear in their direction for the next half-hour, while in another minute or two he could plainly see that a serious engagement would have commenced with the natives on shore, and the sensation this caused was both novel and strange to him.

"The idiots!" he said, in a low voice; "why couldn't they keep to their duties instead of breaking away like this?"

"Because they're just ordinary men," said Briscoe, who was by his side. "They're going to pay pretty dear for their game, though."

"Don't you think that they will be able to get here safely?"

"That's just what I am afraid about. The niggers are better runners than they are, and more at home on the ground, and they could catch up to them at once, only they like to tackle their enemies at a distance. Look!"

"Yes, I see," said Brace, whose breath came and went as if he had been running hard, and his eyes dilated when he saw that, as the men tore off through the various obstacles of rock, bush, and tree, the Indians suddenly began to slacken their pace and prepare their bows.

"Ah, we must put a stop to that, gentlemen," cried the captain. "Give them something to put an end to those games."

A low murmur of acquiescence arose, and guns were levelled, but no shot rang out.

"Can't fire yet, skipper," growled Briscoe. "I could pick off a man or two with a rifle easily, but I'm not loaded with ball, and these buckshot scatter so. I don't want to hurt any of our own chaps if I can help it."

"And they're too far off from us as yet," said Brace excitedly.

"Well, they'll soon shorten the distance," growled the captain; and then he clapped his hand to the side of his mouth and yelled to his mutineers: "Now, run, you lubbers! Don't go to sleep. Run as if you meant it."

Taang!

"Bah! he's got it," cried the captain.

There was the dull half-musical sound of a bowstring, and to Brace's horror one of their flying men made a spasmodic jump into the air and came down upon hands and knees, his nearest messmates passing on some twenty yards before they could check their speed; and then, in the midst of the thrill of excitement which ran through the occupants of the boats, the retreating party paused, and dashed back to help their fallen mate.

An involuntary cheer of encouragement rang out from those in the boats.

"Good boys—good boys!" yelled the captain. "That's true British, Briscoe. There, I forgive 'em all for that. Oh, if they only had something in their fists they'd drive the beggars back to the woods. Pick him up, boys, a leg or a wing apiece, and run again. Oh, Lor' a' mercy, gentlemen, can't one of you shoot?"

For in those exciting moments the Indians, who had come bounding forward with a triumphant yell on seeing the white man fall, hesitated and stopped in fear and surprise when they saw that their flying enemies had halted and dashed back to rescue their messmate.

This, however, was only a momentary pause, for, recovering themselves, they yelled again and rushed forward.

It was the opportunity wanted, and almost together three guns flashed out their contents, sending a little storm of buckshot amongst the runners, who turned on the instant and began to retreat towards the woods.

"Missed!" cried the captain.

"Hit!" cried Briscoe.

"No: there's not a man gone down," cried the captain.

"But plenty of hits," said Briscoe, setting the example of reloading. "Look at them rubbing their coppery hides. The shots wouldn't penetrate at this distance."

"Never mind: it's stopped them, anyhow," growled the captain. "Bravo! Good boys!" he cried, as he saw his mutinous lads carefully raise their companion, while two of the party armed themselves with big pieces of stone and formed themselves into a rearguard, backing slowly, their faces to the hesitating enemy.

"Bravo!" continued the captain. "My boys are the right stuff after all."

He sprang over the boat's side, gun in hand, as he spoke, and, influenced by the same feeling, Brace and Briscoe followed, the former thrusting his brother back.

"No, no, Free," he cried. "You're not strong enough yet. Stay in the boat and cover us with one of the rifles."

A look of resentment rose in Sir Humphrey's eyes, but he accepted the position, dropped back into a seat, exchanged his double fowling-piece for one of the rifles lying ready, and sat watching the progress of the three, who were at once supported by Dellow and Lynton, the men on board cheering as the party of five splashed through the shallow water to meet the mutineers, who were compelled to come slowly on account of their load.

The support was none too soon, for, recovering themselves, and enraged at seeing their intended victims escaping, the savages were now advancing once more at a run.

"Make for the boat, boys," cried the captain, as he led his party past the mutineers, and then, setting the example, levelled his piece. "We three will give 'em this taste, gentlemen," he cried. "You cover us while we reload. Now then, all together—fire!"

There were the dull flashes, the puffs of smoke, and a yelling from the enemy who, at fifty yards away, received the stinging volley and were checked, Brace and Briscoe standing fast while the captain and the two mates followed the retreating party with their load.

"Two of the enemy down," said Briscoe coolly. "Old skipper will think he and his men are better shots than we are."

"Let him," said Brace. "They're up again. Look out: they're coming on."

"Stand fast, then," said Briscoe. "Let 'em have it this way. Can you let 'em come on till they're five-and-twenty yards nearer?"

"Yes," said Brace, immediately following his companion's example and dropping on one knee to take aim.

"Aim low, Brace," said Briscoe. "Let's try to cripple their legs. We don't want to kill any of them. Aim right in the brown, as you English sportsmen say."

"Right," replied Brace, setting his teeth and kneeling firm as a rock, while the Indians came on at a trot, grimacing and yelling to frighten them into flight.

" The guns went off together."

But they had the wrong stuff to deal with, and their eyes dilated and rings of white appeared round the irises in theft utter astonishment at seeing the two white men calmly awaiting their onslaught, Briscoe with the stump of a cigar in his teeth, mumbling out:

"Twenty-eight—twenty-seven—twenty-six—twenty-five—fire!"

The guns went off together, and the pair sprang up and ran after their companions, to find fifty yards nearer the boat the captain and his officers down on one knee waiting to cover them.

"Well aimed!" cried the former. "You two halt to cover us just at the water's edge. That'll give the boys time to get aboard, and then we can laugh at the copper-skinned vermin. Look sharp and reload: they're coming on again."

Brace and his companion continued their retreat, overtaking the sailors with the wounded man, whom they now saw to be Jem, and had endorsement of the fact in the tones of his voice, for he was growling and abusing his bearers.

"Put me down, I says, and go and help the old man. I tell you I can get to the boat myself without any help."

"Hold your row," said one of the men; "if you don't we'll bump you."

"Don't talk, my lads; hurry on," cried Brace, who was busy reloading. "Look sharp and get aboard."

"Ay, ay, sir," cried the party cheerily.

The next minute they were at the water's edge, where their defenders halted ready, just as the captain's voice was heard to shout:

"Fire!"

Three shots rang out, and, covered by the smoke, the captain and his mates ran on, to begin reloading.

"Look sharp, boys!" panted the captain; "get to the boats, each man to his own, but put the wounded man in mine. You're ready, Mr Brace—Mr Briscoe?"

"Yes."

"That's right: we won't row away and leave you. Forward, my lads, and get under cover of the boat's side. Hoist the sail half-mast, and keep behind it. They'll begin to shoot directly. We'll get on board first, gentlemen, to cover you from the boats. Stand fast till we're all in if you can, and then give 'em all four barrels and make a dash for it before the smoke rises."

These next were anxious moments, but Brace did not flinch, and his companion went on talking with his eyes fixed upon the approaching enemy, each man holding an arrow to his bowstring, but unaccountably refraining from winging it home. He seemed to be in every case watching the muzzles of the guns in wonder and fear as he slowly approached.

"I want to cut and run horribly, Brace," said the American, in a husky voice; "only I suppose we mustn't. We shall look like porcupines directly — full of arrows, I expect; but keep up your spirits: I daresay we shall each have a fair share."

"I say, don't!" said Brace. "It is too serious to joke about."

"And no mistake. Are they all aboard yet?" asked Briscoe.

"Don't know, and can't look round. I must face them. It would be ever so much worse to turn our backs."

"Ten times," said Briscoe. "Look out! I say; that's a fresh party — twenty or thirty of them, coming out of the woods a quarter of a mile away. They ought to be too late to reach us."

"Our men are all on board, and the Indians are going to rush us," whispered Brace.

"That's so," said the American. "Be ready. I'll say 'Fire!' Then wait till the smoke lifts, when I'll give the word again, and then it's a rush through the water to the boats. Bet you two cents I get most arrows in my back."

"Steady!" growled Brace hoarsely.

"Fire!" shouted the captain from the boat, and, in spite of the order upsetting their plans, the covering party obeyed and sent their little shower of shot amongst the yelling enemies' legs.

"Let 'em have it again," roared the captain from the second boat.

The remaining two barrels rang out, and those who fired sprang up and dashed through the water to reach the larger boat, where they were seized and dragged in and under cover.

None too soon, for a little shower of arrows came aboard and through the sails, which were shivering in the brisk breeze.

The next minute, in response to a thrust or two, and a touch at the tillers, both sails half-filled, and the boats were gliding swiftly away from the shore, the arrows coming more and more seldom, till the last two failed to reach them, but fell into the water twenty yards astern.

Then the captain, who had been tending the wounded man, rose up and said, loud enough for those in both boats to hear:

"There we are then, my lads, quite out of danger now, and nothing to mind but a few canoes up stream and a few more down; but look here, I've just got this to say to you all: if you'd had your way there'd have been a big fire ashore to-night and a general collection of Indians to the biggest roast they had enjoyed for years. After it was over everyone of those copper-skinned gentlemen would have been going about with a good big bit of my crew in his inside. That's quite true, isn't it, Mr Briscoe?"

"Oh, yes," said the American: "these people are cannibals still when they get the chance."

"That's so," cried the captain; "and now you know, my lads. There, you've had your touch of the gold fever, and if we get back on board I'll give every man-jack of you a dose of quinine. But now I shall say no more about it, for I see you're all sorry for being such fools, and are going to fall back into your work."

There was a low murmur of assent at this, and the captain spoke again:

"What say, Sir Humphrey?"

"I say, we seem to be leaving the canoes down the river well behind, but those up stream are bearing down upon us fast."

"Then," said the captain, "they'd better look out, gentlemen, and keep out of our way, for I mean to rush right upon them full sail. The prows of these boats are pretty sharp, and their dug-outs don't take much to send them to the bottom. I say, you Dan," he went on, "you'd better serve round some biscuit and bacon to the lads, for they must be getting peckish after what they've gone through. I say, Sir Humphrey, what do you say to making a hand-grenade or two out of pound powder-tins and pieces of rag?"

"To throw on board the canoes?" said Sir Humphrey: "horrible!"

"Quite true, sir; but it would be more horrible still if these savages should manage to get the better of the crew of the 'Jason' brig. What do you say to that?"

"I give up," replied Sir Humphrey. "I hate the idea of slaughtering the poor ignorant wretches, but self-preservation is the first law of nature."

"Exactly so, sir. If we kill it won't be for the sake of killing."

"How is Jem's wound going on?" said Brace anxiously.

"You take no notice about that, sir," said the captain, with a peculiar look. "He has got a hole in his leg made by an arrow, and I've doctored it up just as I did your brother's, and laughed at him and told him it served him right. You gentlemen had better take the same line. If he sees that we look serious about it he'll take and die right off: he'll kill himself with the belief that he's shot by a poisoned arrow."

"Is he?" said Brace, in an eager whisper.

"I didn't see the arrow made, sir, and I didn't see it dipped in anything. What's more, I never saw the arrow at all, for the boys pulled it out and chucked it away. Maybe it was poisoned; but you see these arrows are only meant to kill birds, and what might kill a bird won't do much harm to a man. I've done all I know for the wound, same as we did for your brother's. He got well, and if we laugh at Jem he'll get well too."

"The niggers are coming right down upon us, sir," said the first mate from the other boat, "and evidently mean to fight."

"All right, Dellow; be ready for 'em. I shall lead. We mean to fight too."

Chapter Thirty Two
The Way to Nowhere

The long light canoes of the approaching Indians were well manned, and as they came nearer Brace could see that most of the occupants wore a kind of tiara made of the tail feathers of parrots or macaws. Several held spears or bows, but the major part were busy paddling, and they came down with the stream, evidently full of fierce determination to destroy or capture the strange intruders upon their solitudes, striving hard to increase the speed of their canoes, which were in a well-kept line.

There was no time for the discussion of plans, for the distance between the brig's boats and the enemy was rapidly growing less.

"One wouldn't have time to prepare anything if one wanted to," said the captain, after a sharp glance forward. "Will you leave it to me, gentlemen, to do my best?"

"Of course," said Sir Humphrey, and Briscoe nodded from where he knelt, with his double gun held ready in his hand.

"Then here goes," said the captain. "Ahoy there, Dellow; clap on all you can, take the tiller yourself; and run one of the canoes down. Let your lads knock all over who try to board you."

"Ay, ay!" came back in answer from the second boat.

"Now, Lynton," continued the captain, "steer for that canoe in the centre. We're going faster than they are. You, gentlemen, don't shoot, but use the butt-ends of your rifles if we should happen to get to close quarters. Every man take an oar or boathook, and use 'em like as if they were whaling-lances. Ready? Look out!"

Their boat, with the sail straining at the sheet, was now rushing through the water, the side not two inches above the surface, as she raced for the centre of the line of canoes.

"Sit fast!" roared the captain. "Down with you, Mr Brace, or you'll be overboard."

Brace, who had risen in his excitement so as to be able to club his gun, dropped down on to the seat at once.

Then from in front as their own boat seemed to be standing absolutely still and the line of canoes dashing rapidly at them with the paddles churning up the water on either side, there was a fierce yelling, a gleam of opal-rimmed eyes, a crash which made the boat quiver from stem to stern. The sail jerked and snapped as if it were going to fall over the side, and then they were past the centre canoe, sailing on as fast as ever.

Lynton had done his work well, steering so that he drove the boat's iron-protected cut-water right upon the centre canoe's bows diagonally some six feet from the front, when for a few brief moments their progress seemed to be stopped. Directly afterwards the occupants of the stoutly-built boat felt her gliding right over the canoe, which rolled like a log of wood, and then the men were cheering as they looked back at the glistening bottom of the long vessel and six or eight black heads bobbing about in the water.

Crash, grind, and there was another canoe capsized, literally rolled over by the second boat, which seemed to those in the first to rise and glide over the crank dug-out, now beginning to float broadside on with her crew swimming to her side.

A hearty cheer rose now from Dellow and his men, which was echoed from the first boat, as the distance between the party and their fierce enemies rapidly increased.

"You did that splendidly, captain!" cried Brace excitedly.

"Tidy, sir, tidy," was the reply; "but these boats weren't built for steeplechasing in South American rivers. Let's see what damage is done. I don't suppose we're much hurt."

The captain stepped from thwart to thwart as he spoke, and, getting right forward, he leaned over the bows and carefully examined as far as he could reach, before raising his face again and turning to Brace, who had followed him, to now meet his eyes with an enquiring look.

"Right as a trivet," he said. "Took off some of the varnish; that's all that I can see. Ahoy! what damage, Dellow?" he roared to the mate in the boat astern.

There was no reply for a minute or so whilst the first mate examined his boat.

Then came a shout, in Dellow's familiar tones:

"Twopenn'orth o' paint gone, and a bit of a splintery crack in the top plank."

"Any leakage?"

"Not a doo-drop, sir," was the reply.

"Well done. Keep close up abreast," shouted the captain; and, now that the safety of the boats was assured, attention was directed to the canoes, which were being rapidly left astern.

"They seem to be trying to right their craft," said Sir Humphrey, who, like Briscoe, was making observations with his pocket glass.

"Yes," added Briscoe, "and they turned them over quite easily, but their sides are down flush with the water."

"The men have got in again, and they appear to be splashing out the water with their paddles," said Sir Humphrey.

"That's right," said Briscoe, "and the other canoes have ranged up alongside. I can see quite plainly: there's a canoe on each side of the injured ones to keep them up."

"It's my belief that they may bale till all's blue before they get 'em to float. Those dug-outs are worked till they get 'em as thin and light as they can, and if we haven't cut a good gap in each one's side, it's a rum one," growled the captain. "What are they doing now, sir? It's rather far to see, but it seems to me that they're trying to get the sunken canoes to the shore."

"Yes: that's just what they are trying to do," cried Sir Humphrey. "Oh, yes, I can see that plain enough."

"Then they won't follow us up to-day, gentlemen," said the captain; "and perhaps we may not see them again. Might like to sail back, p'r'aps, Mr Briscoe," he continued, "and give the copperskins a friendly word about hope they're not damaged, and then settle down in the shallows for a good afternoon's gold-washing."

"Not to-day, thankye, skipper," said the American drily. "It might be teaching the savages how to catch the gold fever, as you called it, and be bad for their health."

"P'r'aps so," said the captain, with a peculiarly grim look and a glance round at the crew; "and they'll be better employed gumming up those holes in the sides of the canoes."

"Do you think they'll pursue us, captain?" said Brace.

"Most likely, sir," was the cheerful reply. "They'll be wanting to bring us the bill for damages. I'm thinking it would be the safest thing to try and drop down by 'em after dusk. This part begins to be rather unsafe."

He looked at Sir Humphrey as he spoke, and the latter turned to his brother.

"Well, I don't know, captain," he said: "the wind holds good, and we seem to have passed the danger. I don't like to give up yet. What do you say, Mr Briscoe?"

"I think it would be a hundred pities," was the quick reply. "The country is getting more and more attractive. Who knows what we may discover, eh, Brace?"

"I feel exactly as you do, and think we should proceed," said the latter quickly.

"We've got whole skins now," said the captain dubiously, "all but one of us."

"You think it running too much risk to go on?" said Sir Humphrey.

"Well, I can't say that, sir," was the reply, "because we may sail on for weeks and weeks and not see another Indian, while if we go back we are sure to see some."

"Exactly," said Sir Humphrey; "but I can't help thinking that we are getting now into a more uninhabited part of the country, perhaps where travellers have never been before."

"Then I say let's go on," said Briscoe, "and we may find El Dorado, after all."

"El Dorado or no El Dorado, I say don't let's give up yet," said Brace. "Let's keep on till we are obliged to go back to the brig for stores; and by that time we shall know whether it is worth while to come up here again."

"That's good advice, sir," said the captain, smiling at Brace as he spoke. "I don't want to give up: I like it as well as you do. There's only one thing wherrits me."

"What's that?" said Brace.

"My brig. I lay awake for a good ten minutes last night thinking about what we should all feel if we got back to where we left her and found that the old 'Jason' had dragged her anchors and navigated herself out to sea."

"Oh, but if she had dragged her anchors, captain," said Brace, "they'd lay hold again somewhere lower down."

"Yes, sir," said the captain drily; "that's what comforted me. All right, gentlemen. On we go then. I'm thinking now that after the lesson we gave those gentlemen to-day they mayn't care to meddle with us again."

"Do you think any of them were killed?" said Brace.

"Hardly, sir. Certainly not with the buckshot. If any of them lost the number of their mess it would be just now in the river."

"Drowned?"

"Oh, no. They swim like seals. It would be through some of the natives below: old friends of theirs."

Brace felt a shudder run through him as he glanced down over the side, where the water glided deep and dark now from where they were sailing to the tree-clothed shore.

But the conversation took another turn then, the captain proposing that a good midday meal should be eaten now, and no halt made till a suitable well-screened resting-place was reached about an hour before dusk.

"Why not keep right on till it is quite dusk?" said Sir Humphrey.

"He means so that we can land and light our fire in the forest, do our cooking, and put it out again before it's dark, when it would show our position to any prowling natives," said Briscoe.

"That's right," said the captain.

These tactics were carried out, a strong wind wafting the boats along mile after mile to a far greater distance than any amount of paddling would bring canoes in pursuit; and fortune favoured them far more, for, just about the time decided upon, the fine river up which they had come suddenly opened out fan-like, offering them five different routes onward.

"Which shall it be, Brace?" said Sir Humphrey, as he stood up with his brother in the bows. "If the enemy is following us he is as likely to take one as the other."

"I don't know," said Brace, with a laugh. "They are all beautiful. That left one seems the deepest, and the stream flows slowly, so I think we had better choose that."

"Best too for the wind," said Briscoe. "There's a ripple up it as far as we can see."

"It's to the left and not to the right," said Brace.

"All the better," said Briscoe, laughing. "You know what you English folks say about driving: 'If you go to the left you are sure to be right; if you go to the right you'll be wrong.' I think we might well stick to that rule in this case."

The left branch was chosen, and they sailed swiftly up it, finding to their surprise that there was scarcely any appearance of current, and soon after a suitable spot for a landing-place presented itself in one of the many bends of the river's sinuous course.

Here they landed, and Dan was soon busy preparing food, while as far as they could make out they were where human foot had never pressed the soil before.

Chapter Thirty Three
The Sound of Many Waters

The fire was carefully extinguished before night-fall, so that no flash or gleam might betray the adventurers' whereabouts to any prowling foe, and watch was set in each boat after they had been moored about twenty feet from the shore. Everything had been made snug, arms issued round and loaded ready, and once more sleep came to all save Brace and his American companion, who sat together for a good hour, gazing into the forest gloom and listening to the many strange sounds which rose among the dense growth.

Then sleep overtook them, just when they were vainly trying to puzzle out the meaning of a strange booming roar, which sounded not unlike thunder at a distance.

"I guess that's what it is," Briscoe had said. "That's the nearest I can get to it. Maybe there's a clump of mountains not very far away, and they've got a storm there."

"We shall know in the morning," said Brace. "If it's a storm the water will have risen in the night."

"Let it," said Briscoe drowsily. "We're in shelter, and the boats will rise, so it will not matter to us."

The next minute both were asleep, and the night passed tranquilly enough till they were awakened by Lynton, who had the morning watch.

"What is it?" said Brace confusedly: "time to get up?"

"Yes, if you don't want to be scratched out of the boat. Look sharp, please. We're going to get the awning down."

It was quite time, as Brace found on getting his eyes well opened, for the boat was tugging at her moorings, the awning rigged up overnight for shelter was close up among the leafage beneath a bough of the tree to which the rope was made fast; and, instead of the water upon which they floated being like that of a placid lake as it had seemed overnight, it was now rushing rapidly by the boat's sides.

"What is the meaning of this?" asked Brace excitedly.

"Storm up in the hills somewhere," replied Lynton gruffly. "Water's rising fast."

"Mind what you're about there, Dellow, or you'll be capsized," shouted the captain to the first mate. "Make all snug, and keep the boat clear of the trees."

"Ay, ay, sir," came from the other boat, and a few minutes later the mooring-lines were cast off, while the men in each boat lay on their oars, and then as they began to drift swiftly with the rushing waters, a few strokes were given to get well clear of all overhanging branches before the grapnels were let go, but refused for some minutes to get a sufficiently good hold of the bottom.

Finally, however, they caught, plenty of line was let out, and they swung head to stream, dividing the water that rushed by and sending it off in elongated waves.

"That's better," said the captain; "but we must be ready, for I doubt whether these little grapnels will hold long."

"Why not let the boats go?" said Brace. "It's all interesting to glide along a fresh river."

"Because we may be swept no one knows where, my lad. Steering's hard work in such a rapid as this. Besides, we may get into bad company—uprooted trees, floating islands of weeds, and all sorts of things that would make nothing of capsizing us. No; it will be best to wait here till the flood begins to fall. I daresay you gentlemen can manage to amuse yourselves somehow."

"I daresay we can," said Briscoe, lighting up one of his long cigars to have as an early breakfast; "but isn't this all wrong?"

"What?" said the captain sharply, for he was fully upon his mettle in a position which called for all his care. "What's all wrong?"

"Why, the way the water runs. It's just the opposite way to which it was going yesterday."

"That's right," replied the captain; "but it's coming down one or other of the rivers we came to last night with a rush and piling up faster than the main stream will carry it off. It must go somewhere, and some of it rushes along here. Strikes me that the whole country will be under water soon. Look, it's rising fast up the tree-trunks. We shall have to take great care, or we shall be drawn right in among the trees."

"Ah, that would be awkward," said Briscoe drily, "to find the water suddenly go down and leave the boats up in the tree-tops like a couple of big birds' nests."

"Ahoy! Look out, Dellow!" yelled the captain. "Stand by, my lads, to shove her off, or she'll break us away. Hah! I thought so."

For the second boat had suddenly been swept from her anchorage and come rapidly down upon the first. The men tried their hardest to ease her off, but she came into collision with so sharp a shock that the bigger boat was jerked free from her moorings and began to glide with the swift current, dragging her grapnel after her, till the captain gave orders for it to be hauled in.

"Row!" he shouted, and the men dipped their oars into the water with a steady stroke, keeping the boat's prow head to stream as she dropped down stern foremost between two mighty walls of verdure, while on either side it was plain to see that the trunks of the huge forest monarchs were being flooded many feet up.

"There's nothing else for it, sir," said the captain to Sir Humphrey. "You'll be seeing what the country's like, and by-and-by as the water drains off I daresay we can ride easily back with the current quite the other way."

"And what about capsizing?" said Briscoe.

"That's my look-out, sir," said the captain gruffly. "Capsizing means feeding the fish, and I've a great objection to being used for that purpose, without taking into consideration my duty to my passengers and men."

He met Brace's eyes as he spoke, his own twinkling with a drily humorous look, and nothing more was said.

The adventure was exciting enough, for the boats rode on rapidly through the forest, the river, which was comparatively narrow, winding and doubling in the way peculiar to water making its way through a flat country. For now all appeared to be one dead level, with the trees on either side much of a height. Every now and then it was as if they had been swept by the heavy stream into a lake whose end was right in front, but invariably as they were gliding straight for a huge bank of trees the river curved round to right or left, opening out into some fresh bend of its serpentine course, but there was no alteration in their rate of speed.

"It can't last very much longer, though," said Briscoe. "Why, we're going along just like two corks in a gully."

"Yes," said Brace, who had been watching the movements of a troop of monkeys passing along through the trees on their left. "It's all very well now, but if this is to go on after dark we are bound to come to grief."

"No," said Briscoe drily. "The skipper won't risk it. He'll pick his place and run us in among the tree-trunks before sunset. He's a dry old chap, but the longer I'm with him the safer I feel."

The American was quite right, for just when the sun was disappearing behind the trees their leader took advantage of a whirling eddy at a bend of the stream, called upon the men to pull with all their might, and, steering himself; he deftly ran the boat right into the gloom amongst the enormous tree-trunks, where the water was running fast, but it was comparative stillness after the torrent-like rush in the open river.

Here they moored the boats for the night, and, after partaking of a much-needed meal, sleep once more came with the intense darkness, all but the watch resting as calmly as if the sound of many waters lulled them through the night.

Chapter Thirty Four
A Question of Supplies

The morning came bright and clear, and the boats were pushed off once more out of the oppressive gloom of the water-floored forest into the sunny brightness of the river, by which they were again swept on hour after hour.

It was when the question of supplies was beginning to assume a serious aspect about midday that there was a change in the monotonous windings of the river, which suddenly forked, and, the branch to the left seeming the more open, the boats were guided into that.

They were carried along here as swiftly as ever for a few miles, and then the branch divided again and again, till they seemed to be passing through a very network of smaller rivers, their last change being into one whose banks, though well wooded, presented a marked change, for in place of flooded forest the banks displayed steep cliffs dotted with verdure, and in whose cracks grand trees towered up; while, after passing for miles through what rapidly grew into the likeness of a mountain defile, the helpless party had the satisfaction of finding that the current was no longer fierce, but glided along deep and dark at the rate of about four miles an hour.

"Hah!" cried the captain; "this is better. Now, gentlemen, you may get your guns ready for anything worth shooting. We can easily retrieve it here, and find a place by-and-by up among the rocks on one side or the other to land and cook whatever you manage to bring down."

"Why, Brace," said Sir Humphrey, as they glided gently along, gun in hand, watching the steep slope of cliff on their left, everywhere beautiful and in places almost perpendicular and awful in its grandeur, "this is the most beautiful part of the country we have seen."

"Don't talk," said Brace, in a low tone of voice. "I seem to want to watch."

"But don't forget about the cooking," said Briscoe, suddenly raising his gun to his shoulder. "Look out, Brace, up yonder, and watch the bushes on that shelf of rock."

He fired twice the next moment, and half a dozen large birds rose to fly across the river, one of which fell to Brace's gun; while, the boat being run close under the rocky face of the cliff, a couple of men climbed out and crept up among the bushes, where they found that Briscoe had shot three large turkey-like birds, which would form a welcome addition to their larder.

During their steady glide on, half a dozen more good-sized birds of similar and different kinds were brought down from where they were feeding upon the fruits and berries, the men's spirits rising with their success as much as from the beauty of the winding gorge, so that the evening's camping was looked forward to with eagerness, while the captain's declaration that they were getting beyond the influence of the flood was received with a cheer.

"You see, gentlemen, it's like this: the flood has been acting like the tide in a river which has kept back the regular flow here, and it strikes me that before we have gone many miles farther the stream will have grown slacker and slacker till it comes almost to a standstill, and to-morrow some time we shall have it against us once more."

"Unless we turn into another stream and so get back a fresh way," suggested Brace. "It is a wonderful network of water."

"Maybe," said the captain; "but we don't want to lose our bearings."

"We couldn't if we kept on going down stream. We must reach the sea somewhere."

"That's right enough," said the captain drily; "but I don't want to reach it somewhere. I want the way that leads by my brig."

"Yes," said Briscoe, laughing. "Why, Brace, we might be getting out somewhere or other in the Pacific Ocean."

"What about crossing the Andes first?" said Brace sharply.

"Oh, that would be all right. I daresay we could keep on rising till we found a way through-place where the watershed runs, as the learned chaps say."

He had hardly spoken before Brace caught him by the arm, gripping it strongly.

"What is it—bird?"

"No," said Brace, in a hoarse whisper. "I caught sight of a canoe gliding along under the rocks on the farther shore."

"Did you?" said Briscoe coolly. "Well, I'm not surprised. The Indians would be fools if some of them didn't come and live along here. It's about the most beautiful place I ever saw."

"I can see it now," said Sir Humphrey, looking through his glass. "There are four Indians in it with feather crowns on their heads. I don't think they have seen us till now, for they are paddling the other way."

"Then I tell you what: let's lie-to under the trees here," said the captain. "There's a level bit about fifty feet up like a shelf in yon bit of a gully. I had my eye upon that directly, and down here we can lie up quite snugly. Let's have a quiet night somehow, and go on to-morrow morning to see whether the Indians mean to be friends or foes. See 'em still, Sir Humphrey?"

"No," was the reply; "they have gone right out of sight."

"Then now have the goodness to use your glass well, and sweep all the shelves up the farther shore to see if you can make out any sign of an Indian village, sir. Seems a wonderfully likely place for people to be living."

At that moment there was a heavy splash as a large silvery fish flung itself completely out of the water and then fell back, while the noise it made startled a covey of ducks, which went fluttering and paddling up stream.

"Must be inhabitants here, I should say," exclaimed the American, shading his eyes with his hand. "A bit shut in and shady, but all the better in a tropical country: why, it's lovely. Here, gentlemen, I'm getting a bit tired of being cramped up in a boat. I vote we call this Golden Valley and come and live here for a year or two."

"To hunt for the Golden City?" said Brace mischievously.

"Oh, no," said Briscoe quietly; "this place makes me feel as if I didn't want to hunt for anything, only to knock myself up a hut, or to find a sort of cave up on one of these shelves, and then just go on living like. Why, it's a ready-made Paradise, and we seem to have pretty nearly got beyond the reach of the flood."

"Then let's lie up here," said the captain, "and set your Dan to work. It is very beautiful, but it will be better after we've had a bit of something to eat."

Chapter Thirty Five
Night in the Cañon

There was a murmur of approval all through the boat, and soon after the lines were made fast ashore, and Brace was one of the first to climb up to the level shelf the captain had marked out. From here he could command a view of the river banks for quite a mile before the narrow cañon curved, and they loveliness of the place was so surpassing that he stood speechless, forgetting everything in the beauty of the scene, green and golden in the level rays of the sun, with every here and there the shadows deepening into violet.

Brace started as if out of a waking dream as a hand was laid upon his shoulder, and he turned to face Briscoe.

"What can you see?" said the latter, in a low voice.

For answer Brace simply pointed along the cañon, and the American took a long look in silence before venturing to speak again.

"Yes," he said slowly; "very pretty, but I'm not a very sentimental man. One minute I feel as if I should like to live here, and the next I feel certain it would be too dull. Can't see any more signs of the Indians, can you?"

"No," said Brace.

"What sort of a place have you got here? Oh! that's all right; quite a cavern there. Do splendidly for Dan and the boys to make the fire in, out of sight, for we don't want it to bring down strangers upon us. Let's have a look."

Brace had not noticed any cavern, but now his attention was drawn to it he saw at the back of the shelf that there was a broad rift in the cliff, some ten or a dozen feet wide and seven or eight high, while upon entering it was to find that they could look forward into darkness of unknown depth, while the roof seemed to rise as it receded.

"Looks big," said Briscoe, raising his gun as if to fire.

"You had better not shoot," said Brace, laying his hand upon his companion's arm. "It would raise echoes all along the cañon, and perhaps bring down the Indians."

"Quite right; but let's see what's here. Might be a jaguar or something of that kind. Aha, there! Rah-rah-rah-rah-rah!"

The cry ran echoing into the chasm far enough, and was followed by the sound as of a rushing wind approaching them. Directly after a cloud of largish birds, somewhat like the British nightjar in appearance, came swooping by, separating as soon as they were outside, and making for the forest patches across the cañon.

"Do you know them?" said Briscoe, turning round to Brace.

"No: some kind of bird that goes to roost there, I suppose."

"Yes; they roost and breed and live there," said Briscoe. "They're night-birds, and we've started them before their usual feeding-time. Those are the South American oil-birds."

"Yes, I remember," cried Brace. "They breed in the caves round Trinidad, I've read."

"That's right. Well, we don't want to try whether they're good to eat. This way, my lads," he continued, as Dan and three of the men came up to make the fire and start cooking. "Make your kitchen right in here."

This was done, and soon after, as the night fell, the interior of the cave glowed brightly, showing something of its dimensions, and that it extended far into the mountain.

The question was discussed whether it would not be wise to make it their resting-place for the night, affording as it did a roomy shelter such as would make a very welcome change for people who had been cramped up so long in the narrow dimensions of the boats.

But the captain objected, wisely enough, to leaving his boats entirely unguarded, so a compromise was come to, and it was decided that half of each boat's party were to remain below, while the others took possession of the cavern.

The settling of the boats close in shore beneath some overhanging bushes occupied some little time, as well as the carrying up of the necessaries required by those who were to sleep above. By that time Dan's frizzled legs, wings, and slices of bird had been made ready for consumption, and he and his mates worked hard to supply the hungry party. At length, all were satisfied, and they divided to seek their resting-places for the night, Sir Humphrey electing to keep the captain and the first mate company in the boats, while Brace, Briscoe, and Lynton were to rest in the cavern with half of the crew.

As a matter of course, everyone who remained on shore was provided with weapons, and they all sat together chatting till the fire gradually died out and the sailors stretched their limbs with a grunt of satisfaction upon the soft dry sand which formed the floor of the cave.

"What do you say to a quiet smoke on the shelf outside, Lynton?" said Briscoe.

"I'm as willing as willing, for I don't feel at all sleepy yet," was the answer.

"Yes: let's have a look at the stars and the river before we lie down," said Brace; and they strode quietly out till they were at the extreme edge of the shelf, with the black darkness below them and the river sparkling and spangled with the reflections of the stars which glowed brilliantly in a long wide band overhead, the cliffs cutting off a vast amount of the great arch.

"I'm glad that fire's well out," said Briscoe quietly, as he looked back. "Indians are not very likely to be about at night, but if a canoe were coming along the river and the paddlers saw a fire up there, you may depend upon it they would land to see what was the matter."

"That's for certain," said Lynton. "Do you think it likely that those chaps we ran down belong to the same tribe as those we saw in the canoe yonder before we landed?"

"It's hardly likely," said Briscoe. "I fancy the natives of these regions are cut up into little bits of tribes scattered here, there, and everywhere about the forest."

"Pst! Be quiet a minute," said Brace, and all listened.

"What is it?" asked Briscoe, at the end of a minute.

"I heard a peculiar noise while you were speaking, but it is still now."

"Birds—night-birds," said Briscoe. "Our friends of the cavern grumbling because we've turned them out."

"Oh, no; I don't fancy it was that," said Brace hurriedly. "It sounded like human voices singing in chorus."

"Our fellows below in the boat," said Lynton, "only they wouldn't be singing."

"Oh, no; it was not that," said Brace.

"Might be anything," said Briscoe, yawning. "Frogs, perhaps, down by the water-side."

"No: I'm pretty well used to the night sounds we hear," said Brace impatiently. "Ah, there it is: listen."

He was silent, and as if reflected from the cliff there came a low musical sound, very soft and sweet, and, as he said, as if many voices were raised far away in a kind of chorus which reverberated from the sides of the cañon, reaching in a soft murmur to where they stood listening.

"H'm!" ejaculated Briscoe, after listening till the sound died softly away. "Can't be any band having a concert on the next street."

"And I should say it isn't a boating party returning down the river from an outing, singing glees," said Lynton.

"I've heard of singing-fish," said Brace. "There's not likely to be anything of that kind in the river, is there?"

"No," replied Lynton decidedly. "I've heard them out at sea sometimes, when we've been in a calm among the islands."

"More like to be a kind of frog," put in Briscoe. "There are some which whistle and pipe in chorus very softly; but—"

The sound came swelling down the canon more loudly, and the speaker stopped short to listen, till the tones once more died away.

"That's not frogs in chorus," said Briscoe decisively. "Anyone would think there was an abbey somewhere near, and the nuns were singing hymns; only it's impossible, of course."

"Impossible, of course," said Brace softly. "There: it is gone again."

The three men stood listening and straining their ears in the direction from which the sounds had come, but there was a faint whispering as of running water down below, a trickling gurgle, and then startlingly loud came the nasal *quant* of some night-heron at the water's side.

This was answered twice at a distance, while again and again overhead there was the flutter and swish of wings, probably those of the oil-birds circling about the mouth of the cavern.

"It's all over," said Briscoe at last, "and it's night-birds of some kind, I believe. Here, I've been listening so intently that I've forgotten my cigar. I'll go in and light it again with one of the bits of smouldering wood."

He left his two companions, and they heard his footsteps as he went softly into the cavern to reach the fire.

"Does it make you feel queer like, Mr Brace?" whispered Lynton.

"Well, it sets me wondering, and makes me a little uncomfortable as to what the sound can be," replied Brace.

"So it does me, sir. Always makes me feel queer if I don't understand what a noise is. I'm a bit of a coward, I'm afraid."

"I've never seen any signs of it yet, Lynton," said Brace, laughing softly.

"Oh, but I am, sir. That sound made me feel hot and then cold. I say, I've lost count about the points of the compass, but that's plain enough yonder across and up the river. That's the east, and the moon coming up."

"That?" said Brace, as he gazed in the direction named. "Yes, I suppose so. It will be very beautiful when the moon rises over the mountain there and lights up the great cañon. I feel disposed to wait till it shines on the river."

"Moon!" said Briscoe, who had returned unheard, smoking vigorously, and looking in the darkness as if a firefly were gliding to their side. "We shan't see the moon to-night. It must have set a couple of hours ago."

"Of course," said Brace, "and that can't be the east. I should say it's the west."

"What, where that—I say, what light is that over there?"

"Yes, what can it be?" said Brace, as he gazed at the soft glow. "It can't be a forest fire."

"No: if it were we should see clouds of smoke between us and the stars, and they're clear right down to the top of the mountain. Why, Brace, there must be a volcano here, and that's the reflection from the glowing lava. I've seen something like that in the Sandwich Islands."

"I'll go and tell my brother," said Brace. "No; perhaps he's asleep, and it would be awkward for him to get up here in the dark."

"And you couldn't get him up in time," said Lynton. "Look: it's dying out fast. There: it's gone now."

"Yes," said Brace, in a very low whisper. "How strange!"

"Sort of afterglow," muttered Briscoe; "only it's a long time after the sunset. Well, gentlemen, I'm for bed. The scene is over and the lights are out. What do you say?"

Brace said nothing, but he followed his companion into the cave and sleep came soon after—the sound, easy sleep enjoyed in the open air, for the night breeze played softly in at the open mouth of the cave, and there was nothing to disturb the party till the fire began to crackle soon after daybreak.

Chapter Thirty Six
The Strange Find

Saving the canoe that they had seen, the events of the night were pretty well forgotten when a fresh start was made, for all were anxious to explore the great cañon and make a wider acquaintance with the beauties that opened out as they trusted themselves once more to the gliding waters which bore them gently on, so slowly now that the powers of the flood-tide were evidently failing gradually.

"We shall have the current against us before long," said the captain decisively.

"I've been thinking so too," said the first mate; "see how calm the water's getting. It will be wrong then, for the wind is dead against us, what there is of it."

"You'd like to go right on up here, gentlemen, I suppose?"

"Certainly," said Sir Humphrey decisively, "till we are obliged to turn back. The scenery here is grand. Don't you think so, Mr Briscoe?"

"Beats grand," was the reply; "but, my word, if gold wasn't a dangerous word to name in these boats, I should like to land with a hammer and prospect a bit up among these rocks on either side. If they're not full of rich ore I don't know paying stuff when I see it."

"Let it rest," said Brace, in a half-whisper. "Don't let the men hear you talking about gold again. You remember what occurred before."

"Right. I won't mention the word; but if the Indians who live in these parts haven't found out and made use of the metal here, the same as the Mexicans and Peruvians did, they must be a queer sort of people. Shouldn't wonder if we see some more of them to-day."

"Neither should I," said Brace, grasping his piece. "Look: that must be the canoe we saw yesterday evening. What are they doing?"

"Fishing," said the captain quickly. "Now then, gentlemen, let's be ready for emergencies, but make no sign, and maybe they'll be friendly instead of showing fight."

All eyes were directed at a canoe in which three Indians were busy fishing, while a fourth sat in the stern keeping the craft straight by dipping his paddle and giving it a swoop from time to time. They were some three hundred yards ahead, just off a pile of massive rounded rocks which jutted out into the river, and evidently gliding with the current in the same direction as the two boats.

One thing was very evident: they were so intent upon their work that they did not look back, and hence were in perfect ignorance of the approach of the adventurers, while at the end of a couple of minutes they glided on in their frail canoes beyond the rocky promontory, which completely hid them from the view of those in the boats.

"Do you think we ought to follow them up, sir?" asked the captain.

"Yes," replied Sir Humphrey, "and keep our weapons out of sight as if we had come upon a peaceful errand."

"I'm afraid they won't understand us, sir," said the captain gruffly; "but we'll try."

The current was running very gently now, so that the approach of the boats to the promontory took time; but at last it was rounded, revealing to the occupants of the boats a scene as startling as it was strange.

There, a couple of hundred yards away, was the canoe they had followed, while at various distances farther on no less than six more small canoes were dotted about, their feather-crowned crews all busily employed fishing, while as the boats glided round the tree-covered rocks the nearest Indians struck up a soft minor-keyed chant which was taken up by the crews of the other canoes, the whole combining in a sweet low melody which floated over the smoothly-flowing river, fully explaining the sounds heard from the cavern-mouth overnight.

In all probability it was a fisher's song which the people imagined had some effect upon the fish they were trying to lure to their nets. Strangely wild and mournful, it rose and fell, and gained at times in force as it seemed to echo from the right side of the cañon, which here rose up like some gigantic wall hundreds of feet in height, barred with what appeared to be terraces, and honeycombed with open doors and windows, row above row, from the lowest, upon which in two places smouldered the remains of fires, right up to the sky-line, which, roughly regular, was carved into something resembling the crenellations of a gigantic castle, extending apparently hundreds upon hundreds of yards.

Brace had hardly swept the face of the strangely-worked range of cliff when the softly mournful chorus ceased, and as if moved by one impulse, on catching sight of the approaching boats, the Indians burst forth into a shrill piercing yell which echoed and re-echoed discordantly from the face of the rocks. The next moment every man had seized his paddle, and they were making the river foam and sparkle with the vigour of their strokes.

" Every man forced the canoes to their greatest speed."

There was no mistaking the effect produced on the Indians by the appearance of the boats: it was the feeling of horror and dread, every man plunging his paddle deeply into the water and striving his utmost to force the canoes to their greatest speed, so that they might escape from the strange beings. In all probability they were seeing white men for the first time in their lives.

"What does that mean?" said Brace: "going to fetch help?"

"No," said Lynton; "because this must be where they live."

"Yes; there are their fires on the banks," added the captain.

"But they are mere savages," said Sir Humphrey, who ceased to watch the retreating Indians, to sweep the front of the towering cliffs with his glass. "This palace must have been the work of a more highly civilised race."

"And is it your opinion that they are at home, waiting to shoot?" asked Briscoe, stooping to pick up his gun.

"At home? No," cried Sir Humphrey: "those are the ruins of some extremely ancient rock city. Look, Brace. Use your glass. It is the work of centuries. I should say every place has been cut and carved out of the solid rock by some industrious race; but it is quite deserted now save by birds."

"Then we've made a find," said Briscoe excitedly. "I say, I wonder whether this is the great Golden City, captain?"

"No, sir," said the captain gruffly; "don't you see it's all stone?"

"Yes, but—look, Brace. Those places farther on look more regular—there where the trees are growing out of the cracks and the creepers are hanging down like curtains. I can't make 'em out very well with the naked eye, but those windows seem to have carving sculpt about them, and underneath seems to be like a stone colonnade and terrace."

"And a great central doorway," said Brace eagerly. "Yes, you are right: the walls are covered with curious figures and ornamentations. It must be either a great temple or the Inca's palace."

"Inca?" said Briscoe. "Yes—why not? Yes; I suppose it would be an Inca, something of the same kind as the Peruvians. But, I say, look here: these must have been something of the same sort of race as the Peruvians."

"No doubt," said Sir Humphrey.

"And the Peruvians were out and outers for getting gold."

"Look here!" cried the captain, banging his hand down upon the edge of the boat: "if you say gold again, Mr Briscoe, you and me's going to have a regular row."

"Then I won't say it," said the American good-humouredly. "I promised you that I would hold myself in; but recollect what I said to you last night about these cliffs. I felt sure that they contained—ahem!"

"Shall we row close up to the bank where those fires are, sir?" said the captain, turning his back upon Briscoe.

"If you think there is no risk of any Indians lying in ambush among those rock-chambers," Sir Humphrey replied.

"I think the place is quite deserted, sir," replied the captain, "and that if there had been any Indians on shore they would have bolted when these chaps yelled."

"Yes; that's right enough," said Briscoe. "They're canoe-folk, and there's no sign of a single person anywhere along the landing-place. You may depend upon it this is a good fishing-station, and they come up here to camp, and we've frightened them away. It's safe enough."

The captain glanced at Sir Humphrey, who nodded, and the men took to their oars, while Lynton steered the heavy boat right up to the remains of a stone-encumbered wharf or pier that had been laboriously cut out of the solid rock. Here the boats were held, and, well armed, half their occupants sprang out to climb over the slippery stones, which had evidently only lately bean covered by the flood-water, whose mark could be plainly seen, reaching up some ten feet, or half-way to where there ran for hundreds of yards a more or less regular broad terrace cut down out of the rock, and from which the honeycombed perpendicular cliff rose, showing now that it was cut into steps, each step being a rough terrace just below a row of window-like openings.

It was all plain enough now: the Indians' camp had been made right and left of the rugged steps leading up from the water. There the fires were still glowing, and about them and in rows where they could be dried by the sun lay hundreds upon hundreds of good-sized fish: the harvest the Indians had been taking from the river; while the state of some which were piled together beneath a projecting piece of rock suggested that the fishers must have been staying there for days.

"They are sure to come back for this fish," said Brace.

"Very likely," said Sir Humphrey. "Well, if they do, let them have it, and we'll give them some present in return for what we have taken. Look here, captain: we must camp here for a few days to explore this place."

"Very good, sir. We can pick out one or two of these caves, or rooms, or whatever they are, to live in. Your Dan would like one of 'em for a kitchen, Mr Briscoe."

"Yes; he's smelling about them now. I dessay he has chosen one already," said the American. "Yes, I call this fine; we may come across some curiosities next. What do you say to beginning a regular explore, Brace?"

"I say: the sooner the better," cried Brace.

Sir Humphrey nodded.

"We'll divide into two parties, captain," he said. "Let half prepare for making a stay; and I should like the others to bring ropes and a boat-hook or two to help our climb, for I daresay we shall need it before we get to the top of this cliff."

"Very good, sir, and I don't think you'll find a soul to hurt you. I'd keep my eyes well opened though, for you may find wild beasts, and you're sure to find snakes. Let's see," he continued, consulting a pocket compass. "Yes: we're facing nearly due south. It will be a warm spot, and I should say that the old inhabitants are now represented by snakes, and poisonous ones too."

Preparations were soon made, the captain electing to stay below and make all ready for the party's return.

Brace led off along the rugged terrace, which was terribly encumbered by stones fallen from above; but the young adventurer's first idea was to continue along to where the palace-like front reared itself up about the middle of the cliff.

Briscoe stepped alongside of him, and Brace noticed how busily his companion's eyes wandered about, taking in everything on their way. Not that there was much to see at first, save that the captain was right about the inhabitants, for everywhere among the stones which lay heating in the morning sun they came upon coiled-up serpents, many of which were undoubtedly venomous; but there were other reptiles as well, for lizards darted about by the hundred, when disturbed, to make for their holes in crevices and cracks of the stonework, their scales glistening as if made of burnished metal, bronze, deadened silver, mingled with velvety black and soft silvery grey.

At the end of a couple of hundred yards Brace stopped.

"This won't do," he said. "We are on the lowest terrace, and the palace is a floor higher. It ought to be somewhere over where we are."

"That's where I reckon it is," said Briscoe, going to the low ruined wall between them and the river, and straining outward to look up.

"See anything?" said Brace.

"No; I can't reach out far enough; the next terrace overhangs. But it must be here."

"Let's get right on towards the end," said Sir Humphrey, "and I daresay we shall find some kind of steps leading to the next floor."

It was some time before anything but a dark hole was found, and that seemed to be only a receptacle for loose stones, so it was passed; but after pushing on for another two hundred yards, with nothing to take their attention but the retreating reptiles and the beautiful flashing river which washed the foot of the clift, Briscoe grew uneasy.

"Look here," he said; "we're losing time. Let's go back, for I'm sure the way up is through that hole."

"Impossible!" said Brace. "There must be a bold flight of steps."

"No, there mustn't, mister," said Briscoe sharply. "This was an old strong place when the people who lived here were alive, and you may depend upon it that the way up was kept small for safety, so that it could easily be defended by a man or two with spears, or shut up with a heavy stone. I say we've passed the way up."

"Let's go back then," said Sir Humphrey, smiling good-humouredly; and they all made their way back to the bottom of the hole, which had evidently been carefully cut.

Briscoe went to it at once; he gave his double gun to the nearest man to hold, and then, seizing one of the stones with which the horizontal oven-like hole had been filled, he shook it loose and dragged it out to stand in the attitude of lowering the heavy block to the ground.

"No," said Brace; "let me."

Brace uttered a warning cry.

"I see my nabs," said Briscoe coolly, as a snake with menacing hiss came creeping rapidly out, raising its head as it glided down; and then its tail part writhed and turned about, for its power of doing mischief was at an end, the American having dropped the heavy stone upon its threatening crest and crushed it upon the stones below.

"That's one," said Briscoe coolly. "I shouldn't wonder if his wife's at home, and a small family as well. Here, you just fish out that next stone with the boat-hook."

The man addressed stepped forward, thrust the implement into the opening, and drew out another stone, when, as the American had suggested, a second serpent came gliding out, to meet its death quickly and be tossed by one of the men over the parapet-like wall into the river.

More stones were dragged out with the boat-hook, but only a lizard appeared afterwards; and as two more blocks were pulled forth light from above came down, showing that the opening was L-shaped, going about six feet in to where a chimney-like shaft rose at right angles, down which the light struck, evidently from the next terrace.

"I thought so," said Briscoe. "Here: I'll go in first."

"A serpent raised its head, ready to strike."

He crept into the hole at once, and found on looking up the shaft that Briscoe was quite correct, for there were foot-holes chiselled out at intervals in the chimney-like place, so that he could easily step up from one to the other, and the next minute his head was on a level with the floor above and his eyes gazing full in those of a venomous-looking serpent, which raised its head from the middle of its coil ready to strike.

Chapter Thirty Seven
Briscoe's Bit of Ore

Brace obeyed the natural impulse to duck down out of the reptile's reach, and his next idea was to lower himself the ten feet or so to the bottom; but he shrank from doing this, for it seemed ignominious to retreat, so he raised his head sharply again till his eyes were about level with the terrace platform, and there, a dozen feet away, was the tail part of the snake, disappearing in a fissure of the stone.

The next minute he was standing in front of one of the openings they had seen from the river, and his companions were climbing to his side.

Here, upon examination, they found room after room with doorway and window all cut out of the soft limestone, and Sir Humphrey and Briscoe were not long in giving it as their opinion that these single rooms, all separate and with their doorways opening upon the terrace, were really the modest little houses of the old dwellers in this hivelike arrangement. There they were, side by side, all opening upon the long terrace, and, after examining many, they found relics of the old inhabitants in the shape of clay-baked rough pots or their broken sherds; and in several, roughly-formed querns or mill-stones, made, not of the rock in which the houses were cut, but of a hard grit that would act better upon the grain they were used to grind.

These remains, though, were very scarce, and scarcely anything else was found, though search was made in the expectation of finding skeletons; but not so much as a skull was discovered in either of the stone rooms they reached: nothing to show how the ancient inhabitants came to an end. Apparently it was by no sudden catastrophe, and probably only by dying slowly away.

"It might have been a couple of thousand years ago for aught we can tell," said Sir Humphrey.

"Yes," said Brace; "but we have done nothing yet. There are hundreds more of these cells, floor above floor, right to the top."

"Well, let's try another floor or terrace, if we can," said Sir Humphrey. "Has anyone discovered a way up?"

"Yes, sir there's a hole yonder," said one of the men, "and it isn't stopped up."

"Well, let's try it," said Sir Humphrey.

"Hadn't we better get to the end here, and see what that better part is like?" said Briscoe. "It seems to me that we shall find behind those carved stones the best part of the place."

"Very well," said Sir Humphrey: "let's try that first; but we have a month's work before us to explore all this. Now then."

Briscoe eagerly took the lead and went on along the terrace, with the little metallic-looking lizards darting away in the sunshine amidst the fallen stones; and cell after cell was passed till the end of their journey was reached in the shape of a blank mass of rock, beyond which they felt certain that the temple or palace remains must be. But there was no means of passing farther, and nothing remained but to ascend to the next terrace.

This was done, with similar experiences, and another step was gained, from which, after looking down to where the boats were moored, they again climbed higher, entering very few of the cells, but directing their efforts towards reaching the central portion.

But failure attended every effort, and, hot and wearied out by what was growing a monotonous task, Brace and the American readily acquiesced in Sir Humphrey's proposal that they should now descend and join their companions in the midday meal, and afterwards take the smaller boat, row to the front of the temple, and try for away up from the river.

The task of descending and going back took considerably longer than they anticipated, but at last they reached the lower terrace, where the rest were awaiting their return, and over the meal they related their experiences.

These were precisely similar to those of a couple of the men who had explored a little on their own account in the other direction; but they had been compelled to keep to the terrace where the fires had been lit.

"The place must have been built by the same kind of people who cut their rock houses in some of the cañons in Mexico," said Briscoe; "only those are a degenerate set, and their cells or dwellings are very rough and primitive. These people must have been greatly in advance. There: I want to get to work again. There must be a way into that temple place from the front."

"Well, let's try," said the captain. "It's a queer place if there is no way in."

The afternoon was getting on when the exploring party entered the smaller boat and had it rowed out into the stream a short distance from the centre of the rock city, just facing the spot where the terraces were grotesquely carved; and as they minutely examined the partly natural, partly sculptured place, they were more than ever impressed by the excellence of the workmanship.

It must have been the work of many, many years, perhaps of generations, of the people who had lavished so much skilful toil on that centre, which was about a couple of hundred feet in width, and rose up terrace above terrace six or seven hundred feet before the plain uncarved rock was reached, in whose clefts tree, shrub, and creeper grew abundantly for a similar distance, while to right and left the cell-like windows right up to the top of the cañon finished off as before intimated, something like the crenellations on the top of a Norman castle.

"It must have been magnificent at one time," said Sir Humphrey. "I wish I were clever with my pencil, so as to be able to reproduce all this on paper. These ornamentations are grotesque and horrible, but wonderfully carved, and the variety of the figures is marvellous."

"Hadn't we better row close in?" said Briscoe, who seemed impatient, and the men took to their oars till the strong rock wall was reached and the boat drawn along by one of the men with a boat-hook from end to end and back, without a sign of any way up being found.

There they were in the deep water, which glided along at the foot of a blank, carefully smoothed-away wall of rock, perfectly perpendicular, and, save where it was dotted here and there with mossy growth, offering not the slightest foot- or hand-hold.

"Why, it must be fully fifty feet high to that carved coping-like projection," said Brace.

"Yes, about that," said Briscoe, with a sigh of disappointment. "Here, I'd give a hundred dollars for the loan of a ladder that we could plant down here in the water and would reach to the top."

"It would take a long one," said Brace, laughing. "I wonder how deep it is."

"Ah, let's try," said Briscoe. "Here, hand one of those fishing-lines and a lead out of the locker, Lynton."

This was well within the second mate's province, and the next minute he had the heaviest lead at the end of a line, dropped it over the side, and let it run down as fast as he could unwind.

"I say: it's deep," he said, as the line ran over the boat's gunwale; and he said so again and again, till the winder was empty and the lead not yet at the bottom.

"How long is that line?" said Brace, in astonishment.

"One hundred yards, gentlemen," said Lynton loudly. "Shall I have it wound up again?"

"Yes," said Sir Humphrey. "We must try and find bottom some other time. The river must be of a terrific depth."

"That's so," said Briscoe. "You see, we're in a tremendous canon, and the bottom is filled up by this river, which seems as if it would hold any amount of flood-water. I'll be bound to say it's full of fish, and that accounts for the Indians coming here with their nets and lines."

"What's to be done now?" said Brace.

"We must try the other end of the place, and see if we can't get into the temple from there," said Briscoe, who had taken out his knife to begin scraping the slime and moss from the face of the rocky wall till he had made a clean patch, which he examined with a pocket magnifier.

"There's time to do a bit more to-day," said Lynton, who was eager to go on exploring, and in obedience to an order the men rowed gently on past the front of the temple, till about a quarter of a mile farther on a similar landing to that which they had first approached was reached, and the party eagerly ascended the rough steps to a flat wharf or terrace like the other where the smouldering fires were found, ascended by another L-shaped passage to the next terrace, to find more and more rooms or cells, and then hurried on back till they came face to face with the blank rock which formed the other end of the temple.

"This must do for to-day," said Sir Humphrey decisively. "Turn back now. To-morrow, if all's well, we will ascend right to the top."

"And look along there for the way into this place," said Brace; "for way in there must be. Lead on, Mr Lynton; we'll follow."

The second mate started off with the men, and as soon as their backs were turned Briscoe stooped quickly and picked up one of the pieces of stone which had crumbled down from somewhere up the face of the cliff.

"What have you got there?" said Brace: "a piece of ancient carving?"

"Look," said the American, in a low tone, and he handed the piece to Sir Humphrey, holding the side that had been downward as it lay on the stone-encumbered terrace, upward where the fracture looked comparatively new.

"Gold!" exclaimed Sir Humphrey, as he saw that the stone was webbed with glistening thready veins.

"Ah! I didn't say the word," said Briscoe, laughing, as he glanced forward at the backs of Lynton and the men. "But that's what it is. I knew it. I'm not going to talk and make a fuss; but that bit you've got hold of would crush and give as much as a couple of pounds of gold a ton."

"You amaze me," said Sir Humphrey.

"It amazes P Franklyn Briscoe," said their companion. "Shall I put this in my pocket, or throw it away?"

"Keep it," said Sir Humphrey, "and we'll show it to the captain. I don't see why we should not take back as much of the richest ore as the boats will carry. Let's see what he'll say."

"Yes; let's do so," said Briscoe; "but it seems queer, doesn't it, that there should have been people living who could make a town like this, and then for hundreds or thousands of years poor simple Indians going on shooting and fishing while all this wealth was waiting in the rocks if they had known what it was worth?"

"They could not have been so advanced a people as the Mexicans and Peruvians," said Brace.

"Seems not," said Briscoe drily, as he thrust the piece of ore in his pocket and followed the men to where they could descend to the boats.

That evening, as the party sat together in front of one of the lower cells, looking at the beauties of the reflections from the river on the far side of the cañon opposite, Brace waited till the attention of the men, who were at a little distance from them, was quite averted, and said softly:

"Show the captain the piece of curious rock you picked up to-day, Briscoe."

"Eh?" said the captain: "bit of curious rock! I picked up a bit too."

He fumbled with his hand in his pocket and drew out something before taking that which the American held out.

"Humph, yes," he said: "mine's just the same. Bit which has come down from the face of the cliff somewhere. I say, there's no mistake about it, Squire Briscoe: this is rich in gold."

"Ah, would you!" cried the American sharply; "who said we weren't to mention that?"

"I said so," replied the captain drily. "Don't talk so loud. But this sets a man thinking, eh, Sir Humphrey and Mr Brace: and, you see, gold is gold, after all."

Chapter Thirty Eight
A Double Discovery

No more was said about the gold ore then, but the captain showed himself deeply interested in the proceedings to further investigate the ruined city. Briscoe, though, made one remark to Brace the next morning after a restful night.

"If this isn't the Spaniards' El Dorado," he said, "it's quite good enough to be, and I'm quite satisfied with our find."

There had been no sign of the Indians, whose dried fish were utilised a good deal by Dan for the men's breakfast, and in good time a fresh start was made, this time with the captain one of the party, the intention being to try and mount to the highest terrace and see if there was any entrance to the central portion of the rock city from there.

Taught by the previous day's experience, the party—led by Brace and Lynton, who both displayed in their eagerness plenty of activity—climbed pretty quickly from terrace to terrace, disturbing plenty of birds, for the most part a kind of pigeon, which nested freely in the cell-like openings. Reptiles, too, were abundant, but all ready enough to make for their holes in the rifts of the rock, the lizards glancing out of sight in a moment, the snakes slowly and resentfully, as if ready to strike at the intruders at the slightest provocation, but no one received hurt.

Upon every terrace the relics left by the old inhabitants were the same: broken earthenware and the much-worn little hand-mills used for some kind of grain, all showing that every terrace had been occupied by rows of narrow dwellings, safe havens that could easily be defended from attack by an enemy; for, if the lowest terrace had been mastered, the people had but to block up the chimney-like approach to the next terrace after fleeing thereto, and defy their foes, whose only chance of gaining the mastery was by starving out those in possession.

Sir Humphrey pointed this out to the others as they climbed higher and higher; but he was directly afterwards somewhat nonplussed by a question put by the captain—one which was unanswerable. It was simply this:

"How do you suppose the besieged people would get on for water?"

The party were nearing the top at last, having, as far as they could make out, only six more terraces to mount, when, as they paused, breathless and covered with perspiration and dust, for a few minutes' rest, they heard a peculiar sound, which came from the direction of the end of the terrace nearest to the great central part.

"Why, it must be water falling somewhere right in the cliff," cried Brace; and, forgetting his breathlessness, he hurried along over the crumbling stones and dust in the direction from which the sound seemed to come.

"It comes from out of here," said Lynton, who was first to arrive at the end of the terrace, and he stopped at one of the familiar open doorways and listened.

There was no mistaking the sound now; it was the hollow echoing noise of water falling into some reservoir in the interior of the cliff; and, upon passing in, they found that, instead of this being one of the ordinary cells, it was the entrance to a wide passage, apparently leading right into the bowels of the mountain.

"Mind how you go," cried Lynton, as Brace stepped boldly in.

"Hullo! what have you found?" cried Briscoe, who came next to Lynton. "Water? Why, they must have dug out a great cistern or reservoir in here, and let in a spring from somewhere above."

"I say, do mind how you go," cried Lynton excitedly. "It's getting dark there, and you may slip down into some awful well-like hole."

"All right," said Brace confidently. "I'm feeling my way every step with the butt of my gun, and I can see yet."

"Precious awful-looking place," said Briscoe. "Here, we must have lights. Stop him, Lynton: he shan't go a step forward. I don't mean for us all to be drowned like rats in a tank."

"You two wouldn't need to be," said Brace coolly, "for you would stop at once if you should hear me go down."

"Oh, of course," said Briscoe, with a sneer: "we shouldn't try to save your life. 'Tisn't likely, is it, Lynton?"

"Not a bit," was the gruff reply; "but I say, Mr Brace, hold hard now. I'll go back and send a man down below to bring up some pieces of pine-wood to burn."

"I have stopped," said Brace, whose voice sounded to the rest of the party hollow and echoing, dying away in the distance like a peculiar whisper. "There's a great pillar here, and the passage branches off to right and left."

"Well, let's have lights."

"I don't think we shall want them if we take the passage to the left, for I can see light shining in through a hole. Yes, and there's another hole farther on. It's a passage going down at a slope. Why, it's all steps."

"Steps?" cried Briscoe, as he heard the tap, tap of the steel plate covering the butt of Brace's gun as he felt his way.

"And so it is away here to the right: steps going down into black darkness. I know! down to the great tank, into which the water falls from ever so high up."

"Then you stop, young fellow," cried Briscoe hoarsely, "or you'll be falling too from ever so high up, and I daresay that's a big stone cistern half a mile deep, and full of water-snakes and polligoblins."

"Listen," said Brace; "I'm going to feed them. Be quiet, everybody," he added, for the passage behind was now being filled up, the captain and Sir Humphrey in front.

"What are you going to do now, sir?" asked Lynton.

"Here's a great mass of stone that seems to have fallen down from the roof close to my feet. Hold my gun."

He passed his piece to the mate, who could faintly make out the speaker's shape by the feeble light which came from beyond him to the left.

"Heavy," panted Brace, "Hah!"

He raised the stone right above his head and heaved it from him, the expiration of his breath being plainly heard by the listeners in the painful silence which followed for a couple of seconds. Then there were sparks emitted from somewhere below, where the stone struck with a crash and bounded off into space.

The crash was echoed, and seemed to reverberate round and round some great vault, and then came directly after a dull, solemn, weird-sounding *plosh*! evidently not many feet below where they were standing.

After this, there were peculiar whisperings and sounds, as if numbers of disturbed occupants of the water were beating and lapping at the walls of the place: then silence once more.

"Be careful, Brace!" cried Sir Humphrey.

"It's all right," said Brace coolly. "There: I've left that place. All of you bear off to the left and follow me down these steps. Hurrah! I believe we've found the way to the great temple at last."

"It's all right, sir," cried Briscoe, who had passed Lynton. "I can see plainly now. There's a narrow flight of steps leading down close to the face of the cliff, and it's lit every few yards by big square holes, only they're most of them grown over and choked by creepers."

"Hi! Look out there, everyone," shouted Brace. "Lie down."

"Brace uttered a loud cheer and stood waving his hat."

For all at once there arose a peculiar rushing sound, and as everyone crouched as low as he could, he was conscious of the whistling of wings in rapid flight and the ammoniacal odour of a great stream of birds passing over them to reach the outlet from the passage into the open air.

"It's all right, lads," shouted Briscoe. "It's only a flock of oil-birds that we have disturbed. Yes, I thought so: some of them have helped to block up these window places with their nests. I can feel several here."

The birds were some minutes before they had all passed through the opening, and then the tramp downwards was resumed, with the result that before long the light grew stronger from below, and at last quite bright, for a peculiar rustling was heard, which resolved itself into the acts of Brace, who had reached a level spot and was now busy with his large sheath-knife hacking away at a dense mass of creeper not unlike ivy.

A few minutes later, and he was out upon an overgrown terrace gazing over a much-corroded carved parapet at the sparkling river below; and he uttered a loud cheer and stood waving his hat to the men far down to his left, two of whom were seated in the larger boat.

The top terrace of the great temple-like place had been reached, and after a few words of congratulation upon their success the examination of the strange edifice began.

They were a good deal checked at first by the growth of ages and stones which had crumbled down; but they were not long making out that the construction of the place was upon the same plan as that put in practice over the openings to right and left; though the cells were much smaller, and suggested that they had been intended for occupation by one or at most two people. There were no traces of domestic implements to be found, and nothing but the dust of the crumbling stones and the nests of birds with which the openings of the cells were choked met the searchers' eyes.

The investigation of this portion of the cliff city was, of course, made in the reverse way, terrace after terrace being explored by the adventurers descending; but the L-shaped shafts were far larger and more commodious, and, instead of holes being made for the feet, carefully-made steps had been cut out of the solid stone.

Feeling assured that if any interesting traces of the old dwellers were to be found they would in all probability be here, Sir Humphrey and his brother headed the search, and one by one every cell was entered and each terrace explored, till, as they looked over the front, they made out that only three more terraces remained, one of which was that below which the great wall of rock went sheer down to the river at the spot where they had cast the line to find bottom.

The party paused now for a few minutes' rest and conversation before descending to these last three terraces.

"It is a wonderful place," said Brace thoughtfully, "and the old people who cut out these cells and did all that carving must have been clever enough for anything. Look at the shaping of this curious-looking monster."

"I admire the way they protected themselves and prepared for a siege as much as anything," said Briscoe. "The manner in which they contrived the water supply is to my mind grand. We must have torches one of these days, and examine that tank, and get up to the top and find out how the spring is led in."

"But it seems strange that there are no more remains left about. They did not possess anything apparently but a few earthen pots and the stone mills," said Brace.

"People didn't furnish much in early times," said Briscoe, laughing. "A man provided himself with a knife, a bow and arrow, or a spear, and a place to lay his head in, and no doubt thought he was rich. He didn't want a van when he was going to move to a fresh residence."

"But these people must have been highly civilised to ornament this temple, or palace, or whatever it was, so grandly."

"Well, let's make our way to the bottom," said Briscoe; "we may find something more interesting yet. Ready, Sir Humphrey?"

"Yes: forward," was the reply.

"He means downward," said Briscoe, laughing, and, the regular shaft being found, they descended to the next terrace and began to explore.

Chapter Thirty Nine
The Temple of Idols

Working now upon a regular plan, the party began at one end of the terrace and examined each cell in turn.

They had proceeded about a third of the way towards the other end, when, to the surprise of all, although the openings like windows continued in a regular row, the doorways ceased altogether, and when an attempt to peer in at window after window was made, nothing whatever could be seen, for within all was deep silent gloom.

They soon found that about a third part in the centre of the two-hundred-feet-long terrace was like this: then the doorways began again and continued right away to the end.

"Here, I want to see what's inside that middle part," said Briscoe. "I propose that I have a rope round my waist, and that I climb in, and you lower me down till I holloa out."

"And I propose," said Sir Humphrey, "that we leave that till another day. Let's go down to the next terrace."

"At your orders, sir," said the American quietly. "I can wait."

The opening leading to the next terrace was sought for after the last cells had been examined, and when discovered it was found to contain nothing whatever but the crumbling dust of ages and the traces left by birds; while, upon descending to this last terrace but one, they saw that the construction was precisely the same as that of the terrace they had just left—the central part being pierced only with windows, doored cells being on either side.

"I feel more and more that I want to see what's inside there," said Briscoe.

"Well, we'll have plenty of time to do so some other day, for we are not going to move away from this place just yet," said Brace merrily. "Wait till tomorrow, and we'll go in together. I fancy that we shall find it is a temple, and full of mummies."

"Like as not," said Briscoe; "and if it is we shall find no end of interesting things wrapped up with them, I should say. I daresay these people did like the Egyptians used to do."

"Now," said Sir Humphrey, as the last cell was examined, "one more terrace, and we shall have done all but this centre, and I propose to leave that till to-morrow."

"No," cried Brace and Briscoe, in a breath.

"I want to sleep to-night," said the latter, "and I can't with this mystery on my brain."

"Very well, then; we'll eat a bit of lunch, and then examine that."

As soon as the party had disposed of their meal, they left the entrance to the shaft, walked along to the end of the terrace, and began to examine the first cell.

Here a surprise awaited them, for the cell was double, had two windows and a door at either end, there being no dividing wall, only a curious construction in the middle, but so crumbled away that for some minutes it was examined in vain, the loose stones about turned over and over, and the dust raked here and there.

"I know," cried Brace at last: "it has been a kitchen."

"Right," said Briscoe: "must have been something of that sort. Let's get on."

The next place was entered, and proved to be also double, but with only one entrance, and that narrow.

Brace was the first to enter, and after a glance round and upward to see if the roof had fallen in, he stood looking down at a heap of stones which were thickly covered with the dust that had crumbled down and accumulated.

"There's nothing to see here," he cried; "and the windows are nearly choked up with growth."

"Yes, come back; these places are all the same," said Briscoe, gripping him tightly by the arm; but, as he made way for Brace to pass him, and the rest went on, he stooped down quickly and picked up a piece from the heap of dust-covered stones and placed it in his pocket.

"Why did you do that?" said Brace, in a low voice.

"Don't ask questions now," whispered Briscoe. "I'll tell you soon. Wait till we're out of hearing of the men."

Several more of the large double cells were inspected, and they all seemed to have been used for other purposes than habitation, for various stone objects lay about, and in two cases their aspect suggested that they had been used for grain stores; but it was impossible to decide.

Then Brace's heart began to beat quickly with excitement, for he felt that they were on the brink of a great discovery. Several windows were passed which were heavily loaded with grotesque ornamentation; but there was no door visible. The centre of the terrace was marked by a perfect curtain of liana-like creepers and vines, which hung in festoons from on high and almost completely hid the elaborately-carved front.

"There must be an entrance here," said the captain. "Out with your jack-knives, my lads, and cut a way through."

It was no easy task, for the various creepers were interlaced and had grown together so that saws and strong bill-hooks would have been more suitable implements than knives; but the men worked away with a will, being as eager as their superiors to get a glance into the strange place which had kept them at bay so long.

A good half-hour's cutting and hacking was, however, necessary, two men working at a time while the others dragged away the greenery, which they tossed over the elaborately-carved colonnade into the river, where it was slowly borne away along the canon.

At last the foremost man was nearly through, and, reaching up as high as he could to divide a pale green strand which had grown almost in darkness, and now hindered his way, he put all his strength out to sever it with one cut, not anticipating that wood which had grown under such conditions would be tender and soft, and, consequently, his knife went through it as easily as if it had been a thick stick of rhubarb, and he fell forward into the darkness upon a pile of dead wood and leafy rubbish.

"Hurt yourself?" cried Brace, stepping forward, half in dread lest the man should have been plunged into some deep pit.

"Not a bit, sir; only rolled down about a dozen steps, and— Oh, yah! yah!" he yelled, uttering a horror-stricken cry; and then, as guns were cocked in anticipation of seeing some savage beast of prey dash out, the man came blundering up, stumbling over the heap of rubbish, and finally dashed out on to the terrace, covered with dust and with his eyes starting in a scared and terrified manner, as he sank down shuddering, and uttered a groan.

"What's the matter? What is it, old matey?" cried one of the men; but Brace, his brother, and the American stood fast with levelled guns and fingers on the triggers.

"What is it, my lad?" cried the captain: "a jaguar?"

"Oh, no, sir; worse than that," faltered the man, wiping the sweat from his face: "worser than that."

"What did you see then? Was it a great serpent? Speak up, lad."

"No, sir; I shouldn't have been skeared o' any serpent. It was a great big Injun who had a lot o' greasy white snakes swinging about all round his head, and he'd got his club ready to hit me. Ever so big, he was."

"'How are you, old chap?' said Briscoe quietly."

"That chap's telling a big lie," said Briscoe coolly, "only he thinks he's telling the truth. There couldn't be any big Indian in there, and if there were he wouldn't have a lot of greasy white snakes hanging about his head. I'm going in to see for myself. Coming with me, Brace?"

"Yes," was the reply, and, holding their pieces ready while their companions crowded round the narrow entrance, the pair stepped boldly but cautiously into the opening.

They found themselves descending rugged stair after stair, encumbered with dead branches of creeper which cracked and snapped under their feet at every moment, till they were about five feet below the level of the terrace, with some dozens of greeny-white darkness-grown creeper strands swinging to and fro from above, and just in front of them they could dimly see, standing with uplifted menacing arm, what seemed to be a hideously grotesque half-human half-animal figure, apparently blocking the way.

"How are you, old chap?" said Briscoe quietly, staring at the figure. "Long time since you've had any visitors, eh?"

"Why, it is a temple," cried Brace, in tones of suppressed excitement, "and I suppose this is the idol the old people used to worship."

"And very bad taste too. Come in, everybody," cried Briscoe, and his voice sounded weirdly strange as it echoed all round.

"No: stop at the entrance," cried Brace. "Did you hear what I said, Free?"

"Yes: that it was a temple with an idol," his brother answered.

"Yes; but we must have more light before we proceed any farther, in case of there being any terrible holes or pitfalls."

"Yes: be as well," said Briscoe; "but I'm beginning to see fairly now. Why, Brace, lad," he continued, as the captain set the men to work at once hacking away the growth of many generations from entrance door and window, "it's as I expected: the temple runs up as high as three or four of the terraces, and look: you can see the light from the upper windows, showing the walls. It's a hugely big place, but I wish it wasn't so dark down here."

"I'm getting used to it too," said Brace, in a voice full of excitement; "but I'm afraid to move, in case of losing my footing."

"That's right; so am I. Look: can you see over yonder?"

"Yes; quite plainly now. There's what looks like an altar, and I can see several more figures standing about."

"So can I. I wish we had a good strong light. Hah! that's right; they're letting in the sunshine. Oh, we shall soon see."

"Look here," said Brace: "the place is very lofty, and there are windows upward to take off the smoke. Let's make a fire of the dead wood lying about here."

"That's a good thought," said Sir Humphrey; and five minutes afterwards a match was applied to the heap of perfectly dry wood underfoot. It caught fire at once and began blazing up, sending forth such a glow of light that the men set up a cheer, drawn from them by the excitement and wonder of the weird scene which confronted them.

Chapter Forty
The Flood Subsides

As all stepped back from the crackling and blazing pile, the smoke rose, rolling up in wreaths, and the fire illumined the whole place, displaying a perfect crowd of grotesquely horrible figures in all manner of menacing attitudes.

To add to the weird horror of the scene, high above and mingling with the smoke clouds were scores of great bats, fully three feet across in the stretch of their leathern wings, with which they silently flapped through the gloom till they succeeded in reaching one or other of the windows through which the smoke poured, and thence the outer air.

"Horrible!" cried the captain.

"It is weird in the extreme," said Sir Humphrey; "but it is interesting."

The men who had been hacking away the vines stood in a group, silent and awe-stricken, gazing at the grotesque figures and the flickering shadows they cast as the fire rose and fell and lit up the strange interior to the farthest corner.

"Well, Brace," said Briscoe, "I don't call this pretty; but I'd have taken twice as much trouble to get here so as to see it. Throw on some more of this dead stuff, lads. There's a good draught comes in and carries the heat upwards, and it will make a clearance of all these birds' nests and rubbish."

"It is horrible," said Brace, as the men hurried to obey the order given, and the flames leaped up and up, revealing the many figures from fresh points of view in the golden ruddy glare. "But I feel like you, Briscoe; I shouldn't have liked to miss this."

"These are the old bogies with which the priests who lived in the cells upstairs used to scare the people and keep them under. I wonder whether they ever thought to light up the place."

"No doubt they did," said Sir Humphrey, who had now joined them. "That square erection at the back there, surrounded by small figures, must have been the altar, and no doubt they burned a fire upon that."

"Think so, sir," said the captain. "Well, I didn't think we were coming up to see a sight like this. Old Dellow will be a bit mad at missing it, eh, Lynton?"

"But he shan't miss it," said Briscoe. "We must light it up again. Say, Brace, I can't see any sign of holes. The floor's covered with rubbish and stony dust, but it seems to me that we can walk right back among those two rows of images to the altar. I want to see what those things are round about it."

"Well, let's take hold of hands and try," replied Brace. "We can try every step before us with the butts of our guns."

"Be careful," cried Sir Humphrey.

"Yes; we'll mind," said Brace. "Let the men throw on more dead dry stuff; Lynton; and only a little at a time so as to keep up a good light."

"All right, sir," was the response, and more flame and light and less smoke was the result, while more light came in from the windows above, for as the hot acrid smoke poured out the leafage writhed and crinkled up, taking up half the space it had occupied before.

There was nothing to hinder the advance, as Brace and Briscoe carefully felt their way between the two rows of menacing figures, till they reached the square elevation, a good ten feet high, and then found that they could ascend a flight of steps thick with powdered stone.

At the broad landing at the top the altar was about waist-high, and now for the first time they made out that at the back there was a big sitting figure, whose breast seemed to be covered with a kind of rayed shield; but everything was indistinct in the flickering light, and the figure was absolutely clothed in dust.

Just then Briscoe stretched out his left hand and laid it upon one of the objects which stood in a row on either side of the altar.

The next moment he began to breathe hard as if he were about to have a fit.

"What's the matter?" said Brace anxiously; "overcome by the heat and smoke?"

"No, no," whispered Briscoe hoarsely. "Touch that thing nearest to you."

Brace did as was suggested, and found that it was heavy, but that he could move it.

"Why, it isn't stone," he said, "but metal. It must be some kind of ornament."

"Yes," said Briscoe, in a hoarse whisper, "and that kitchen place we went in first was a foundry; that next place where you spoke of a rubbish heap was all ore. I picked up a bit, as you know, and it's rich. Brace, my lad, we've found the Spaniards' El Dorado, and these ornaments we have just touched are solid gold."

"Impossible!" said Brace, in an awe-stricken whisper.

"'Tisn't, lad. Look now the light's stronger. That squatting figure with the thing like a rayed shield over his breast isn't only stone, for I'd bet my last dollar that the shield's a golden sun."

"Well?" cried the captain; "found anything?"

"Oh, yes," said Brace, trying to speak calmly; "this is an altar, sure enough."

"Well, I'd give it up for to-day. Come out, Brace," cried Sir Humphrey, "and we'll examine the place carefully to-morrow when the fire has burned out and the air is breathable. I think we shall be able to take back something curious for our pains."

"Not a doubt about it," said Briscoe cheerily. "Yes; we've had enough of it for to-day, and I want something to take the smoke and dust out of my throat. Come along, Brace. Hist," he whispered: "not a word till we get them away from the men."

"I understand," said Brace.

A few minutes afterwards the whole party were out on the terrace, shouting down explanations to Dellow and the men, who on seeing the smoke rising had taken to the small boat and rowed to the foot of the great wall.

"Found anything worth getting?" shouted the mate.

"Well, yes: I suppose so," cried the captain. "It's a big temple full of stone idols. We shall have to take a boat-load back for the British Museum."

"Bah!" said Dellow. "Are you coming back now? Dan's got a splendid dinner of fish and bird roasted and I don't know how you are; we're starving here."

"We shall be with you in no time now," said the captain. "Forward, my lads, and let's get back."

The men started, Sir Humphrey and the captain followed, and Brace and Briscoe came last.

"Yes, that's gold, sure enough," said Brace, looking furtively at the piece of ore thrust into his hand. "But, Briscoe?"

"Well?"

"Suppose the Indians know of all these golden ornaments and things being here?"

"I don't suppose they do; but if they do, what then?"

"Suppose they came now in force and beat us off?"

"Ah, it would be awkward if they came now; but if they did there'd be a very ugly fight before we gave up our hold on what we've found."

"Yes; we couldn't give it up now."

"I say, what about the men?" said Briscoe.

"They must know, of course, and take their share of what we carry away."

"Oh!" groaned Briscoe, "and after finding what has been the dream of my life."

"What do you mean!" said Brace wonderingly.

"Why, we've only got those two boats and can't take much. Brace, my lad, do you think it would be possible to bring the brig up here?"

"Yes, perhaps we might if you could knock down those falls, and do away with all the shallow parts between here and there."

"Of course," said Briscoe, with another groan full of misery. "I forgot all that."

"I say," said Dellow, as they came within sight from the lower terrace once more, "something's happened while you've been away."

"What is it?" said the captain.

"Tide's turned, and the water's flowing steadily the other way."

"That means the flood's gone down then," said the captain. "Well, then, gentlemen, when you've got your images on board I suppose you'd like to be going back, for the stores are running very low."

Chapter Forty One
The Slippery Treasure

"Don't know that I am pleased," said Sir Humphrey, when his brother and Briscoe told him of the discovery; "but it is very wonderful, and I suppose we may claim the right to all we have found."

"Certainly," said Briscoe.

"Well, the first thing to be done is to acquaint the captain, Dellow, and Lynton."

"Of course," said Briscoe, "and the men must know."

"Does it not mean trouble?" said Brace. "I mean with the crew."

"No," replied Briscoe; "the skipper has them all well in hand now, and they must be given to understand that every man will take a share of the gold, according to his position. I vote we tell the skipper and mates at once."

Ten minutes later they were fully acquainted with the facts, and the captain screwed his face up tightly.

"Hah!" he said; "I never aimed at being rich, but I'm not going to quarrel with my luck."

"No," said Briscoe, "and I think we ought to take as much of it as we can carry with us."

"Well, gentlemen, it's a big find, and I suppose it means half a dozen journeys here to fetch it all to the brig."

"We cannot say yet," said Sir Humphrey; "but we ought to get all we can down to the brig at once."

"Yes," said Briscoe, "and leave Mr Brace and me here with a couple of men to guard the rest."

"No," said Sir Humphrey firmly; "we must keep together. I say: let's load the boats as far as is wise and get as much of the treasure as possible safely to the brig."

"And lose all there is left," said Briscoe.

"No," replied Brace. "This gold must have kept here in safety for at least a thousand years, so I daresay it will rest till we get back again."

"Look here, gentlemen," said the captain; "both these plans sound well, but we can settle which we'll try afterwards. I don't feel that we've got the treasure till the two boats have their loads packed in the bottoms like ballast, well covered with leaves. Let's get as much as we can, and then perhaps it might be well for part of us to stop while the others take down the first part."

"The captain is right," said Sir Humphrey: "we'll settle that afterwards: perhaps there is no more than we can take in one journey."

This was put to the proof the next morning, when the men, having cheered till they were hoarse at the wondrous news, the party divided: one portion to make their way to the temple, the other to moor the two boats conveniently under the wall below, the captain and Dellow taking the latter duty, with a couple of men to stow, while as soon as Brace, Briscoe, Lynton, and the rest of the men appeared on the lower terrace communication was made with a block pulley and ropes ready for lowering the treasure, a couple of stout biscuit bags being taken from the stores for sending up and down.

Brace led the way into the temple, his heart throbbing with eagerness; and, lights having been set up in convenient spots, the threatening aspect of the inanimate guardians of the treasure was soon forgotten, and all set to work to sweep the dust from the ornaments upon the altar, and then to carry them out into the broad sunshine ready for lowering down.

A feeling of astonishment attacked Brace as he worked hard, and hardly a word was spoken, everyone busying himself and toiling as if there was not a moment to spare, and a whisper might bring someone to stop them from carrying the treasure away.

It was wonderful indeed, for after the thick coating of dust had been shaken off they found that they were handling roughly-formed lamps, figures of gods with benevolent features, those of savage and malignant-looking demons—in fact, what seemed to be the whole pantheon of the idols who might be supposed to preside over the good qualities and evil thoughts of mankind.

Most of them had been roughly cast in moulds and left untouched; but others had been hammered and chiselled with an archaic idea of art that was surprising.

Then there were ornaments which obviously suggested leaves and twining vines, with rayed flowers sufficiently well executed to show that they had been copied from such as the finders had seen growing on the ledges of the cañon.

But unmistakeably all were of rich solid pale gold, bronzed and ruddy in places with the action of fire, and, setting aside their value as antique works of art, representing a cash value as gold that was almost startling.

Every now and then a figure was attacked and left standing on account of its weight and the party of toilers busy in the weird gloom of the temple paused at last as if half-stunned by the feeling that had come upon them after two men had tried to lift the seated figure of some deity.

"Yes, we can't take that," said Briscoe dismally. "We could carry it out, I daresay, but it would go through the bottom of the boat. We shall have to start that old furnace and melt these big things down."

Just then two of the men who been carrying a load out on to the terrace came back, bearing a message from the captain.

"He says, gentlemen," said one of the men, "that it will be as much as he dare take aboard when we've let down all we've got waiting outside."

"Nonsense!" cried Brace; "why, we have ever so much more to send out yet. We can't leave all these small things."

"How much weight do you think you have taken out, my lads?" said Sir Humphrey, who was working hard with the rest.

"'Bout half a ton, sir, I should say," replied one of the men.

"Let's go out and have a talk to the skipper," said Briscoe. "I say, chaps," he added jocosely, "fair play and fair sharing; no pocketing either of those big images while we're gone."

"All right, sir," said one of the men: "we won't; but to speak square and honest, I was longing to collar that biggest one at the back there, him with the sign of the sun on his front."

"We must fetch them another time," said Briscoe; and he followed the brothers out on to the terrace, where, dully gleaming in the sunshine, quite a couple of hundredweight of the strange objects connected with the ancient worship lay waiting to be lowered down.

"Well, captain," said Sir Humphrey, "what does this mean—you can't take any more?"

"I'm going to risk what you've got out already, sir," was the reply. "According to the men there's about three hundredweight to lower yet."

"At a rough guess, yes," said Brace.

"That's the very outside then, and we shall have to beat and hammer a lot of these together with the axeheads to make them take up less room. Look for yourselves."

A long and earnest look was directed below, where the boats were packed beneath the thwarts and fore and aft with the treasure, and presented a strange aspect.

"Yes, he's quite right," said Briscoe, with a sigh. "Oh, if we only had one of those coal-barges that I've seen lying at anchor in your Thames."

"Let's be content, Briscoe, and get these figures aboard. We must not run risks and lose all."

"That's wisdom, Sir Humphrey, and I've no more to say. Keep on lowering down, my lads, while we go back. Oh, dear, I wish we hadn't burned all that green stuff that hid the door."

"It will soon shoot out and grow again," said Brace; "but we must come back for another load."

They went back into the temple to take a look round, lanthorn in hand, and then had literally to drag themselves away from the sight of the vast treasure they were compelled to leave behind.

"It's of no use," said Brace. "Come along. The more we look the more unwilling we shall be to leave."

"I feel as if I can't leave it. I must stop and take care of the rest, even if I stay alone," said Briscoe.

"No," said Brace; "that would be folly. It will be safe enough till we return."

"But look here: suppose we build a raft, and load that? We could tow it down with the boats."

"Yes," said Brace, "and end by upsetting it and sending all to the bottom."

"Look here," said Sir Humphrey: "I am going to set you both a good example."

He hurried out into the light, while after another glance round Briscoe said slowly:

"Yes, a raft would end by shooting it all off into the river. Let's make sure of what we've got."

And, rushing out, he set steadily to work helping to get the objects still waiting down to the boat, and then he was the first to lead the way and mount from terrace to terrace to the slope and by the way to the great tank, where the water was making a strange reverberating sound.

"That noise is enough to keep the Indians away," he said to Brace, as he paused with him till all the men had passed. "It's as good as a safe."

When all were down, the L-shaped entrance was carefully blocked with stones and covered with rubbish, earth, and growing plants, so that there was no sign of the place having been disturbed, and by that time the boats were back at their moorings, with the captain shaking his head at them.

"More than we ought to take," he said; "but we'll risk it, and hope for fine weather. Now, gentlemen, as we've made our fortunes, let's have the good dinner Dan has got ready for us, and then I say: all traps aboard and down stream for the brig."

"Ready to come up again for another load," said Briscoe.

"Well," said the captain slowly, "if we can."

The dinner was eaten, and various cooking-articles were replaced in the boat.

"Now then," said the captain; "all aboard!"

"Three cheers first, lads," cried one of the men; "for we shall have our gold now without washing for it."

They gave three hearty cheers, and as the last was echoing from the opposite side of the cañon every man stood as if petrified, for it was answered by a savage yell which seemed to come from a couple of thousand throats; and as there was a rush to where, from the water steps, they could gaze up stream it was to see quite a fleet of small canoes, each of which held four or five Indians, bearing steadily down for where the boats were moored.

Chapter Forty Two
Found and Lost

"Now, gentlemen," said the captain firmly, "what is it to be: turn this into a fort and fight, or into the boats, hoist sail, and go down stream? You see it runs our way now."

"Take to the boats," said Sir Humphrey decisively, and the captain gave the order.

"Slow and steady, my lads," he said; "they can't reach us for some time yet, and by then we shall be sailing steadily down."

The canoes seemed to be coming on very fast, but the captain was correct.

The sails were hoisted as soon as every man was in his place, and, to the satisfaction of all, the heavily-ballasted boats began to glide down stream before a pleasant breeze with a steadiness that was all that could be desired.

But by the time they were well moving the first of the canoes was very near, and their occupants started their savage yelling again and began to paddle with all their might, till, seeing that the boats were leaving them behind, they dropped their paddles and seized their bows, to let fly a shower of arrows.

At this the captain gave the word, and a little volley was fired, followed by another.

The walls of the great cañon took up the reports and echoed them to and fro till, startled by this novel thunder, the enemy paused in confusion, many of the canoes being paddled back.

"Anyone hit?" cried Brace.

"No, sir," came loudly from both boats, and the next minute they glided round the promontory they had passed in coming up, and the rock city disappeared.

A few minutes later and the last of the canoes was seen.

The wind being favourable and the night following lit up by a full moon, the retreat was kept up so as to get well beyond danger.

It was far on into the next day before a halt was made to light a fire and prepare a meal.

The flood had passed away, and with wind and stream in their favour, and a total absence of danger, the two boats glided down and down from river to river till after many days the adventurers came within hearing of the falls.

They ran the boats safely aground just above where the river made its plunge, and then came a long and toilsome task.

But the boats were safely unladen—for the men worked with a will—run ashore, and up and down the two slopes, to be re-launched and all the stores and treasure replaced by dark one night.

The next morning at daybreak a start was made for the brig, which was found a mile lower down, where it had been swept by the flood, but was safely re-anchored.

In due time the men were cheering loudly again, for the treasure was safe on board.

"Now," said Briscoe, "one day's rest, and then we'll start with three boats, skipper, and stouter tackle so as to handle some of those big images better. We ought to take three or four planks."

"Then you want to get some more?" said the captain, smiling.

"More?" said Briscoe, staring; "why, man, it would be a sin to leave that treasure wasting there. What do you say, gentlemen?"

"Well," said Sir Humphrey, "I can't help feeling as you do, Briscoe. What do you say, Brace?"

"I don't want any more gold," was the reply; "but I should like to get those curiosities to England. It would be such a shame to leave them up there."

"And so say we," said Dellow and Lynton eagerly.

"But what about the men?" said Brace; "would they go?"

"Would a dozen ducks swim, sir?" said the captain scornfully. "Ask 'em."

The men were asked, and their answer was a tremendous cheer.

"Of course, sir," one of them cried. "We must clear out the lot."

"Very well," said the captain. "I shall stay on board here with two men as guards, and you shall start with three boats to-morrow morning."

There was another tremendous cheer at this, and then Dellow threw a wet blanket over all.

"I dunno," he said slowly: "I don't think it will be to-morrow, for there's some weather about. Look at that lightning playing away to the west'ard."

The first mate was right, for that night there was a frightful storm to announce the breaking-up of the season.

The next day the river was in flood, and in spite of all the captain's skill the brig was torn from her moorings and borne rapidly down stream.

The days passed, and the weather grew worse and worse. Efforts were made to moor or anchor over and over again, but the river rapidly became like one vast lake with the water extending for miles on either side.

After terrible vicissitudes the captain at last breathed freely when at the end of some weeks the "Jason" was rising and falling in half a gale well out to sea.

"Hah!" he said; "this is something like. I can turn in now for a rest without expecting to be capsized by being swept over a clump of trees. There's nothing like the sea, after all."

"But what about going up the river again?" asked Briscoe.

"It will be in flood for months to come, sir, I should say, and my advice would be for us to get safe home with what we've got, and make another trip next year."

The captain's advice was taken, and to a man the men volunteered to go again the next season.

That trip was made, and proved to be quite a blank, for the brig was never got up to the falls.

The next year, though, the party started with high hopes, for the weather was magnificent, and they reached the falls; but not without finding that the course of the river had been a good deal altered by two seasons of tremendous floods.

But there were the stupendous falls and one morning, leaving the brig snugly anchored in a bay of the river to wait for her golden freight, three boats, with the men well armed, started for their journey up stream.

The course of the river below the falls had been greatly altered, but that was as nothing to the complete change in the network of rivers higher up.

Let it suffice to say that they rowed and sailed for days which grew into weeks, and then to months, from river into river, and then in and out of what was a great watery puzzle; but the cañon with its golden city might have sunk right out of sight, for in spite of every effort the party were driven back at last when the torrential rains set in.

The next year the captain said he had had enough of it, and Brace and his brother declined to go, the latter saying that the proverb was right: "You can buy gold too dearly."

Briscoe then declared that he would freight another brig and go by himself.

He went, and, at the end of six months, returned, visited London, and called upon his old companion.

"Haven't found it yet," he said; "but there's a lot of gold there, and I mean to try till I do."

Brace met him again and again as the years rolled on, but he had not found the gold.

"No," he said; "there's something about that puzzle place of rivers that I don't quite understand. I can't find it, and the longer I live the more I feel, Brace Leigh, that we ought to have eaten our bread when it was ready buttered, and brought the stuff away upon a raft."

"Why don't you be content with what you had for your share?"

"Oh, I am," said Briscoe: "just as contented as you are, but I want to find the rest of that treasure all the same. You see, old fellow, I'm this sort: I'm Amurrican, and I don't like being beat."